To Jess, the daughter of my heart.

The Scent of Freedom

With blessings and good wishes

Happy Reading

Alan T. McKean

Dec 2016

Alan T. McKean

BLACK ROSE
writing™

This is a work of fiction. Names, characters, businesses, places, events and incidents
are either the products of the author's imagination or used in a fictitious manner.
Any resemblance to actual persons, living or dead, or actual events is purely
coincidental.

ISBN: 978-1-61296-774-5
PUBLISHED BY BLACK ROSE WRITING
www.blackrosewriting.com

Printed in the United States of America
Suggested retail price $17.95

The Scent of Freedom is printed in Perpetua

The Scent of Freedom

CHAPTER ONE

Honeymoon Interrupted

The revolving doors in the Martello Hotel in Rome had thick, dark-red curtains on each side. *Victorian overkill*, I thought. I went through the door first and Marie followed. I assumed she was a couple of compartments behind me. We had only been married two hours and were eager to enjoy our first night together as husband and wife.

I heard her delighted giggle just before the door jammed and I caught a glimpse of a hand throwing a vial of something into the revolving door. The vial shattered and smoked. My head spun. I crashed to the floor. When the door opened into the foyer, I was helped to my feet.

"Perhaps Signor has had a little too much champagne," the manager said with a chuckle as I wobbled on my feet and slowly regained my wits. Looking around wildly, I gasped, "Where is she? Where's Marie? Where's my wife?"

The manager looked perplexed. "The lady who was right behind me," I explained, in an attempt to sound patient and reasonable and to quell my mounting alarm. "Where is she?"

The manager shook his head and repeated. "Definitely too much champagne. Signor arrived on his own. There was no one with you. But there are plenty of beautiful girls in Rome." He smiled suggestively.

My eyes searched frantically for Marie. The manager added, "I swear, Signor. You arrived alone."

Inhaling a deep gulp of air into my lungs to restore my breathing and still the rising panic, I told the manager, "The booking was made for two. Drew and Marie Faulkner."

The manager shook his head. "No, just you, Signor. But here! I have a telegram for you."

A telegram! No one knew where we had gone on honeymoon except my Vanguard time travel boss, Colonel John Carlisle.

Smiling politely, the manger handed me the telegram. I ripped it open. A deep chill, for which there was no warmth or cure, invaded every part of my body as I read: "*Lost something, dear boy? Tut tut! Very careless. Should not it have been ladies first? Will be in touch. Have fun without your new bride. Reynolds.*"

I stared at the telegram, reading and re-reading it. The words didn't change. Neither did the circumstances. The only way Vanguard nemesis Professor Reynolds could have known that Marie followed me into the revolving door at the hotel was if he had time traveled here before Marie and I had arrived. He had left the wedding in Scotland in 1867, before the service began. This I knew, because Angus McTurk, my fellow agent and also my best man at the wedding, had noticed him. I had stupidly thought nothing of it at the time. Reynolds was the mastermind of PATCH, an enemy time traveling organization that sought to go back in history and change events to fit its own agenda.

Vanguard was a counter time traveling organization. Our main goal to date had been discovering and stopping PATCH's evil plots before they did tremendous damage to world events. If Reynolds had been to the hotel before Marie and I—and in time to send a telegram—it meant that PATCH had traveled forward and not just back in time. I must alert Colonel Carlisle immediately.

The manager hovered politely at my elbow, watching me with concern. "Your luggage has been taken to your room, Signor. First floor, Room 32."

Luggage! I thought. *Marie's things will be there and I will find this is nothing more than a nightmare. Perhaps Marie is already there waiting for me! Possibly she's playing a game with me…if so…I am not amused.*

Clutching the key, I bounded up the blue-carpeted stairs from the ground floor to the first floor two at a time. *Dear God*, I thought, *the wedding was only a couple of hours ago.* My colleagues, Mike and Hera, had married at the same time. Such a joyous occasion…and now…this…surely, no! Surely I was overreacting and everything was okay.

Two cases were on the bed—a single bed. There should have been four cases and a double bed. Marie couldn't be responsible for this horrific attempt at humor. I remained unwilling to believe it could be anything more sinister, in spite of the evidence of Reynolds' telegram which I still grasped in my hand. In spite of her shyness, Marie was a passionate woman. She had looked forward to our first time making love as much as I had—or so she had assured me. I searched the room. Finding no trace of Marie, I opened the suitcases on the bed. My clothes. Just my clothes. Nothing of Marie's. Dumbstruck, I stared at the clothes and around the otherwise empty room. Then the angle of the sun slanting through the curtained window changed and something on the floor glinted. I swooped down and grabbed it. Marie's amulet!

Marie's amulet had at one time contained Kairon , the substance that made time travel possible. My uncle, Professor Adrian Conroy, had removed the Kairon and given the amulet back to Marie as a gift. I clutched my wife's amulet against my chest. So, I had not imagined everything! Reynolds *had* kidnapped Marie. The hotel manager and he must be in cahoots for Reynolds to have made it up to the room with Marie and remove her cases before I regained consciousness. It was likely that Marie had deliberately dropped the amulet to leave a clue for me. But how had PATCH known our honeymoon plans? *Arrive'derci Roma*—Goodbye, Rome suddenly took on a whole new meaning and urgency. I had to get back to Vanguard Headquarters and enlist the help of my fellow time-traveling friends to rescue Marie!

Vanguard's whole reason for existence was to stop Professor Reynolds and PATCH from time traveling with the purpose of changing history. We had stopped PATCH from getting England to enter the American Civil War on the Confederate side. We had saved Queen Victoria's life from an assassination attempt. And we had foiled many other PATCH attempts to rewrite history.

Reynolds was clever, dangerous, devious—and was now armed with a fearsome new weapon—my lovely wife. Marie, with her haunting eyes and clouds of dark hair, had been blind when I met and fell in love with her. She played the piano like an angel. We were already engaged when Vanguard financed the operation that had restored Marie's sight. In a way, she had earned the right to that expense by saving my life. Even blind, she had shot the two PATCH operatives who had broken into our home to kill us.

Only burning anger held back my tears. I left the hotel and walked out into the sun. All around me, people went about their daily lives in Rome. Eating, drinking, and reveling in love…experiences that I had dreamed of sharing with Marie.

Angus used to say to me in training, "Don't lose your temper in a fight; you lose control and it affects your ability to think and form a solution."

I must leave Rome immediately. Nobody at headquarters would know what had happened until I made it back.

I tried to shut the malevolent reasons for Marie's kidnapping out of my mind. Reynolds always had a reason for everything he did. He was a crook, but an economical crook. He never wasted anything. He was angry over his failed attempts to change history. It made sense that he would now use Marie as a human shield—but where? And more importantly—when and why?

* * *

Turning my back on Rome and closing my shattered heart to her timeless allure, I journeyed back to Vanguard headquarters at Bellefield, a large house in its own grounds on the road between Aberdeen and Huntly in Scotland. The time car took me to the basement. The two guards stationed there were shocked to see me. "Major, you're supposed to be on honeymoon! Where's your wife?" Jock asked.

"She's been kidnapped, Jock."

Shoulders slumped, and no doubt looking like a dispirited, retired racehorse, I stumbled over to the desk and buzzed Colonel Carlisle. "It's Major Faulkner, sir. Can I come see you?" I added, "I'm alone."

There was a stunned silence before the colonel's voice replied, "Come to my office immediately, Drew. I think this is not a domestic argument between husband and wife."

I shuffled from the basement up to the familiar surroundings of the colonel's office.

"Come in," he said. "Take a seat. Coffee or something stronger?" We waited to speak until the coffee I had requested arrived. I took a huge gulp, ignoring the scalding heat. I had not realized how thirsty I was, or how shocked. Now, back at the familiar HQ, it hit me hard. Unable to control the shaking that seized control of my body, I set the coffee down on the desk to keep it from sloshing all over me.

With a voice that conveyed kindness and genuine concern, Colonel Carlisle ordered, "Start at the beginning."

Realizing the need for immediate action to rescue Marie, I quickly told the colonel all I could remember and handed him the telegram from Reynolds. Without wasting time asking questions I couldn't answer, Carlisle rang my uncle, Professor Adrian Conroy, Vanguard's chief scientist. Adrian had been a colleague of Professor Reynolds before Reynolds had gone rogue.

"I will have this analyzed," Adrian promised, taking the telegram from me. "Blast it, Drew! I'm sorry. So sorry. And how stupid and empty those words sound at a time like this."

I nodded my acceptance of his words, hoping he didn't see the tears swimming in my eyes. This was the second time I had lost a wife before we had even had the chance to go on our honeymoon—both losses courtesy of PATCH.

My first wife, Lucy, had been murdered on our wedding day—shot by Caleb Bryant, who was then Reynolds' second in command. Bryant had been insanely jealous because he had wanted Lucy for himself. He murdered her in cold blood because he wanted to hurt me. When I closed my eyes I could still see my lovely Lucy lying in my arms, the front of her bridal gown covered in blood. I still missed her, even though I knew she was safe in Heaven. Bryant had pulled the trigger that had killed Lucy, but he had been employed by the same evil individual who now had Marie—Professor Reynolds. Reynolds seemed to feed on other men's jealousy and hate, cruelly twisting it to fit his own advantage.

It was obvious Uncle Adrian didn't know what to say to me. After slipping the telegram in a protective envelope so he could carry it to the laboratory, Adrian thumped me on the shoulder in an effort to console me and shook his head. "Marie is still alive. I can stake all I have on it," he said. "We must act quickly to rescue her. Reynolds is not a mindless thug like Bryant. He's arrogant and wants to show us how clever he is. In Reynolds' world there is only one person of importance—Reynolds."

Word had spread quickly. Angus McTurk was next to join us. Gripping my shoulders in strong hands he said, "Son, I am so terribly sorry. I feel responsible. I should have gone after Reynolds in the church when I spotted him at the wedding." He sighed. "Hindsight is a great thing."

"Right," the colonel sighed. "We have always gone on the rule; *nobody gets left behind.* I have sent word to Hera and Mike. If we can reach Meryl, we'll let her know, too. The team would want that, and were the shoe on the other foot, you and Angus would do the same thing. Drew, go now and get some rest while we sort this out. But I think you would be wise to tell Mi-Ling what's happened, and Libby, as well."

Mi-Ling was my adopted Chinese daughter. God had helped me rescue Mi-Ling from a nightmare existence in a child brothel in the port of Foo-Chow, China. Libby, about Mi-Ling's age, was Caleb Bryant's daughter. I had taken responsibility for her welfare when Bryant was killed attempting—once again—to kill me. Like Mi-Ling, I now considered Libby as my daughter. Both girls were looking forward to having a real mother. Both girls had saved my life, and the lives of other team members…but that was another story. Now, while Marie and I went on our honeymoon, the girls were staying in Adrian's flat at HQ with Adrian's wife, Victoria, who was Lucy's mother. Victoria and Lucy had been reunited when we traveled back from 1867, winning the Foochow to London Tea Clipper Race the same year. I now thought of that heady adventure as *The Scent of Time*. I thought of the time travel adventure that had brought Libby into our lives as *The Scent of Eternity*. It had been Victoria who helped me cope with Lucy's murder. That had meant a lot of crying on her shoulders, in spite of the fact that she had lost her daughter when I lost my wife.

I knocked at the flat door. Mi-Ling opened the door. Her face lit up when she saw me, then switched to puzzlement. "Papa," she said, hugging me. "Where is Mummy Marie?"

Victoria came to see who was at the door. The fact that I was back from the honeymoon early and Marie was not with me caused color to drain from Victoria's face. I prepared to answer Victoria's unvoiced question and Mi-Ling's voiced one. Fortunately, to circumvent delivering the bad news yet again later, Libby joined us, carrying a great mug of cocoa, and we all sat together in the front room. I sat on the couch with my arms around a daughter on each side. Victoria slipped into Adrian's comfortable recliner across from us and sat forward, waiting for the news that she really didn't want to hear. I shared the facts with my three listeners. They all knew about Reynolds and I could see Libby getting angry. I didn't blame her. Reynolds' actions had led to the death of Libby's father, Nantucket sea captain Caleb Bryant—who had no doubt once been an honorable man. The girls wanted to go with me to rescue Marie. When I explained to them gently that they were still a bit too young for time travel, they wanted to leave Adrian and Victoria's flat and come home with me.

"Someone will need to put Papa's cornflakes in a bowl," Mi-Ling reasoned.

"And make him cocoa in the morning," Libby augmented.

Back at our place, the girls sat with me. "Mummy Marie would want you to get some sleep," Mi-Ling said. "She would be giving me a telling off for keeping you awake."

I got a kiss on both cheeks from my two girls. They left me to go get ready for bed. I sat by the dying embers of the fire and cried…cried for Marie, and for me, and for the girls. Both Mi-Ling and Libby had looked forward to having a real mother. Both were reaching the age where a mother could instruct them on important topics about which I—as a man—was ignorant. Would I ever see

Marie again? It seemed impossible, yet I had seen God do many miracles both inside and outside the heart.

Mi-Ling came back to the room and sat on the couch beside me. She gently slipped her arm around my shoulders and stifled my sobs. "It's alright, Papa. Mi-Ling is here and loves you. Sleep and rest. There, there, there."

My lovely petite daughter cradled my head against her shoulder. I drifted off to sleep with my daughter's arm around me and her gentle, soft, soothing voice—like a whisper of her heart—repeating, "There, there. I'm here. Rest, my Papa."

* * *

"Major," the voice over the intercom said. "Would you join us in Briefing Room One in thirty minutes? The rest of the team is arriving."

By the time I reached the briefing room, the Vanguard Alpha team was fully assembled. They had come from various ages and times, but worked well as a team and were completely loyal to each other and completely capable and trustworthy. We all hated Reynolds' organization, PATCH, for its many attempts to change history for evil purposes that would not be apparent until years later. PATCH operatives were time travel terrorists. If people outside Vanguard knew some of what PATCH had planned, they would have been petrified with fear. Thankfully, we at Vanguard had so far always succeeded in stopping PATCH. To be afraid of PATCH was wise—not wasted emotion.

Meryl was the first to speak. She had helped recruit me into Vanguard. In fact, we had fallen in love and would have been married had she not met a Native American named Kitchi in a time travel adventure I now thought of as *The Scent of Home*. To Kitchi we owed much, for he was an expert tracker and had helped us find Mi-Ling and Meryl when they had been kidnapped. Funny thing…although Meryl had broken off our engagement and gone to live in 1759 with Kitchi, she had never given me back the engagement ring I had bought her. Probably just an oversight. Time traveling is a dangerous business with unexpected events that can easily rob one's memory, if not his or her life!

"Drew," Meryl said sincerely. "I am so sorry about what's happened to Marie. I want to help you get your wife back." I nodded to my lovely blonde-haired, blue-eyed time traveling companion. What is it Kitchi called her? *She with Sun in Her Hair.*

"Major," said Hera, who had been rescued from a 1st century Roman gladiator arena. "I pledge my sword and my heart to get back the woman you love." Hera was the kind of girl you wanted to have watch your back in a fight. I had seen her fight and win when she was greatly outnumbered. Hera practiced every day against skilled opponents and using different swords. She had never lost.

Sebastian was a slave from 1863. We rescued him on a visit to Gettysburg during the battle. He had proven his worth many times over. Sebastian pounded me on the back in his usual unaffected greeting. "Major, you shore nuff got my backing. Let's go!" He looked around the room at the others. "What are y'all waiting for? We've got to get this man's wife back."

Anton Devranov was a Russian from 1867. He had the Russian poetic soul and loved the company of beautiful women, who also seemed to like him. He was a great guy in times of trouble or when there was diplomatic work to do. He also was a fountain of *Old Russian Sayings*.

There was a younger girl at the table. She must have been new to the organization, because I hadn't met her before. If I had, I would have remembered. She was tall and lithe with long auburn hair flowing over her shoulders like a fountain splashing in a breeze and bright blue eyes that seemed to notice everything. She looked wise and scholarly in spite of her obvious youth.

Colonel Carlisle motioned to her. "Major, the young lady is Jayne Grewer. Jaguar to her friends. Her story is most interesting. She discovered another way of time travel. Through a trip she and her friends made to 6th Century Byzantium, we learned that there have been Monks time traveling since the 6th Century. She is our newest operative and already has a dangerous mission under her belt. She can think on her feet when presented with a difficult situation."

I remembered having heard snatches of conversation about Jayne. "So you are Jaguar?" I crossed the room to shake her slender hand, noticing the long tapered fingers and the sensible unpainted fingernails. "Glad to meet you. Good to have you on board."

"Mike Argo is busy with unfinished business," the colonel explained when I noted his absence. Mike was a Marine Commando and Kendo expert. He and Hera had shared the same wedding ceremony as Marie and I, turning it into a double event. I was rather surprised that Hera was at HQ without Mike. Like Marie and I, they were newlyweds. I wondered if they had even managed a honeymoon before being interrupted by urgent business—my urgent business of a kidnapped wife.

Colonel Carlisle coughed and everyone stopped talking. "We are all very sorry about what happened to Marie Faulkner, and we want to get her back. To get her back, we need to catch Reynolds and make him talk."

Hera said in her dark brown voice, "I volunteer to assist in making him talk." That might not have sounded like much of a threat to those who didn't know Hera, but if I were the object of that threat I would be heading for the hills in Australia.

The colonel hid a smile and continued. "This parcel came this morning. Inside was this drawing of a flower." He passed the drawing around the room. "Anyone know what kind of flower this is, or what it might mean?"

We looked. No one spoke at first. Then Jayne said in a soft voice, "I think it's a violet, sir. Where was the packet posted?"

The colonel read the address. "Braine-l'Alleud, Belgique. Our address is hand written in almost copperplate writing." As the colonel turned the package around to show us the writing, something small dropped to the floor. On closer inspection, it appeared to be crafted from some kind of ceramic material and resembled an insect.

Anton observed, "I think it is a bee. The kind that makes honey."

The colonel hung his head and sighed. "Reynolds is teasing us. He knows we will come after Marie, but he prefers to give us clues than to tell us where she is."

"Sir," Jayne asked. "What is his real reason for doing this? Is it just to get back at Major Faulkner? Or are we are so tied up with responding to the bait that we miss his real intent? He has all time and history to hide Marie, but if we go off on the wrong trail, he will just wait and let us suffer in our agony and frustration. It seems that he wants to show us that his intelligence surpasses those of us at Vanguard."

I smiled at Jayne in agreement. "You are voicing the same opinion my uncle did yesterday, Jaguar. Professor Adrian Conroy is my uncle. Reynolds needs Marie alive." Then I turned to Colonel Carlisle. "Sir, does Marie look like any historical character? Could we not run her picture through our data banks of photographs and paintings and see if any matches come out?"

Uncle Adrian slipped into the room just in time to hear my question. "Drew, my boy. I can get onto that pretty quickly, but the results will all depend on who we have in our files."

"Okay, people," the colonel said. "No one wants to sit still. I know that. We are of one heart and mind to rescue Drew's wife and get her back to him as quickly as possible. But Jayne is right: Reynolds has all of history at his fingertips to use as a hiding place for Marie. So, for now, we wait and see if there are any results. This is not the first time that PATCH has tried to use doubles, or doppelgangers, or people surgically altered."

His words reminded me of General Robert E. Lee's double in what I now thought of as *The Scent of Home*. I felt a momentary pang as I remembered that it was in following the scent of home that Meryl had found her home in Kitchi. "Stay available," the colonel concluded, "until Professor Conroy and his team get back to us. Dismissed."

Hera, particularly, looked disappointed. She was always ready for action and righting wrongs.

The colonel turned to me. "Major, I am sorry this is moving so slowly, but we don't want to go off in the wrong direction. Please be careful. I wouldn't put it past Reynolds to come up with some dangerous scheme—especially if he blames you for Bryant's death. We will help you keep a close watch on the girls."

"Thank you, sir," I replied dispiritedly. "I'm trying to trust Marie to God, but it's hard. I miss her so much that I feel as if I've ripped in two. In actual fact, I feel numb. I want to see this through, and with all due respect, sir, before you ask…no! I don't want to leave this to the others."

With the danger alert high, Mi-Ling and Libby were immediately sent back to Adrian and Victoria's flat. I was advised to follow when I left HQ. We would all bunk there together because it offered maximum protection. If it hadn't been for the girls, I don't think protection would have been a priority for me. With Marie gone, I kept getting the sinking feeling that there was nothing left worth living for. When I got back to the flat, Libby was lying on the couch with a book on her knees.

That's when one of these God-incidences happened. I sat by the kitchen table trying to work things out. It's true that sometimes you can't see the forest for the trees—or even the twigs.

"Father," Libby said.

"Yes, kitten?"

"Mummy Marie's picture is in this book."

I only half-heard what Libby said, but I got up and went to look at the book she held. It was about Emperor Napoleon I of France. When I looked at the picture, I finally realized it was not my Marie—but I had to look two or three times to be sure. The caption underneath read, *Marie, Countess Walewska, 1789-1817*. She had been Napoleon's mistress and had borne him a son, Alexandre Florian Joseph, in 1810.

"Good work," I told Libby. "The resemblance is remarkable. Do you know if Napoleon had a favorite flower or was known by a flower? Is that in your book?"

"Yes," Libby replied without the slightest hesitation. "The violet, a pretty flower, but it always looks so sad. When Mr. Reynolds used to come to Papa's ship, he would bring me a bunch of violets. The flowers were nice, but I got nervous when he gave them to me because he had funny eyes. Creepy, as if they could turn you to stone."

"Kitten, does it say in your book if Napoleon had some kind of an emblem or something he was known by? You know, like *Snoopy* from *Peanuts*. When you think of Snoopy, you think of his doghouse. Was it a bee that people knew Napoleon by?"

"Yes," she said in excitement. Her head nodding up and down gave her dark curls a life of their own as she searched through the book for the right picture. When she found the picture, I nearly cried. Tears welled up in my eyes. I pulled Libby to me and kissed her. "Thank you, daughter. I've always been proud of you and Mi-Ling, but I think what you've just found in your book might help bring Mummy Marie home."

I contacted the colonel to request a meeting. An hour later, we were all back in the briefing room. I shared the information from Libby's book. It was reinforced immediately in the computer files when Marie Walewska's picture popped up as a close match for Marie.

The colonel nodded. "And from our other research, we've learned that the postmark on the letter is from the area where Waterloo was fought on June 18, 1815."

We sat in silence, each chewing over the questions: *Why? How? For what reason?*

Anton spoke up, "Does this mean that Marie has been kidnapped and taken to Waterloo?"

"If so, what part?" Jayne asked. "There were three battles in total, but only one directly at Mount St. Jean, which is about three miles from Waterloo village."

"So we go charging in find Marie and miss why Reynolds did it in the first place?" Meryl asked.

"Remember, at Gettysburg they wanted to put in a false General Lee. We stopped them. Suppose they want to change Napoleon for a genetically modified look alike with the mind to win at Waterloo," Angus suggested.

Sebastian thought and said, "Suppose they want to kill the British General before the battle starts? Catch him off guard…then wham, or bang, and Napoleon's done got himself a big head start."

"I think we need advice from a Napoleonic expert," Colonel Carlisle said. "Someone who would welcome hands-on experience."

"You mean someone to come with us once we find where Marie is?" I asked.

Angus reflected, "Was Marie really the target from the start? If not, who is their target? Or is it both Marie and someone else? By the looks of what Reynolds has sent, Marie is where the French are."

"Which by dint of common sense is not where Wellington would be," Jayne said.

"We know," Adrian added, "that Wellington survived the battle no matter how close it may have been. Any danger to him has to be engineered by Reynolds or a couple of his stooges."

"Right, people," the colonel said. "We have a lot to think about, but from what I can see it looks like we need two teams: one to protect Wellington and one to find and rescue Marie."

"Old Russian saying," Anton offered, "*Do not open the Vodka until you lock both house doors.*"

We stared at him and he shook his head. "Wellington is the front door. Blucher is the backdoor. You have to know at which door the wolves are waiting."

Angus mused, "Anton has a good point. Take out Blucher and Wellington doesn't get the help he needs."

"Right, people," Colonel Carlisle repeated. "Think and talk it over. And get some rest. Rest is of paramount importance."

Before we could end the meeting, Sergeant Cathcart entered the room, saluted, and handed the colonel a note. "Beg pardon, sir, but this was handed in at the gate by a young lady on horseback. If I am not mistaken, she had an American accent. Said she would be back for the reply."

"Did she give you a name?" the colonel asked.

"Elouise, sir, and very pretty she was, too." Cathcart saluted and left. The colonel read the note, then handed it to me as the others were leaving.

I read it.

Capitaine Antoine Métier 12eme Regiment de Cuirassiers:

It was related to me that you planned to somehow come from the future to kill or assassinate our beloved Emperor Napoleon. Monsieur, I now know this not to be true, but the one who tricked me had me convinced that I was to go with him and have you killed in a duel. Then I learned that the lady he wishes to marry is already your wife. She will not have him while you are still alive. Therefore, you must be killed.

Major, I am a soldier of the Emperor—not an assassin hired to kill one who is only trying to find his wife. I believe I have somehow moved into your time and when I would not obey Reynolds' wishes, I was told I would be kept here and put on trial to be judged by the new empire, the new government called PATCH. I have given back the gold I took from him (I had debts of honor to fulfil). Now I ask as one soldier to another for your help to get me back to 17 June 1815. I know where your wife is, Major. I also know her name is Marie Waleska, but she insists it is Marie Faulkner. I can take you to where she was the last time I saw her. She is well, but her heart is shattered. She has been told you abandoned her in Rome just before your wedding night. She cannot believe you would do such a thing, and neither can I. I have seen her, Monsieur, and to abandon such a beautiful woman on her wedding night would make you heartless and cold.

Monsieur, get me back to live or die with my regiment at Mount St. Jean, back to my Emperor and my France. I will take you to her though there may be danger, but what is that to us, my comrade in arms?

The one who brought you this letter is a friend: she knows where I am hiding and I give you my word that what I speak is the truth. Send your reply by the young woman, Elouise, who is my traveling companion. Although we are not lovers, she enjoys my protection.

I have done something shameful and been made foolish. At least I can wipe my name clean and, as you English say, wash the slate. Send me your reply tomorrow.

Vive L'Empereur–Antoine Métier

So Reynolds had put a contract on me based on a lie. Would it twig with Marie who her 'suitor' was? A night's sleep would help alleviate the deep pain and despair that impaled me so cruelly that I gasped at times for no apparent reason. The doctor gave me something to assist me. The girls thought I needed rest, as well. The following morning after Mi-Ling made sure I had eaten enough breakfast, I met with the Colonel and Anton.

"Well, it looks like we have his attention and have maybe even found his

Achilles' heel," the colonel said.

"Yes, sir," I replied, "so I do believe. But do you realize that every time I get a girlfriend or wife, someone else comes along to take her? I'm getting a bit fed up with that. Anton, what do you think about this?" I passed the letter to him.

"You sound petulant, brother. Old Russian saying: *From a distance a wolf can look like a dog. It is only close up you feel the teeth.* In Russia, we have big wolves."

"What do you mean, Anton?" the colonel asked.

"Either he is a genuine French officer from Napoleon's time, or he is lying to us. Marie is the bait if Reynolds is after Drew. He has control of one of the three people in the world Drew really cares about."

"Sir," I said, "I've got to try. This is all we have."

"I'm willing to help," Anton chimed in. "I speak good French, probably better than their Russian."

"Reply to him," the colonel instructed me, "and meet as he suggested along with the young lady. Mention there may be a couple of other people there, but better not say that Anton is Russian. I hope your French is up to it, Major."

I had been doing a computer revision course in my spare time...but I hadn't had much spare time. "Sometimes we have to take risks, sir." I pointed out.

"Tell me about it," the colonel replied, running a hand through his hair and groaning.

Elouise would soon return for the answer. I hoped she was not being followed. Sergeant Cathcart was the only one who had seen her, so he would have to alert me when she arrived.

Meanwhile, it was decided that for the mission to rescue Marie, Meryl, Jayne, and Hera would travel ahead of us. Their job was to concentrate on protecting Wellington in Brussels and at the village of Waterloo. Where the rest of us went would depend on what Capitaine Métier said.

I met Meryl in the canteen. "Drew, I'm so sorry you're going through all this. You must be missing Marie terribly."

I took her hand and the words of the Abba song came to my mind... *you and I can share the silence finding comfort together the way old friends do.*

"Meryl, I just don't care anymore. I am empty without Marie. If anything happens to her I think I would crack up."

She squeezed my hand. "Drew, quit blaming yourself. And don't tell me you're not; I know you too well to believe that lie. I think if I saw Reynolds I would kill him. He has left an unending trail of misery and unhappiness. And for what? For his ego: *I am right and you are all a bunch of peasants in comparison to me.* Drew, I can't give you any more comfort than just friendship. We both know that would be wrong. I would have to face Kitchi and you would have to face Marie."

I sighed. The scent of coconut from her hair was getting a bit too close for comfort. It made me think of the love we had shared so passionately and eagerly in the past. But she was right. The past had ended long ago.

"Drew, we've through bad situations before."

I nodded in reply. Mi-Ling's face surfaced in my mind. We had taken her safely to Jesus for healing just in time after all medical remedies in our time and place had been exhausted. "*The Scent of Eternity.*" I mumbled.

Meryl looked at me, puzzled. "Drew, just get the letter written and leave it with Sergeant Cathcart. Then pray." She kissed my forehead lightly and I inhaled deeply of the fragrance that was exclusively Meryl. "You know all of us at Vanguard are working to help you get Marie back so you can get your long overdue honeymoon. That should knock your blood pressure down a bit! All this will seem a distant dream someday soon, my friend."

I kissed her cheek, then headed off to write my reply and check on Mi-Ling and Libby. Abba still played through my mind…*the way old friends do.*

I drafted the reply to the letter in my best copperplate handwriting and gave it to Sergeant Cathcart, who seemed to need little sleep. I found Libby and Mi-Ling playing *Scrabble*. They let me pick a rack of tiles. We had fun arguing over American spelling, and when we totted up the score, Libby won. Mi-Ling quickly got over her disappointment that we had not allowed her to use English versions of Chinese words. "I would have beat you and Papa with my words," she told Libby. Then she hugged her. "But I'm glad you won, sister."

The girls wanted to play another round, but we were interrupted by a brisk knock on the door.

"Major, sorry for disturbing you, sir," Sergeant Cathcart said, "but there are two people at the gate. One is the young lady what brought the letter. The other is a tall gentleman on horseback covered with a light blue cloak. He is fearsome-looking cove, sir, if you don't mind me saying so."

"Thank you, sergeant. Please stable the horses for them and show our guests into Room One. Then inform the colonel and the others. Oh, and get Lieutenant Meryl to meet with the young lady. She may need a chaperone."

The colonel contacted me almost immediately and requested that I come to his office before going to see our guests. When I got there, I was met by a tall man in his late thirties.

"Major," Colonel Carlisle said, "let me introduce Professor Jude Savant, the Napoleonic historian."

I nodded and shook hands with him. Professor Savant was well known for his programs about the Napoleonic Wars. He made the subject come alive. He was fluent in French, even the French of Napoleon's time. There had been Germans at Waterloo, too, and Savant also spoke German, Russian and Spanish.

"I am amazed at the possibility of going to Waterloo in 1815," Jude Savant told us eagerly. "It will be fantastic to be able to see what happens—even just a small part of it. I am still trying to wrap my mind around time travel."

I smiled at his eagerness. "It happens, and it generally doesn't turn out the way you think it will," I told him.

"I am sorry about your wife, Major, and I will do anything to help to try to get her back from 1815." Then he said under his breath, "1815, who could believe it?"

"With due respect, Professor Savant, the first thing you will notice about time travel is the need for staying alive. Staying alive needs to get your full attention, closely followed by watching what you eat. I hope you can load and fire a musket and pistol and use a sword? Sometimes historical characters are not kind to those who are just learning."

"Understood, Major."

"Now," I told him, "We are about to meet a real Cuirassier from 1815. He's very much alive and well. His desire is to get back to the battle of Waterloo. Of course, he doesn't know the result and he must not. That's another paramount rule of time travel: we can do nothing to change the past. That includes giving away the ending before the beginning."

"I understand," Savant replied. "Mum's the word, or in this case, Maman."

"Right," Colonel Carlisle said, breaking into the conversation. "Let's go and meet our guests and the rest of the team."

We entered Room One. Savant's eyes popped open so widely that they rose up and nearly touched his bushy eyebrows. He exclaimed in French, "A real live Cuirassier."

CHAPTER TWO

History Comes Alive

"I'm glad to see you well, Capitaine," Savant managed, in spite of his obvious amazement.

Métier replied in English, "I have found that being alive is infinitely preferable to the alternative. Capitaine Métier at your service." The huge man bowed gracefully.

Fight a duel with this guy? I thought. *I wouldn't have a snowball's chance! With guys like this on the French side, how in the blazes did we win at Waterloo?*

"I present to you my traveling companion Mademoiselle Elouise Leppard," Métier said, motioning to a stunningly beautiful woman.

"*Enchante, messieurs,*" she said.

The size of Capitaine Métier was impressive, but the sight of Elouise Leppard took my breath away. Her astonishing beauty exceeded adjectives I had in my repertoire to describe her. It was an effort to get a grip on myself.

"I'm sorry you've been caught up in this trial, Mademoiselle," I told her. "We hope to get you back as quickly as possible."

It's a good thing I had spoken quickly, because when she turned and looked directly at me, words froze in my throat. Her violet-colored eyes sent me to another planet and it took all my effort to return to reality. When she lowered the hood of her cape, corn-colored hair flowed around her head like a dream. I noticed that Anton seemed unable to take his eyes off her. It was hard to tell what Angus McTurk thought. He was unusually silent. Because he and I were such close friends, the ordeal I was going through with my kidnapped wife had hit him hard. His sympathy was almost concrete.

Meryl, who had been standing next to Elouise, frowned slightly and said, "I'm going to get Elouise some food and show her where she can freshen up. Showers will be a new experience for her."

"Of course," the colonel said. "Quite right." But he, like the rest of us, continued to stare at Elouise.

I couldn't speak at all.

"Thank you for taking care of Mistral, my palfrey," Elouise added with a slight curtsy. "It has been a long ride. She, too, needs to rest." When Elouise left with Meryl, it was like seeing the last swallow of summer depart.

"Well," the colonel said to Capitaine Métier. "We better get you something to eat and drink and...er, a bath."

Métier took off his breastplate, which was part of his protective covering, and dropped his sword and pistols on the table. He laid his helmet beside them. "I need to get back to my regiment before I am missed. You can put me back at the right time, major, and I will show you where your wife is."

"We will do our best to get you back," I assured him, "but we must also go to Mount St. Jean on an undercover mission. We know how the battle ends, Capitaine, but my wife being there was not part of the original history."

Métier slumped into chair and speared us with a fierce look. "Answer me one question, just one. Is the emperor killed in the battle?"

"No, Capitaine," General Carlisle replied. "Napoleon survives the battle. The man who brought you here to this time is cruel and dangerous. He was going to leave you here 200 years after the battle. Away from your country and your family. You would have been labeled as one who fled before the battle. He would have made you look like a coward when that is most certainly not true. We will get you back. What you do in the battle will be dictated by real history. All we want is the major's wife back safely. We also must make sure the battle finishes according to recorded history."

"It is how France finishes. That is what is important," he replied.

"France is a democratic republic," Carlisle assured him. "Liberty, equality, and fraternity still apply."

Métier smiled and said, "Perhaps I could have some food, sleep, and a bath before we go back...if that will still get us there on time."

"I have an idea where things are now," Savant interjected, "and it would be a good opportunity to ask some questions about the revolution and life in Napoleon's Army. Stuff like this for a historian like me does not even come along once in a lifetime." He addressed Métier and explained, "I am a historian. Maybe we can share a bottle of wine? And you can answer my questions?"

"Vodka," Anton murmured to himself. "Russian vodka is always the best."

Métier grinned. "Back in my time, some asked too many questions and ended up at the guillotine." He made a gesture across his throat, then inclined his head at Savant. "As your name is French, you may ask away."

As they were leaving together, Savant said something to Métier. Métier responded, "In Russia it was so cold in 1812 that it froze your bones and your words. The poor horses, they went into Russia stallions and came out geldings...." The two walked out together, with Savant soaking up every word. I wondered how he would succeed when we actually got to 1815.

Anton was nodding as if he, too, had experienced that severe a degree of cold. I wondered if he would pop up with one of his 'Old Russian Saying' remarks, but he remained quiet and thoughtful. I wondered if he, too, felt my grief at having lost Marie. Angus still had not moved from his perch on the edge of Colonel Carlisle's desk, although his eyes had roamed the room and scrutinized the occupants.

Adrian Conroy joined us. "We hate to burden you down with kit, but here's one extra bauble. The girls have theirs. These are not just watches: they are fob watches. Only ladies wore wrist watches back then. What happens if you are in a hurry to get home and you can't find the time car control unit? You are stuck unless you're lucky. These watches ..." he indicated a small button in the back, "will send out a signal to the time car unit, causing it to flash and emit a whine." He produced a unit and put it at the other side of the room, then pressed the button. Sure enough, it began to glow and emit an annoying whine. "Press the button twice more," he directed, "and it will stop. Though who knows how far this can be heard in the noise of battle? You will get to field test that, so to speak."

"What is the range of this?" Anton asked with interest.

Professor Conroy thought. "Hmm...about 500 meters for the light and about 750 for the sound. We thought it might be useful."

Anton responded with an eager nod. "I have the same effect on beautiful women. When they see me, they light up and make beautiful noise."

"Sounds good," Angus responded, ignoring Anton's comment and dream-like trance. "We have been fortunate so far not to lose a unit or have one stolen."

Now that Meryl, Elouise, and Métier had left, we sat around a table. Colonel Carlisle produced folders, handing one to each of us. "You will be on horseback," he directed, "members of the Elite Gendarmes. Joseph Fouche was their boss and chief of police, so the scrolls in your folders are passes signed by him. They should open doors. The paper has been treated to make it waterproof. The acquisition department of Vanguard did well."

"Interesting sounding department," Anton said. "I have quite a few friends with irons in various fires. But this I know of Fouche—he was a dangerous man. If any of our operatives get caught, they could lose their lives."

The colonel lowered his head and sighed deeply. "They did. One was my nephew Peter, but he got these out to us before he was apprehended."

We were all shocked at the colonel's words and made ineffective attempts at sympathy. Meryl returned and immediately picked up on the air of sadness. "What's happened?" she asked in alarm. "Somebody has been killed, haven't they?"

The colonel looked up at Meryl, which gave me a view of his profile and the unshed tears sitting heavily on the rim of his eyes.

"My nephew, Peter," Colonel Carlisle explained.

Meryl was visibly shocked. Being a woman, she did something that none of the rest of us had felt comfortable doing. She crossed over to Carlisle and hugged him tightly. "I'm so sorry, Colonel," she whispered, blinking back the tears in her own eyes.

The colonel straightened in his chair. "Gentlemen, could we continue this in the morning? I fear it's late and a lot has happened today. Take your files with you and familiarize yourselves with them."

The colonel looked tired. I could read the look Meryl sent me over the top of his head. *Drew, you and the others leave. He needs rest. I will tell his wife.*

Meryl's look proved as effective as words. We all rose to leave, stopping to pat the colonel's shoulder somewhat awkwardly. He dropped his head into his hands. Meryl slipped her arms around his shoulders and rubbed his back. It gave me the impression of a daughter helping her father in the middle of a troubled dream. I could imagine Mi-Ling doing the same for me.

All of us loved Colonel Carlisle. He had done so much for us. His sacrifice and care for us over the years had been nothing short of miraculous and amazing. He had woven all of us with our different weaknesses, strengths, and personalities, into a tightly knit family. He was quick to correct us when he thought we were wrong, which had often saved lives and engineered successful missions. This was our chance to make this mission work to rescue Marie, but equally as a dedication to Peter's memory.

As I was walking back to my room, I met Clarissa Carlisle on the way to see to her husband.

"Mrs. Carlisle, I left Meryl Scott watching over the colonel. I hope you don't mind."

I had not seen much of the colonel's wife, but her support of her husband was evident in her face and body language. Then she hit me with a bombshell. "Me, mind? Why should I mind a daughter looking after her father?"

She laughed at the shock registered on my face.

"You could not possibly know, could you, Drew? I'm John's second wife. Meryl has a middle name—Carlisle—which somehow got left off the birth certificate. Her mother stole her away from John after the divorce was finalized, then abandoned her. John didn't know where Meryl was and didn't find her until years later. Scott is the last name of her adopted parents. By the time John discovered where his daughter was, she was so happy with the Scotts that he thought it would be heartless to try to get her back and rip her out of the arms of the only parents she had ever known. It was John who helped and supported Meryl in her fencing career and paid for her education. Her adoptive parents couldn't afford the additional expenses—but they were never short on love. Meryl has no idea that John is her father, or about what he has done for her. It's probably been better that way. He loves her dearly and is always glad to see her back from a mission, but he tries to treat her no differently than any of the other operatives. You must know, Drew, it's not just a job to John—he loves all of you. It takes a lot of courage to send the one you love the most into danger." She looked at me in a kind of motherly way and put her hand on my arm. "I had better give you time to let that information sink in. And Meryl must be tired. She's been helping the new woman who just showed up here—Elousie, I believe her name is. Drew, please don't give the show away unless it's absolutely necessary. It's only fair that John has a chance to tell his daughter himself."

I sighed and nodded. Feeling somewhat ashamed, I said, "I really wanted it to work with Meryl and me but...well, it didn't happen. I really loved her. I suppose in a way I always will."

Clarissa smiled. "Then Kitchi happened, and you know the first rule of time travel; *expect the unexpected*. It is fine making rules until they affect you."

"You are very wise, Mrs. Carlisle. You remind me of Lady Constance Gray, the wife of the British ambassador in Foo-Chow back in 1867. She couldn't be your sister, yet you are very like her."

Clarissa smiled the perfect enigmatic smile and laughed softly. "Remember the first rule of time travel, *expect the unexpected*, does not apply only to pretty young girls. Good day to you, Major. I must go and tend to John."

God has a sense of humor, I realized. Lady Constance and her husband Sir

Charles Gray had helped me so much during *The Scent of Time* tea race between China and London in 1867. Their love for Jesus Christ had been part of their lives. They had given me confidence and a belief that with God nothing was impossible. I had always since found that to be true even though some of the roads on the journey had been scary, fraught with danger and filled with close escapes from death.

I hurried, eager to see the girls, who were safely installed in Victoria's flat. After the barrage of hugs from Mi-Ling and slightly more restrained ones from Libby, Victoria brought us hot chocolate and cookies. We sat cross-legged by the fire. Mi-Ling snuggled up to me and then came one of these moments in your life that bypass everything else and hit you right in your heart. "Daddy, thank you."

"Sweetheart, I haven't given you anything. Why are you thanking me?"

The look in her eyes said, *One day, Daddy, you will understand.* "Uncle Anton said Old Russian saying. *The most important gifts are those not brought with money.* Like the things Father God gives us. He gave me you."

Why do your eyes seem to leak at the most awkward times? I asked myself. Mi-Ling looked at Libby who was sitting slightly apart from us with a book. Libby loved reading. It was funny, but history books seemed to be her favorites.

"Come on, sister. Daddy's arms are big enough for both of us." It might have been imagination, but I could swear that at that moment I saw Jesus. He was smiling.

Libby looked up from her book hesitantly. Mi-Ling looked into my eyes and indicated Libby with a nearly imperceptible nod of her head.

"Libby," I said gently. "I might not be the best father. I make mistakes. I get things wrong. Sometimes I even get nervous around people I love. But even so, with all of my flaws, would you consider letting me...."

The blackbird's nest of curls bobbed up and down enthusiastically. "I accept! You can adopt me! Yes! I would like that most above all things." Then she tossed her book to the side and joined Mi-Ling and me in a group hug.

So there I was with two adopted daughters, both 150 years older than me, and to each of whom I owed my life. Well, what was the first rule of time travel? *Expect the unexpected.*

With the cover of the book facing up, I noticed that Libby's book was a history of Napoleon. She saw me looking at it. "Father, the man who came to the Allegheny, my first father's ship, he mentioned a place that is in this book. Look." She opened the book and pointed to Plancenoit.

"Are you sure?" I asked.

"Yes," she said with assurance. "It took me while to learn to say it properly."

I had done a bit of enquiry about Waterloo. Plancenoit was one of the most well-documented battles. It had been total carnage, which made me shudder when I realized that Marie might at this moment be trapped in a deadly event. What was Reynolds thinking? Did he even know how dangerous it was? Yet, his plan was apparently to get us to come and search for her. Why had he sent such nebulous clues and no specifics? Did he want to kill or kidnap Wellington, or was he after Napoleon? Maybe even to introduce a genetically altered look-alike that made none of the mistakes the emperor had made on those fateful three days of battle.

"Come on, you two. Teeth and bed. You don't want bags under your eyes from no sleep."

Mi-Ling hugged me. "Don't worry, Papa. Soon it will be hugs for you and Mummy Marie, too."

Libby followed Mi-Ling's example and hugged me gladly.

"Don't worry," I told both girls, "it will be alright. I love you both. God bless."

It was funny, but all my life I had wanted to be free. But since these two came into my life, I was beginning to realize what freedom meant, and it wasn't at all what I had always thought.

* * *

The following morning Capitaine Métier decided that he would like a long lie-in. He had eaten quite a bit for breakfast—in fact, it looked as if he had not seen food since 1812 in Moscow. The rest of the team met to discuss our next move.

"Libby recognized that Reynolds had mentioned Plancenoit to Bryant several times," I told them. "That might be where he's hiding Marie. Marie looks like the paintings of Napoleon's mistress, Marie Walewska."

"You can't all go," Colonel Carlisle said.

It was Meryl who first noticed the change in the colonel's uniform—from Colonel to Lieutenant General. "Congratulations on your promotion, sir, we are all very proud of you."

"Thank you," he replied in his usual humble manner.

"A general needs to know how to handle a sword," Hera ventured. "I am willing to teach you, sir."

The general smiled. "Thank you, Hera. I will give it my utmost thought."

I wonder if Meryl has been teaching her dad swordsmanship? I thought, remembering that she was a fencing expert.

"I propose we split into two teams," Carlisle told us. "One to go to Waterloo and the Duchess of Richmond's Ball to protect Wellington, and the other to the dangerous part at Placenoit."

Anton took a deep breath and said, "Sir, I happily volunteer to go to the ball. After all, one of these beautiful women may try to harm the duke. I will do my best to restrain her from so doing. A smile from me has been known to disarm a beautiful woman—in fact, several at one time."

We all grinned and the general continued, "Thank you, Anton. Your willingness to make such a sacrifice is noted. But just now, we need your other talents, including your expertise in French."

Anton shrugged his shoulders. "The spirit of sacrifice is part of the Russian character, sir."

"Professor Savant, I have no doubt, would like to go to Plancenoit. I propose sending him there along with Major Faulkner, Lieutenant McTurk, and Anton. Then the ladies can go to Waterloo. Meryl, you will lead. Hera and Jayne will go with you. There will be a separate briefing for you. There will be back-up from Sebastian. He is perfecting his coach driving skills just now. The details are in your files."

Professor Savant remarked, "I am due some leave from Texas A&M University. I can see the Aggies charging at Waterloo—had they been around then. This will be a wonderful experience! Any knowledge I have is at Vanguard's disposal. All I can say is that I hope we come through the challenge. Hands-on history! Who would have believed it?"

"We broke down in 1757 once," I told Professor Savant. "It didn't look as if we were going to get back. Then we found some crude Kairon and made it back by the skin of our time-traveling teeth."

"I suppose it would be alright living in 1815," Jayne speculated, "but I don't fancy the dentistry from then very much."

"Hmm," said Professor Savant. "The teeth of many of the bodies at Waterloo became a source of false teeth after the battle."

The general coughed. "I hate to interrupt this fascinating history lesson, but let's concentrate on getting you there and back."

Elouise had been quiet. "Will I get to go to Plancenoit? I have a feeling my brother's regiment will be there. I've come a long way to find him."

"We will do our best to reunite you with your brother, dear lady," Anton promised.

"Professor Savant," the general said. "We have an unwritten rule in time travel—*nobody gets left behind*. I will expect you to help if any of my people should get into trouble."

"Of course! It is a bit like the motto of the Dumas book, *The Three Musketeers—all for one and one for all*," Professor Savant agreed.

"Let's hope there is no Lady de Winter," Jayne said softly.

"Apart from Meryl, Jayne, and Hera, you get to take horses with you. I am tempted to say, if you see Reynolds, shoot first and don't bother with the paperwork. However, one of you reminded me that unless there is a clear and valid reason for assassination, carrying it out makes us no different from PATCH."

Hera asked thoughtfully, "If we see him, could we not have a gun go off accidentally?"

We smiled in amusement at Hera's idea, but nodded in agreement with Carlisle. For my own part, I had learned by now that if one did not do things the right way—God would not provide His blessings. Still, the thought of a *time drone* passed through my mind. Sadly, there would be no way to control it from one-time era to another.

"You go by horse, as you know, so it is good you have kept your riding skills up. You will probably meet Reynolds' men. We can risk a Glock and maybe a few grenades. Also some explosive charges for opening doors when the fellow on the other side doesn't want to let you in. Any questions so far?"

There were none and he continued. "I think that if Reynolds is in with the French, he will want to appear as normal as possible—not too far out of the ordinary. As Elite Gendarmes, and armed with passes from Chief of Police Fouché, you can go pretty well where you need to."

Professor Savant said, "That should get us past the problem of the Gendarmes' Commander Capitaine Dyonnet. He was supposed to be a tough customer."

The general continued, "You and your horses will transport together. If there are Prussians where you come out, I suggest you come back. Professor Savant will be able to tell you who is friend and who is foe."

Anton responded, "Old Russian saying: *He who shoots at you, it is normally because he is out of vodka*."

Elouise laughed and asked, "Is he normally this humorous?"

Anton put on serious face. "No, dear lady. Only on a Tuesday and Thursday—and today, sadly, is Wednesday."

Métier said, "I will show you the building where Marie is being held. How you get her out I leave to your expertise."

"What about Elouise?" I asked.

Professor Savant replied, "She can name her brother's rank and regiment. In their eyes, she is one of theirs. She should be safe, at least from the French."

Elouise produced two small flintlock pistols from her dress, as if to further assure us of her ability to stay alive.

Hera looked at the guns and said, "You should take a dagger with you. Your weapons can be affected by rain, but you can kill with a dagger whether it is raining or not."

We were dismissed so we could finish our preparations. Out in the hall, Meryl spoke to me. "Drew, be careful. Guard your heart with Elouise."

I shrugged my shoulders. "She just needs help. That's all there is to it."

"It's the way you look at her. I remember you used to look at me like that."

"No," I countered, trying not to be angry. "I'm just concerned that she finds her brother."

"Just words of care," Meryl replied, "from an old flame who doesn't want to see you get burned again."

"We get the two of them linked up and the job is done," I said. "Simple. Look, I miss Marie. I'm not looking for or at anyone else. How would you like to start out on honeymoon and have your new spouse evaporate? And, don't forget; this is the second marriage for me that ended before we could even get to bed together."

She shook her head. "How do you think Marie is feeling? What do you think that pig Reynolds is telling her? She is alone and afraid, and Reynolds is no doubt chipping away at her self-confidence. Having been blind for so long before she recovered her sight, I'm sure her self-confidence is shaky at best. Three other people are risking their lives to help you get your wife back. You can at least stop thinking 'poor me' and try to put yourself in Marie's place. All of us want to see Reynolds stopped. We're going to Waterloo to protect Wellington. Angus, Anton, and Savant are going to help you rescue Marie."

Oh, hang it all! Why did Meryl have to be so right? I had forgotten what Marie must be going through. I *had* been feeling sorry for myself, forgetting that there were two people concerned in a missed honeymoon.

"Drew, help Elouise find her brother if you can. Then let her go."

I nodded my head. "You're right. I was losing the plot. I'm married to Marie and she's the other half of the missed honeymoon—and heaven forbid whatever else might be happening to her in the meantime."

Meryl smiled at me. "Drew, I know you. I know that you once you get back with Marie, you will become an insufferable man. It will be, 'Marie said this,' or 'Marie said that,' or Marie did this, or brought this.' And you will go around holding hands and kissing often, scared to let each other go. And we who are your friends will be so happy for you both."

Capitaine Métier came clunking down the corridor in his huge boots and said he was ready to return. We would get him back to the regiment and he would take us to Marie. Then we would get Elouise to her brother, who was in the 7th Hussars, who were engaged in the battle. Her brother's first name was Guy.

"Hey, *mon ami*. Are you ready to go to a real battle? *Eh bien*, your wife must be on your mind. It is important that she learns you are alive, but that she keeps that information to herself. "Métier laughed. "It will be hard for her, will it not? She will want to rush into your arms."

"Have you ever seen Reynolds?" I asked.

"If I saw him, he would not be breathing. But we will try not to hurt him until your wife is back with you. There is something romantic about the French soul."

I noticed he was drinking from a bottle of Dr. Pepper, of all things. He waved the bottle at me. "This is good, whatever it is, but it does not taste of pepper. Now, I propose a toast to wives and sweethearts—and may they never meet. Ha!"

Mi-Ling and Libby had promised me they would get the flat tidy for Mummy Marie's homecoming. They had showered me with hugs and "I love yous." Mi-Ling had given me an envelope with Lucy's photo. Lucy had signed the back. Mi-Ling explained, "It is the only photo I have that Mummy Lucy signed. You can bring it back to me, and while you are away, you can both look after each other until you find Mummy Marie."

I hadn't looked at Lucy's picture for a long time, but when I closed my eyes it seemed like just yesterday…which in time travel terms it was. I remembered gathering her limp, blood-soaked body in my arms and holding her while the color drained from her face. She was happy in heaven and I had two girls and a wife who needed me. Yet, why had Lucy had to die? However, if I trusted God at all—I must trust Him for everything, including the tough places. And thinking about trusting God brought to mind an old Chinese saying: *A journey of a thousand miles begins with one footstep.* Our journey was about to start.

Hera was disappointed by her assignment to attend the ball at Waterloo instead of taking part in the battle. "Can I not take part in the battle after the ball finishes?" she asked.

Métier studied the former female gladiator and remarked quietly, "I am happy she is not fighting on the English side."

Meryl hugged me. "Be careful, my dear friend, you are precious to many people." She touched my lips briefly with hers, then quickly turned away. This was the first time we had gone on separate missions.

In the time car, Elouise said to me, "You must be sorry to leave that girl who kissed you behind, for she surely loves you."

I didn't try to explain, but said instead, "We are just good friends."

Elouise spoke one word in French. "*Vraiment.* Really, Major?"

"*Allons mes braves* to Waterloo. Glory awaits," Métier declared cheerfully.

CHAPTER THREE

Waterloo

Village of Plancenoit,
Battlefield of Waterloo,
June 17, 1815: about 1:30 p.m.

Capitaine Métier and I disembarked from the time car at what should be the Bois de Paris, closely followed by Anton, Angus, and Professor Savant. All we heard was birdsong and the thump of an axe against a tree. We had to be sure that we had arrived during the time when Capitaine Métier was absent. If he happened to meet himself, it could result in confusing fight of honor with dire consequences for them both. Métier had left with Reynolds at 1.20 p.m. and had found himself in Scotland at 1:30 p.m.; therefore, the current time seemed like a good bet. Probably no one had missed him yet.

One thing we had overlooked, as Professor Savant reminded us, was that although the Prussian Infantry would not arrive until about 4 p.m. on June 18, the light cavalry troops such as the hussars were a different matter. They could move fast, appear from nowhere, strike, and vanish before their target knew what had hit.

If infantry formed a square, they were generally safe. But if the cavalry caught them in a line, it was serious because they were then considered battle ready. The other thing we had to be aware of was that another task of light cavalry, or hussars, was to capture prisoners for interrogation. That could be a nasty experience for any soldier in any age, but if they captured Elouise, I shuddered to think of what would happen to her.

We formed up, putting Elouise in the center and the rest of us around her as we headed toward Plancenoit. Then, as I passed a tree, a bullet slammed into it, followed by another that whined off into the woods.

Capitaine Métier looked around and pointed. "They are Prussian Hussars.

They must be a forward patrol. Some of them may be armed with rifles and not musketoons."

First, there seemed to be about five of them, then it jumped to ten. "Savant," Métier shouted, "head for Plancenoit fast! We'll try to hold them off."

Anton said, "We will form a diamond-shaped echelon and charge." Angus nodded his agreement.

Ten-to-four odds like that have a habit of increasing, I realized. *How many of these guys are there?*

"Lean forward over your horse," Métier directed. "You will be a smaller target." Métier shouted, drawing his cavalry saber, and the odds against us instantly increased. Métier started to lead off, then whirled his horse around and ordered, "Get to the brush and trees. It will break their charge! If we charge into them, we will be killed."

I was worried about Elouise. If these Prussians caught her, she would be gang raped, probably passed around repeatedly until she died of her injuries. Savant was making heavy weather of his own horsemanship, let alone helping Elouise's palfrey. I fingered the Glock. I would shoot Elouise rather than let her get caught, because we would be overwhelmed anyway…. but I just couldn't do it. Suddenly there was a loud order from behind us, "*En avant*," followed by the rasping sound of an unknown number of sabers being drawn.

Savant got knocked off his horse. One of the Prussians grabbed the bridle of Elouise's horse. I leaped from my horse to rescue her, except that the commander of the French Hussars had seen the danger, and wow, could he shift! Two of them charged ahead of the others. The man who held Elouise's horse never knew what hit him. His mate, who tried to back him up, fell to the second Frenchman's sword. The other Prussians had seen the flood of green uniforms heading toward them and decided that discretion was the better part of valor.

Savant waited until he saw French uniforms. Then he jumped up, seemingly uninjured and unflustered.

The young capitaine rode up to Elouise, vaulted off his horse, and looked at her searchingly. "ma'moiselle, are you alright?" he asked, as the other hussar who had taken out the second enemy horseman reined in behind him.

She smiled at him. "Thank you, Capitaine, for your prompt action."

"Allow me to present myself. Capitaine Guy Leppard at your service," he said, bowing and removing his hat. Released from the cover, his fair hair blew in the breeze. "May I know the name of such a fair lady who finds herself in the middle of a battlefield?"

The color drained from Elouise's face. Tears ran down her cheeks. She tried to speak, but could only shake her head wildly.

"Oh, ma'moiselle, we must get you to our camp, but what is your name?"

"My name is Elouise," she gasped.

He smiled. "A fine name. I have a sister named Elouise…" He looked at her more closely, seeing now the rippling corn-colored hair that was much the same color as his. He fell silent.

"My second name is Leppard. Elouise Leppard."

Now the color drained from his face, as well. Elouise produced a letter from their mother. Guy walked away to read it. When he finished reading, tears tracked down his face. He dried them with his red gloves.

"Maman, is she well? How is my family?"

Elouise ran to him and put her hands on his shoulders. "Mother was well when I left, as was everyone else. Now, my brother, let me look at you." After a moment of searching each other's eyes, they fell into one another's arms, hugging and talking. There are some conversations that it would be dishonorable to repeat, and the conversation between this brave woman who had come thousands of dangerous miles to find her brother, and that same brother—a leader of men, but also her big brother—fit into that category.

Javel, Guy's second in command, who had aided him in rescuing Elouise, said, "Maybe we should get out of here in case the hussars come back with some lancer friends, Capitaine." Guy agreed, and we followed them toward their camp, Anton and Savant behind me, and Angus bringing up the rear and keeping a close watch for unexpected attacks.

Capitaine Métier left alone to see if he could pick up any information about the 12th Cuirassiers. As we headed back, Lieutenant Javel asked me what we were doing there. I showed him the pass signed by Fouché and said we were trying to recover a kidnap victim taken by a French officer by the name of Reynolds, as he was half English.

"With Fouché's paper, there has to be a valid reason behind your presence here. Besides, you reunited the Capitaine with his beautiful sister."

"Capitaine Métier knows where the kidnapped lady is being kept," I told Javel. "He will return and take us there. We aren't sure who is keeping her captive and why, but who is going to argue with an angry captain of the guards when he gives orders?"

"You walk in high circles, my friend," Javel observed. "With your friends, you could have avoided being here and just sent someone else. What is the lady's name?"

"Marie Waleska."

He spun around to stare at me. "The emperor's Polish wife?"

"No, although they look similar. This lady is Marie Waleska. The lady of whom you speak is Countess Marie Walewska. If I am not mistaken, Lieutenant, you were brought up in America. Your accent betrays you, and it is an easy mistake to make. Reynolds intends to try to use Marie to gain access to the emperor and somehow trick him."

He smiled. "*Eh bien*. Nothing gets past the gendarmes and Chief of Police Fouché."

"Marie Waleska knows nothing of the plot. Reynolds is trying to convince her that her husband is dead and that her only hope is to fall in with his wishes."

"Mmm…" Javel said thoughtfully. "The choice between following what this Reynolds wants or poverty and prostitution to make enough for food and clothes are compelling for any woman. Do you know if her husband is dead?"

"No, he's not. I'm her husband. And Anton and Professor Savant," I pointed to them as they rode closely behind us, "can verify that. If Reynolds sees me, he may kill her rather than have his plans spoiled and lose her again." I left out the time traveling part in recounting these things to Javel. I didn't want this level-headed soldier think he was talking to a crank.

"Our aim is to rescue Marie," I explained, "and get back to Paris. We are happy that Mademoiselle Leppard has met up with her brother. She is a courageous lady and deserves to be protected. Will you or Capitaine Leppard notify your commander, Colonel Liegeard, of her needs?"

"You are well informed." He laughed. I shrugged my shoulders in true Gallic fashion…well, inasmuch as I was able while trying to hold reins and keep my horse on track.

We got to camp, but we left the saddles and bridles on the horses. We didn't want to get caught out by a Prussian lancer attack. We gathered round the campfire and Javel lit a cheroot. I asked him, "Have you ever thought what you are going to do after the war is over? For I believe you have been fighting for our beloved emperor since '05?"

Guy and his sister crowded under a hastily erected canopy as it started to rain. Even though we were strangers, the French soldiers shared their food with us. I found myself thinking about Métier. I hoped he had found his people.

Javel's eyes grew distant as if he were visiting a place I had never been and couldn't follow him to as he answered my question. "The *Capitaine* and I grew up together near New Orleans. I promised his mother that if we went to Europe, I would, what is the expression? Ah, yes. Watch Guy's back. That's, as you saw today, a full-time occupation. We are still American citizens, but we haven't been home for a long, long time."

I declined a drink from his wine flask and asked, "If the emperor wins tomorrow..."

"If? Surely it is when," he objected.

"When the emperor wins tomorrow, it will only be a matter of a few weeks before we are fighting the Austrians, then maybe the Russians. Both have major armies on their way here."

"It is a soldier's joy to fight!" Javel exclaimed earnestly.

I looked at him by the light of the campfire and felt deep sorrow because I knew things he would never understand. "Yes, it is a soldier's joy to fight," I agreed, "but while you and Guy are fighting France's enemies, what is Elouise going to do? Live in some garret in Paris until you both get killed? Javel, Elouise has come several thousand long weary miles to find her brother. How is she going to get back? It was a miracle of God that got her here safely, but maybe you and Guy are God's miracle to get her back."

I sighed and shook my head, wondering how much to say and how much to withhold. "Javel, if I have read Guy correctly, he is going to be torn apart as to what to do next. America is a land of promise, but she needs men of the quality of Guy and you. You could go home with honor. Get Elouise back home. Then you and your families could all work together to make America a great place— a place where people will want to come to work and build a life. If Napoleon were to lose, or if the Prussians capture Napoleon— just for argument's sake—then Louis XVIII will be restored. For loyal soldiers of the emperor, France will be a hellhole for many years because the Bourbons will try to reverse everything the emperor has achieved.

"What you and Guy have been fighting as a war for glory will become a civil war with a country that isn't even yours tearing itself apart, brother against brother. You know what happened in America in 1776. You were fighting to become a free nation. Now the only thing that could enslave America is other Americans whose hearts are not true. Here, it will be a fight for who rules. Javel, this is not your country. America is and she needs you. Someone has to pick up the torch of liberty before it is extinguished again."

"What will you do if we lose?" he asked, which took me aback.

I thought for a moment. "My wife has family in Poland. We would probably go there. Or else we, too, would go to America."

"Let me think on what you have said," Javel replied, nodding. "But first you have to get your wife back."

A high-ranking officer rode into camp. When Javel and Guy saw him, they scrambled to their feet and saluted. I quickly followed their example.

"Colonel Liegeard!" The colonel strode to the fire, looking around as he walked. He noticed Elouise

"What is this, *Capitaine?* The eve of battle and you have this beautiful woman with you? You rogue!"

"May I present my sister, Elouise?" Guy asked.

The colonel kissed the back of her hand. She withdrew her hand quickly and I wondered if his huge moustache had tickled it.

"Enchanted, Ma'moiselle Leppard. To travel from America to here must have been quite a journey. You must be as tough as your brother, and you are a thousand times more beautiful."

Elouise had guessed Liegeard's significance. "Thank you for your kind words, Colonel. I thank God that I have found my brother."

"God? God? You were lucky to find him. The luck of a pretty woman."

She flashed her disarming smile and replied, "With all due respect, Colonel, in my journey I have found God to be a more reliable source of help than luck."

Colonel Liegeard coughed slightly and then brightened. "I bow to your wisdom, Ma'moiselle. I never argue with a beautiful woman. Capitaine, it is the duty of every hussar to protect beautiful women, and I am sure Lieutenant Javel will agree. Capitaine Penchant can lead the squad should you gentlemen decide to escort the lovely lady home."

Elouise looked at Javel. Her face broke into a radiant smile, and I swear as far as I could see in firelight, Javel blushed. Maybe he could see into the future and the future with Elouise Leppard did not look too bad.

Well, maybe our job was half done, but I still had to find Marie. Colonel Liegeard told us to get on with it as people were starting to come in from Quatre Bras and the battle that took place there. Colonel Liegeard joked with me. "Capitaine, this time try and hold onto your wife. The hussars may not be there to help you get her back the next time! Ha!"

That's the trouble with the military, I thought, *sometimes you have to put up with superior officers' bad jokes and pretend to laugh*. Anton, Professor Savant, and Angus all attempted to humor Liegeard by laughing. If Liegeard could have looked below the surface, he would have found that we were actually somber, knowing that we had to get to a place where we could all—except for Métier and Elouise—travel back to modern times.

After we found a place to put the horses, along with some fodder we had brought through with us, all we could do was to pray that the horses would still be there if we needed them in a hurry.

Angus, Anton, Savant, and I met to discuss Métier's brief visit after he had reconnected with his squadron. He had pointed out an inn called *Les Trois Etoiles*, The Three Stars. It was just down the road from St. Katherine's Church, the church at the center of the village that presided over the village from a small hill. The church, we knew, would become deeply involved in the fighting when the French occupied it and the Prussians attacked. There was a red brick wall around the church and a view from it that covered most of the roads leading up to it. Because it was raining, we donned our cloaks, which enabled us to hide our faces as we passed the inn. We would be just four nondescript soldiers.

We decided that the best French speaker was Anton. He had a commanding presence. Presenting his pass from the chief of police, Anton would ask to see the lady whom the guards thought they were protecting—Countess Walewska—and give her a note if she were free. The two soldiers at the door were privates. We had no way of knowing who else was inside. It was a guess, but we thought that if there was a possibility of danger, cowardly Reynolds would not risk his precious hide. There was a wall around the inn, but we saw guards lurking at the entrance.

Because it was still fairly light outside, if Marie was on the first floor and came to the window, she could see me, but pretend she had not. To do this, she would have to be a skilled actress. If by chance there was a piano in the room, she could play some consummately sad music. If there was a fire in the room, she could burn the note or give it back once she had read it. We had to move! If Reynolds was about and still sending clues to General Carlisle, he would not be expecting us. In time travel, you expect the unexpected.

We decided I would wait across from the inn where Marie could see me. Angus would provide back up. Savant wanted to mingle. Even if Savant did take a photograph with a microcamera, when he produced pictures taken on the eve of the battle of Waterloo in 1815, who would believe him? They would think it was one of the many reenactment groups, not the real battle.

The first stage was to let Marie know we were outside the inn and that I was still alive. The second part of the plan was to figure out how we could get her out and to a place where the time car could pick us up.

I wrote the following note:

Sweetheart, go casually to the window. You will see me on the path opposite. Act calmly. We have come to get you out. Until then, play along with Reynolds. Soon, my love, soon! Destroy this note or return it to Anton. All my love, Drew.

Anton took the note and, with a masterful air of command, walked up to the soldiers. He showed them what looked like the document from Fouché. Knowing that it would be raining, all three of these documents were waterproof and the ink would not run, which was comforting. The guards snapped to attention and Anton disappeared inside.

Oh, Lord! I prayed. *You who made blind eyes see, make seeing eyes blind.* Anton was out again in a few minutes. He handed the corporal at the door a bottle of wine. They were not Reynolds' goons; Reynolds was kidnapping on the cheap. Had they been from PATCH, they would not have been so easily fooled and bribed.

Anton sauntered nonchalantly back to where we waited, blending into the background. Suddenly, trying to be as calm as possible, Marie appeared at the window. She saw me, smiled joyfully, and then turned quickly away. For us, we needed to move to part two immediately—getting Marie out before Reynolds stopped us.

Professor Savant, dressed in his French uniform, hurried back to us as quickly the dignity of his rank would allow without raising suspicion. "Bad news! Napoleon's coming for an inspection and to offer encouragement. He is not far behind me."

"One day," Angus had once warned me, "you will find yourself in a situation where you know you have to work for your corn." I guess that day had just arrived.

CHAPTER FOUR

You Shall Go to the Ball

Part 2:
Meryl's Account—Brussels, June 15, 1815

The night before we left for Brussels, I dreamed fitfully. It was as if many of my dangerous adventures came back to haunt me. I relived the sword fight in Foo-Chow and woke up in a sweat. I had nearly been killed and would have died had it not been for Drew carrying me back to the time car.

Drew had prayed that I would not, must not die, and his prayers were answered. I remembered the mixture of fear and anxiety in his voice. I don't think I had ever before felt so much love. Then I dreamed I was back at Balmoral where I was kidnapped when I was caught off guard. I knew Drew liked to call that mission we had shared *The Scent of Eternity*. Kitchi found me and rescued me, backed up by Drew. When my guards were overcome, the expression on Kitchi's face turned from anger with them to the sweetest tenderness towards me…even though I was a mess of bruises. When Kitchi put his arms around me, I could feel his heart beating and my own sped up in response. The look in his eyes and his gentle touch were like balm to my wounds. I thought we belonged together. Even though it hurt Drew dreadfully, I knew the kindest thing was to leave him.

Yet, months later, I was off again. This time there would be no Kitchi and no Drew; just Hera, Jayne, and me. I thought I should be a good girl and just settle down with Kitchi and live my life around him. Still, there was within in my spirit something that craved excitement, even though it had nearly cost me my life. It was the challenge of pitting my wits against the odds. I had been caught out in Balmoral because I had been vain, wanting to prove myself capable by stopping PATCH single-handedly. These dreams and thoughts mingled with the present mission, which was to stop anything from happening to Wellington before he became the conqueror of *the conqueror of the world*, one of the name for Wellington.

It was a good guess that Wellington's attacker would not be Reynolds, but rather some poor soul who had been lied to, bribed, or hired to neutralize the duke; not necessarily to kill him, but at least to prevent him from getting to the battlefield at Mont St. Jean in time. Suppose the assassin was quicker and faster than we were; then one of us could end up with 'killed in action' after our name at headquarters. After some herbal tea, these thoughts were sublimated to taking some paper tissues with us tomorrow, because toilet paper would not be invented for another 70 years. I was to find that the same idea had occurred to Jayne, and after a helpful hint, to Hera.

We had been given our briefing and the procurement department of Vanguard had done well. Somehow, they had managed to get us three invitations to the Duchess of Richmond's Ball, which took place on the evening of June 15, 1815. Wellington had attended this ball, and with a crowd of people milling and dancing, it would be all too easy for an assassin to make an attempt on his life.

General Carlisle said at the briefing, "We know Wellington turns up to the ball, but he is unaware of how close Napoleon is. He arrives about 10 p.m. Use your charm to dance with him. Keep an eye on him. Take care...of yourselves, and of him."

"But there is no record of an attempt on his life," I pointed out.

"Yes," the general agreed, "but how many things are not recorded in the history books? That's the reason nothing beats actually being there. Remember your cover story—three girls caught up in the excitement. Jayne, you can be excited about your first ball. If too many questions are asked, follow the dancing line...you know...the young girl at her first dance. Just think Cinderella."

Jayne smiled her enigmatic smile and said, "With all due respect sir, Cinderella was not trying to stop someone from getting killed."

"Quite so," the General replied. "Besides, we can't do glass slippers. But to any observer, none of you is married, so it's only natural you would go to a ball with all these fine young gallants there."

Jayne smiled with just the slightest shimmer of stardust in her eyes, but Hera could not see anything attractive about the prospect of dancing with strangers; she was a fighter, not a dancer, and newly married besides.

"Remember, too," Carlisle added, "that back then, officers liked to be gallant. So be careful how you respond to remarks. It would not be the first time that some poor soul had been called out—challenged to a duel—over any question of a lady's honor."

Hera snorted. "I do not need any man to fight for me. With one sword I can take care of any fighting necessary."

"Lieutenant," Carlisle rebuked her gently. "Remember, your heart may be that of a lioness, but it must appear to be that of a shrinking violet."

"Why a shrinking violet? In Greece, violets bloom. They do not shrink."

The general seemed at a loss to explain what he meant to Hera, who did indeed have the heart of a lioness.

"It's okay, sir," I assured the general. "I will explain to her later. I promise. For some things she gets…err, enthusiastic."

General Carlisle nodded in relief. "Remember to guard your conversations. Don't mention Facebook, the Internet, or Twitter. None of them have been invented yet." He chuckled. "Sorry, I was just trying to imagine Wellington's face if you said 'I will tweet this.'

"After the duke leaves the Richmond's Ball, presuming nothing happens, you head outside to the neighboring street, the Rue du Parc. Your rooms are there, your kit will have been sent, and the bill paid in advance. To my understanding, the owner of the house, Madame de Stael, was very much in favor of this idea of advance payment. Outside, there will be a blue coach to take you to your inn from the ball. The driver will be Sebastian. He will take you to the inn at Waterloo village. There may be danger from French cavalry vedettes—small French cavalry patrols, so there are arms in the coach."

"Suppose something happens to me?" I asked.

At my question, a look of pain crossed his face, which both puzzled me and touched me. I knew the general was good to all of us and treated us as family, but I hadn't expected that look of pain.

He cleared his throat. "Then Jane and Hera must come back, but…" He followed that with something right out the blue. "You are coming back, Lieutenant, if I have to come and find you myself." I had the strangest vision in my mind; that I was a little girl sitting on his lap with my head against his chest and he was reading me bedtime stories. Suddenly, I felt safe and wanted.

He continued our briefing. "You must change out of your ball gowns in the coach. May I suggest you do so with alacrity. Remember, your mission ends once Wellington heads safely out to the battlefield on the morning of June 18. With the narrower vector targeting scanner on the time car, you should be able to pass from the night of June 17 to early morning of June 18 at Waterloo within a few minutes. Keep a weather eye open. When Wellington is leaving the inn and heading to the battle, he will be vulnerable in the village. That's the time for extra vigilance."

Jayne asked the general, "Will it be all old men at the ball? Will there be some younger ones, as well?"

The general handed her a picture of a painting of Lord James Hay, a handsome eighteen-year-old. "He will be there. Sadly, he is killed at the battle of Quatre Bras the following day."

I saw the look on Jayne's face: *How sad! Why does such a beautiful boy have to die so young?*

The General added, "Jayne, I know you have seen death before, but not on the scale you will see it soon. Maybe you being there will give some young officer even a brief moment of happiness before he leaves for duty. These battles happened in real time, but what they don't show you in the movies are the huge numbers of wounded, thirsty men…sometimes minus arms and legs. Thirst is a terrible problem after gunshot wounds. This was at a time when medical facilities were primitive, despite the advances made by Barron Larrey, who was Napoleon's chief surgeon, and a doctor ahead of his time. There is no shame if you want to call the mission off. We can get a replacement."

"No, sir. I want to go. I have to learn. I think it is called experience."

Sebastian had entered the room in time to hear the general's question and Jayne's plucky answer. He smiled at Jayne. "Experience is what you gets when you don't get what you wanted. Now, we would consider it a favor if you would give us the kind of experience that involves you not gettin' killed. Besides; them young dudes at that ball are gonna be queuin' up to dance with you when they claps their peepers on you."

"Any questions?" the general asked.

Then like the Von Trapp children going to bed, it was time for "*So long farewell, auf Wiedersehen, good bye,*" and we were off. I was glad Sebastian was coming with us, even though his main job was to find and drive the coach and watch our backs.

"I'm scared," Jayne whispered. "Suppose I mess up?"

"Jayne," I told her, "there is not one of us who has not been scared or messed up sometimes."

"Keep your eyes on me," Hera replied. "If anyone hurts or upsets you, I will kill them." When she made the statement, I thought, *that gives a whole new meaning to the phrase, 'I will get my big sister onto you.'*

We were supposed to be three shrinking violets while in the heart of one violet—there was a hussar waiting to come out. Trouble with Hera was, you never knew when it was going to happen.

Brussels: June 15, 1815

The targeting scanners had improved. We ended up in the Brussels Park about 4 p.m. We found that we were nearly opposite the place where we were supposed to be staying with Madam de Stael. We would use the extra time to 'glam up' as one of my girlfriends would say. Get on our finery and head for the ball. There was a small glitch—we had come out at the opposite side of the park fence and it wasn't clear where the gate was located. I had climbed fences dozens of times, but in an 1815 long day dress, it presented a problem.

At that point, three young British officers, judging by the scarlet uniforms, which advertised themselves from under their cloaks as they headed down the street in our direction, arrived.

"Sirs, oh, sirs!" I cried in distress.

The three officers stopped and looked at us. "Are you ladies alright? How may we assist you?"

"Please, sir. We're due to go to the Duchess of Richmond's Ball tonight. We need to get to our room to change, but we're on the wrong side of the fence. We can't find our way out of the park."

"Please, sir, if you can help us," Jayne added in her best girlie voice. "It will be my first ball, and I should so hate not to get there."

Hera said nothing, but I could see she had caught positive attention from at least one of the three officers. She was an outstanding looking woman in any century.

The one I took to be the leader said, "I am Captain Iain Montgomery." He bowed with a serious face. Then his face relaxed into a sweet smile and the corner of his eyes crinkled around hazel-colored eyes. I didn't know whether to be alarmed or complimented when I realized that Captain Montgomery was appraising me as if I were a priceless painting.

"This is Lieutenant Anthony Meldrum." Meldrum touched his hat in a salute as he was introduced. "And last, but not least, the youngest of our group, Ensign Lord James Hay. We have the honor to be in His Majesty's 1st Regiment of Footguards."

Jayne's blue eyes opened wide and she let out an involuntary gasp.

"Are you unwell?" Lord Hay asked Jayne anxiously. "Did I do something to upset you?"

"No, no, sir," Jayne assured him. "I, err..." She disposed of words and flashed him a winsome smile instead.

Lord Hay returned Jayne's smile. "I was looking at the flowers as we were walking down here. I have a large garden on my estate." He stared at Jayne, embracing her with his eyes. "Yet, how ugly they seem now."

I thought I should interrupt them—for which one of their sakes I wasn't sure. "I'm Tilly Monroe," I told the officers, "and this is my sister Jayne. The tall girl is my cousin Constantia from Rhodes." I cast a glance in Jayne's direction and discovered that her eyes were still fixed on Lord Hay. I could almost read her mind: *by this time tomorrow, that beautiful boy will be dead and I can do nothing about it.* I saw her head giving an involuntary shake and knew that she was hoping and praying in her heart that somehow history had got it wrong.

Lieutenant Meldrum said, "Your cousin doesn't say much. Can she speak English?"

"She is very shy. You'll have to excuse her. She's much more inclined to action than words. She's a swords woman."

Hera spoke. "In Rhodes we are raised differently. It is not all baking and babies. We are taught to use the blade."

"So long as you don't cut yourself," Lieutenant Meldrum joked, then laughed. Hera fixed him with her grey eyes.

"Well, probably you will not cut yourself," Meldrum said rather nervously.

"A jest, Hera," I explained quickly. "Just a joke."

Captain Montgomery said to Hay, "Ensign, you go in that direction for ten minutes seeking a gate. Lieutenant, you go in that direction." He pointed in the opposite way. "Meet back here in ten minutes, or sooner if you locate a gate. We must get the ladies to safety."

After the two officers had left, Montgomery attempted small talk, but his eyes kept returning to my face. "We also are going to the Ball at the Richmond's. I hope may see you there."

Lord Hay returned within a few minutes. "There's a gate just along here." We waited for Lieutenant Meldrum to get back, then we followed Lord Hay. Perhaps I should say we followed Jayne and Lord Hay, for they walked together, and for him, no one else but Jayne existed.

"May we escort you to your front door?" Captain Iain Montgomery asked after we had passed through the gate.

"No, thank you, I replied. "We will see you at the ball." I placed my hand on his arm. He took a deep breath. "Then if you will favor me with a dance at the ball, my day will be enriched." I smiled at him, tilting my head to one side. "Until tonight, *parting is such sweet sorrow*," he murmured, embracing me with a lingering look. He turned and walked away with the others. I felt a tingle run up my spine.

We walked to our door and breathed a sigh of relief, except for Jayne, who watched Lord Hay disappear with his comrades. I remembered myself at 19, and how stars had found their way into my eyes with amazing frequency.

We knocked at Madam de Stael's door. A lady opened it and said, "*Oui*, what can I do for you?"

I gave my best smile and said, "I am Tilly Monroe. This is my sister, Jayne, and our cousin, Constantia. I believe we have a room reserved with you where we might get ready for the Duchess of Richmond's Ball tonight."

Madame de Stael sighed and said, "Of course, the ball. All these handsome young officers. Who knows what may come out of you going to the ball. Come in and I will show you to your room. Your things are there already. I put in an extra cot in case you need to rest. Ah, rest. Who rests when they can dance? Especially in such company. Day is for resting. Night is for dancing and love." We followed her upstairs.

Jayne said to me quietly, "I bet she was a real firecracker in her time."

Our things were on the bed. We thanked Madam de Stael and started to get ready.

I had dressed in many uniforms and dresses, but never a ball gown like this. I thought of Gettysburg in 1863. My brief time as a Southern Belle had been amusing, but I quickly realized that it hadn't prepared me for this. The Empire line fashion of 1815 was so light you forgot it was there. I was glad for the cloaks provided for outside. We had to be careful about jewelry. It wouldn't do for anyone to think we were trying to compete with any of the ladies and grand dames who might be attending. We had to be part of what was going on, but we were there to take care of the Duke of Wellington so he would be able to keep history on its proper course over the next few days.

My gown was silver and gray, enhanced by a silver necklace of swans. Jayne wore jasmine with a necklace of blue stones. They might have been sapphires, but when you looked like Jayne, you didn't need much help. Hera was in dark red with a necklace of rubies. With her hair was up, she reminded me of Tolstoy's *Anna Karenina*. I wondered whimsically if there would be a Prince Vronsky at the ball.

I slipped my .22 in my reticule and a flick knife in the lining. Jayne had her flick knife and a small tap pistol in her purse. Hera carried a knife up her sleeve, which was tied by ribbon and could be undone in seconds. Tissues, a dance card, and small pencil, along with a few personal necessities, made up the kit. I also carried a small vial of knock-out drops guaranteed to put a rhino to sleep for a week. We repacked, putting a change of clothes at the top of our cases for after the ball. What I could not have done with a good pair of Levi jeans!

As it was starting to rain, I wondered how we were going to get the short distance to the Rue de la Blanchisserie without ending up looking like drowned rats.

Madam de Stael let us out. "Oh, *mes enfants*, you will be soaked by the time you get there—your hair, your gowns, and dancing slippers."

To our relief, the coach was parked across the street, pointing in the right direction. Sebastian lit up like a ray of sunshine finding its way out of a dark cloud when he saw us. "Ladies, your carriage awaits. Y'all shall go to the ball." He held the door as we climbed inside, then announced, "Next stop the duchess' house."

There were some soldiers in the street and an officer was arguing with a family who was trying to load furniture into a wagon. Obviously some people knew more about Napoleon's whereabouts than the duke did. Some people were not willing to take chances just in case the French got to Brussels. Sebastian drove us to the ball. When the coach pulled up, a footman opened the door for us. We had to walk through the house from the back to the ballroom. We stopped and deposited our cloaks and showed our invitations to two liveried footmen who examined them and passed them to another footman, who beckoned us to follow. This third footman, I guessed, by the way he dressed and moved with elegance, was the next rung in the ladder of footman ship.

It was a smaller ballroom than normal, but we waited and when the music stopped, we were announced. "Mesdemoiselles Tilly and Jayne Monroe, and Mademoiselle Constantia Vassilites."

The hall was where carriages were normally sold, so on the far side of the room away from the house there were large opening windows running down to the floor. If someone did buy a coach, they had to be able to get it out of the showroom. Only tonight the showroom was draped in white muslin curtains. Mirrors hung on the wall spaces between. Candles burned in front of the mirrors and free-standing candelabras were on the floor. All around there seemed to be candles, and I was not sure I liked the way the muslin was blowing, sometimes perilously close to the flames. As well as muslin, there were swathes of scarlet, gold, and black cloth cascading down from the rafters and curved around vases of flowers, mainly roses.

Somewhere in among the growing number of guests there could be an assassin. Would it be a man or woman? Armed with knife, poison, or pistol? All one would have to do, as Jayne reminded me, was to make sure that Wellington couldn't reach the battlefield. Perhaps drug him, put something in his champagne. We were supposed to go and stand with the other ladies and wait to be asked to dance. The older women sat down and crocheted or did some kind of work from their reticules. The younger girls seemed to be doing a shuttle service, which involved dancing with various handsome young men—all officers, some of quite high ranks. We could not afford to wait. Hera went to one side and I went to the other. We began to circulate around the room.

Jayne literally was bombarded with offers; her dance card was filled with names. I was not in the least bit jealous…really, I wasn't. Well, not much. The waltz had just started and Lord Hay escorted Jayne to the dance floor. When you looked at the two of them together, they might have been the only two there. It was getting increasingly hard to concentrate on what we were supposed to be doing. What would I do if I were Reynolds? As for assassins, maybe a man and a woman—a mixed team, one to act as back up?

Still circulating around the room, I was surprised to spot Hera dancing now, with the tallest soldier I had ever seen. Much to my surprise, she was even smiling.

When the dance stopped, the officer bowed and smiled, the epitome of cool. Hera moved toward me. "He speaks perfect Greek!" she said with admiration. "He knows Lord Byron, who is apparently an English poet who fights for a free Greece." She then resumed her circuit of the room, but as I watched her, her feet fluttered into occasional dance steps.

At that point, and while I was still attempting to survey the room, I felt a hand touch my arm gently. Iain's voice drifted into my ears. "I do not understand my colleagues or any of the other officers in this hall. How could they leave you without a dancing partner?"

51

I turned as gracefully as I could to find Iain was in front of me. He looked at me with those soulful eyes and said, "May a poor, humble foot guard crave a dance from the fairest lady in the room?" He smiled and I felt that tingle run up my spine again. He placed his arm around my waist and extended his other arm to the side and I put my hand on top of his. I was thinking, *Just one dance, or two at the most. I have a job to do. Now, don't look into his eyes. Look anywhere in the room, but not into his eyes.*

"Do you know I have an estate in Perthshire?" he asked. "Do you like to walk among the hills, Miss Tilly? You can walk for miles and miles and we could see…sorry. It's just you can see so much beauty and hear the sound of birds like a cascade of heavenly music. You make me want to enjoy every moment." His voice drifted around me like a sun-lit cloud and his face became animated as he told me more about his estate. *From all the killing he had seen*, I thought, *and all he would see…he wanted life.*

"My aunt could act as chaperone. Your sister could come also if we can tear her away from Lord Hay." I knew what would happen to Lord Hay, but as for Iain, I did not know.

"If there is a battle soon," he confided, "I would have a reason to come back."

I danced a few more dances with Iain before we broke apart. The officers were obliged to dance with several ladies.

I saw Lord Hay slip a ring on one of the fingers of Jayne's right hand. The metal looked like gold, pure and bright. Lord Hay might only be eighteen, but he was a fast worker. "Jayne," he was saying, "please wait for me. When I come back, we can move the ring from the right to the left hand."

Jayne smiled. Her face glowed. But the look of misery in her eyes gave her real feelings away. She knew that Hay would be killed at Quatre Bras. Maybe, I thought, that that is why God normally keeps such knowledge from us.

"Yes, we have all the time in the world," she replied. I realized that Jayne wanted Lord Hay to live his last hours with some assurance of a future. The only trouble was that he had picked the only girl in the room who knew that, for him, there was no future.

Suddenly, the stains of music changed to announce the arrival of an important person and there he was, His Grace, the Duke of Wellington. He looked better in reality than in paintings. He took off his cloak and handed it to a waiting footman. I had to look away because if the assassin was going to strike it was going to be now. I sidled up to Hera and asked quietly, "If you were going to kill the duke, how would you get into the ballroom?"

Hera replied, "I would be outside the windows on the opposite side of the house where the carriages leave. I would have someone open the door in the glass quickly and let me in. All the eyes, like now, would be looking at the Duke."

We examined the windows at the back of the room and as people crowded forward to see the Duke, one on the doors in the windows opened, then closed. If we had not been expecting that, we would have missed it. We fanned out as best as two people can and assumed that it would be someone with a cloak. He would have to put the cloak someplace so as not to be dressed differently. It was difficult to search through the moving figures and swirling ballgowns. Then, behind a large stand of roses, we saw a man in uniform working the priming pan of a pistol while attempting not to draw attention to his actions. It is amazing what can go on unnoticed in a crowd of people.

The man was damp, proving he had just come in out of the wet. He wore the uniform of one of the Nassau regiments and it was kind of French looking. I palmed the .22 and wandered over to him with a glass of champagne in one hand.

"Tonight is a night for dancing."

"Your husband will be looking for you. Please leave me alone," he snapped, pocketing the pistol. Sometimes the direct approach is best, but if I was wrong, I would land in more than the soup.

"Le Reynard—the fox Reynolds—has left you high and dry," I told the man and was rewarded by jerky body motions and wide, startled eyes. "If you kill Wellington, you will hang...slowly. You are not Dutch, but French, and therefore a spy. They will hang you. While your comrades fight for the emperor's honor, you will be tried by a drumhead court martial and you will die having failed. But that won't happen, because I will kill you first if you do not stop. My pistol will not be heard."

"I will be a hero," he countered, sounding uncertain.

"There is going to be a battle tomorrow. What is your rank?"

"Lieutenant Andre Soubris, 9th Infantry Regiment of the Line."

"Are you married?"

"Yes. Celeste will be proud of me."

"Would you not be better off leading your men to glory tomorrow? There is no honor in being an assassin, and you may survive the battle. Think."

"You have to shoot me to stop me."

"Don't be dramatic. Leave your pistol on the table under the roses and leave. Get back to your regiment."

"Why are you doing this?"

"Because I can put myself in place of your Celeste and I know what I should prefer. Someone to keep me warm at night, and love me, and help with the children. You can't hug a memory. A memory doesn't keep you warm when it is cold at nighttime."

He slid the pistol under the roses and left to the sound of music to find his place in history. From his name and the information, the general had given us, I later found that he survived the battle and was promoted to Capitaine. Celeste and he had seven healthy children. A captain with seven children—now where had I heard that before?

Someone had let him in. I hurried to Hera and Jayne, who were taking a break from dancing, and told them.

"These dancing slippers are pinching my feet," Jayne remarked. She cast a look around the crowded room. "I suspect we are looking for a woman as the Lieutenant's partner."

"Why did you let him go?" Hera asked.

"Because if I had turned him in, it would have put us in the history books as having saved Wellington's life. Besides, he was no assassin…and he was good looking."

Jayne smiled. Hera looked at me and shook her head.

Wellington was dancing with various ladies, one of whom was obviously pregnant. She must be Lady Georgiana Lennox. I was getting thirsty; the heat off the candles was prodigious.

Iain found me and asked for a dance. He told me more about his estate and his servants. It sounded wonderful, but it brought back too many painful memories of Drew and Bellefield before Bryant's attack. Bellefield was now the Vanguard HQ. It also was the place from which Drew had set out to marry Lucy, and the place where Marie had shot two assassins to save Drew's life, while she was still blind. The church where Drew had married Lucy and then Marie was close to Bellefield, although in a different time. I had experienced enough of estates, but Iain was a sweet man, determined to put my comfort before his own desires.

"When we fight tomorrow," he said looking deeply into my eyes, "I will have a reason for coming back." The spine tingle again. I had to change the subject. "Can you introduce me to the duke?" I asked.

His disappointment was obvious. "I am only a captain, not a general. I cannot guarantee anything." He left me as he sought for an opportunity to stop the duke on my behalf. I didn't want him to put me down as a gold digger and I didn't want to hurt him, either. Before Iain returned, my attention was caught by a woman in a blue ball gown. She was keeping a professional-looking eye on the duke. She looked like the kind of woman with whom the duke might dally.

She hovered next to a tray of filled champagne glasses, glancing around furtively. A ringlet of hair had fallen over my face, which was a pest, so I pulled out a small mirror and pushed the errant curl back in place. This action also gave me an opportunity to observe this femme fatale. She tipped the contents of a ring—at least I thought it was a ring—into one of the glasses and swirled it around. Then she helped herself to a second glass, from which she took a sip. Elegantly, she shimmered toward the duke. He was surrounded by several people. She waited a short distance from them.

I eased up behind her and took out my dagger. I jabbed it into her back and put my hand around hers. I have a strong grip. Fencing helped develop it. I said to her, "I have a knife at your back." I prodded her so she got the point. "You will drink the contents of that other glass. If you don't, I will kill you, and people will think you have fainted. By the time the truth is discovered, I will be long gone."

I thought that if it was a knock-out drug, it would work quickly and she would probably sleep for a long time. If it was poison, then it would be retribution for her deeds. My action seemed justified; I had to do something.

"Drink," I whispered in her ear. She did. Whether her obedience was forged from an element of surprise, or the feeling of my knife in her ribs, I never knew. The drink worked quickly. She lost her balance and I caught her and managed to get her over to a vacant couch. I put her head against a cushion.

"Is your companion well?" a voice asked, and I turned to find myself looking into the handsome, concerned face of the Duke of Wellington.

I curtsied and said, "You know what it is with these young girls, your Grace. First ball, too much champagne, and feeling the heat. Suddenly the spirit is willing, but the flesh does not match up to it. Thank you for your concern."

"May I escort you to the floor? It seems such a pity to let a dance go to waste."

I smiled and replied, "Of course, your Grace. This will be a memory to tell my grandchildren about someday."

He looked at me, puzzled, and asked, "You have grandchildren? You do not look old enough."

I laughed. "You are right. I have neither children nor grandchildren at the present. But when I am an old woman and the time of champagne and ball gowns is past...I will remember the night I danced with his Grace, the Duke of Wellington, at Brussels."

He smiled. "I could have used you on my diplomatic staff in Spain." We finished our dance and he bowed to me and kissed the back of my hand.

"God keep you safe, your Grace. If there is a battle tomorrow, I fear it will be a terrible one."

He smiled and said, "Let us hope that it will be not too terrible." Then my dance with history walked away into the immortal pages of time. It was probably a good idea to leave before the sleeping beauty on the couch woke up.

I got Jayne and Hera. We hoped we could find the coach and Sebastian. It had been quite a night. Would Reynolds know that his attempt had failed? If he did, there may be another attempt at Waterloo.

Iain caught up with me. "I saw you dancing with his Grace, Tilly. I can face French muskets or cavalry, but time is short. Just give me hope that I may see you again...and more than that."

What could I do? I looked into his puppy-dog eyes so filled with hope and found I could not hurt this lovely man. If he were killed tomorrow, at least he would die believing that one would grieve for him and would be comforted. But what if he survived, or was wounded or crippled? I tried not to think of that.

"Let's wait till the battles are over," I said. "Just come back, Iain. It's been a long night and I'm tired." I didn't want to wait around long enough for sleeping beauty to awake and get up from the couch. That would be certain danger. Hopefully, she wouldn't wake up until after Wellington left. Suppose it had been poison in the glass? In that case, I had just killed someone. No, I thought, a bit comforted, poison would have caused more symptoms than just falling asleep, surely.

Iain received a message to report to some superior officer. Having received the same summons, Lord Hay left Jayne. I looked at her standing there and realized that in spite of her ballroom finery, she suddenly looked like a lost little girl. Hay swept back to kiss her and I couldn't help overhearing his words. "Wait for me, my love." Then he joined the others, making his reentry into a man's world of smoke and death and that elusive commodity...glory.

Hera was easy to locate. I signaled to her to head for the door, or at least to get our cloaks back. When we got outside, somehow Sebastian had managed to get the coach fairly close. He saw us coming and jumped out to help us. Sebastian had amazing patience. He opened the door and we piled in. "Y'all get yourselves inside and pull down the blinds and try and get into something more practical for travel."

One of the dangers we could face was meeting a French cavalry vedette out patrolling to see what they could steal. Part of their job was to take people for interrogation, we tried not to think about that. We closed the blinds slowly as the coach moved forward. Soldiers were starting to fill the street, but it was nowhere near as crowded as we reckoned it would be later. We decided to pull on culottes in case we had to do any fighting. Long skirts could trip you up if you stood on a hem. Culottes were more suited to action while still providing the ability for us to be shrinking feminine violets if necessary. Well, for at least two of us. The only time Hera would fit that bill was when Mike was around. At those times, it was just amazing how gentle she could be. I guess we could all be like that with the right man, but the challenge was to find him. "The right guy" seemed to be as elusive as the proverbial hen's teeth.

We rumbled along on the road to Waterloo Village. The coach had fairly good suspension, but I was glad our liquid refreshment did not need glasses or cups. We drank small beer from stone bottles to quench our thirst. The water wasn't safe. Dressing and getting hair down from ballroom style to something more practical took time. Sebastian suddenly knocked on the small trapdoor on the roof of the coach.

"Reckon we've got company," he warned right before shots were fired. The coach rocketed along the road, but I realized the shooters would soon catch up. They were more than likely French. I didn't want Sebastian hurt. But if he stopped, all we had for firearms that I was aware of was my .22. I didn't fancy our chances. If they caught up with us, they would kill Sebastian. I could guess what would happen to us. I had forgotten about the arms in the coach. "Seb," I shouted up to him, "any weapons in this thing?"

"Yup." He shouted back. "Take the cushions off your seats and look under them."

There were two blunderbusses. These were like shotguns, but with shorter range and a wide spread of fire. They were common on coaches at the time to protect against highwaymen. There were also two double-barrel pistols and two swords. Hera took one of the swords and a blunderbuss. I took the other sword and the other blunderbuss. Jayne grabbed the pistols.

"Lie on the floor," I told them. "Stay as low as you can."

The horses came to a slow halt and Sebastian said in French, "I rely on your gallantry to protect these defenseless women. They are very frightened."

My stomach was stuck in a knot. We didn't know how many men were outside the coach, but if it was a vedette, there were probably about five. There was a scuffle outside.

"They are probably ugly," a male voice speculated, "but it's worth a look. Besides, I'm cold and I could do with warming up, Lieutenant." He laughed.

The idea of rape stinks in any language—men who think it is a God-given right to use power and fear to dominate women.

Two of them flung open the doors of the coach, and because the lamps inside the coach were still burning, I placed the muzzle of the blunderbuss in the face of one and said in French, "Any sudden moves and you won't have a head. Nod gently if you understand." His nod intensified the smell of garlic and sweat.

Hera, on her side, did not need to say anything. She pointed the gun in the face of the other cavalryman. At that range, she couldn't miss, but what added to the man's terror was Hera's appearance. She held a dagger between her teeth. I was even scared.

Hera said through clenched teeth, "I will fight any one of them in exchange for letting us go free."

"Lieutenant," I shouted to the men outside, "one of us will duel with one of you. If we win, we go free. If you win, we are yours." I was thinking of Jayne. There was no way overly protective Hera would let Jayne be injured or taken.

The lieutenant, when I stepped outside with my hostage, bowed and commanded, "Gros Louis, you will fight this…err…lady for the privilege of keeping us warm tonight."

"Fight a woman, Lieutenant? Ha! What an insult! What are we going to fight with—fans? We hit each other with fans and the first one to break down and cry loses?" The man laughed uproariously.

Hera stepped out with a sword in one hand, the dagger in her teeth, and her pistol in the other hand. Jayne kept an eye on her hostage. Hera, in serious fighter mode, was seriously scary. Gros Louis decided that laughing was no longer wise.

The other men were impressed, Louis was not. He said in French and with bravado, "Oh, Lieutenant, I have loved plenty of women, but I have never killed except with passion!"

Hera stood, slowly spinning the sword. Jayne held the blunderbuss and had a pistol stuck in her belt for easy access.

"I will have to teach you a lesson, missy," Louis said, pulling a dagger from his boot.

In French, the Lieutenant said, "Gros Louis, she will kill you." The others nodded.

The warning failed to stop Louis. He underestimated Hera as so many had done before. He swung mightily and Hera sidestepped. He tried again, a bit handicapped on foot because he was trained to exert his full force into the sword from the back of a horse at speed. Hera swung. He leaped back, but not quickly enough. The sword cut a deep gash in his arm. He moved quickly, swearing loudly. He threw his dagger. Hera sidestepped and kicked it out of the road. Then they exchanged blows; thrust, parry, block. Hera threw her dagger into the trunk of a tree. With amazing speed, she rolled over and came up behind him with the blade right between his shoulder blades. He dropped his sword. "Yield," Hera ordered. Louis, I thought, had been lucky.

"Parole," he replied.

Hera turned to face the lieutenant. He nodded and shrugged his shoulders.

Unfortunately, Louis did not like losing. He grabbed the dagger, moving faster than I thought he could, and was about to throw it at Hera's back when there was a shot out of the dark from the opposite side from which the French had come. Louis fell forward. I guessed he was dead. The remaining French looked around. I was about a dozen feet from the lieutenant when on the outskirts of the trees behind us came foot soldiers in dark green uniforms.

The lieutenant jumped off his horse. Before I knew what was happening, he kissed me, not an unpleasant experience. "Unhappily, we must go. C'est la vie." He vaulted back on his horse and what was left of the vedette shot off into the night, easily outpacing the footmen. One of the cavalry conducted a Parthian shot with his musketoon, turning right round in his saddle. He hit one of the riflemen in the leg. Somehow, I wanted at least the lieutenant to get away.

The officer wearing a green uniform ran over to me and saluted. "Lieutenant Bernard Pointer, miss, 95th Rifles. Are you hurt?" I shook my head.

"No, we are all fine. But we are relieved to see you." The music from the television series featuring Bernard Cornwell's books about Richard Sharp of the 95th Rifles passed through my head.

"The effrontery of that French cad kissing you! If I had arrived minutes sooner, I would have stopped that."

I smiled at him. "Thank you, Lieutenant, but we ladies are used to the hardships of life." I added a resigned sigh at the end of my sentence.

He said to Hera. "That was fine swordplay, miss. Where did you learn to fight like that?"

"The Roman arena of life," Hera replied. I thought to myself, *Hera is getting philosophical in her old age, or perhaps it's being a married woman.* The lieutenant was impressed.

"I should be disposed to imagine you are heading for Waterloo? You were unlucky to meet a French vedette."

"Yes, and thank you for your gallant rescue. On the off chance, do you have a Lieutenant Colonel by the name of Sharp in the regiment?"

He shook his head. "No, miss. Sorry. No officer of that name. Friend, is he?"

"Childhood sweetheart," I replied. *Oh well,* I thought, *you can't have everything.*

Sebastian had been strangely quiet. We were all relieved that he had not been hurt in the incident. "All of y'all ladies," he informed us with a gallant bow as he helped us back into the coach, "did a right fine job."

Once in the coach, Hera said, "I can't believe I got careless." Then a rare smile appeared on her face. "The French officer had a pleasing aspect." High praise, indeed, from Hera!

Jayne quickly fell asleep. It had been a long night for her. The poor girl must have been all done in. If she were to write down what she had seen, I wondered where she would start.

As Jayne slept, a tear ran down her cheek, a silver yearning for a too-soon lost love. It did not take much to guess who her dreams were about. How did that song go? *The joys of love are but a moment long; the pain of love endures a whole life long...*"

CHAPTER FIVE

Waterloo, June 16, 1815

We arrived at the village of Waterloo. I had been to Waterloo 200 years before this. Only the smell was different. Time travel gives you a different connection with places. The rooms we had booked at the Bodenghien Inn on the main thoroughfare were almost opposite the large round domed St. Joseph's Church with the Chapel Royal at the back of it. The church was a perfect place for a sniper. A one-shot professional could kill or cripple Wellington. Such a sniper either would be in Reynolds' pay or be an upset Frenchman who thought that Napoleon was not quite the commander he used to be and wanted to even the odds by stopping Wellington before the battle.

At Brussels, the people Reynolds had sent had been in pairs. If the same held true for here, where would the first gunman or woman strike if the pro was in the dome of the church? Until we got our bearings and could figure out our next move, Sebastian turned the coach into the Bodenghien Inn. Our rooms had been booked, but there were still empty rooms.

We unloaded our kit and turned into two-and-a-half shrinking violets. Jayne should have received an Oscar for the performance she put on when we found the patron and he seemed surprised by our arrival. I reminded him that rooms for the Monroe sisters and their cousin from Rhodes had already been booked, but he seemed to have grown forgetful. We persevered, telling him it would be a long way back to Brussels and we were tired. I smiled and batted my eyelids, as did Jayne. Then I plopped a gold coin into his hand. It was amazing how quickly his memory returned. He got the register.

"Ah, yes, of course. Two rooms on the ground floor."

"And," I told him, "if another cot could be put into the bigger of the two rooms, we will take just one room and you will be free to let out the other." I rotated the second gold coin in my hand. Coupled with a smile and bat of the eyelids, that request quickly proved successful. I had come to the conclusion on our adventures that if you are a woman, a smile and fluttering of the eyelids can get you a lot—but gold gets it for you even quicker. We decided to rest for a few hours. It had been a long night. We had learned that when you are tired, you get careless. We got to our room. Now, with the additional cot, we could be together and had a sort of headquarters.

After resting, we realized we were famished. Pork was on the menu. We chose instead a well-cooked beef stew with vegetables and a hot fruit pie. Hera ate with relish. "As a gladiator," she explained, "you ate when you could. I think we should do same. If we have to fight, we need to eat first."

We sat at a corner bench and sipped beer made from fermented cherries. We were all thirsty, but made sure we ate quite a bit to help absorb the alcohol content. A cheery fire danced in the huge fireplace even though it was warm outside. The military presence had increased. Tobacco smoke waltzed with smoke from the fire. Sometimes the best place to discuss things is in the middle of a noisy venue. Our thoughts were interrupted by a couple of soldiers who had seen us and had started into gin early in the day.

"Hello, love, how about giving a couple of brave soldiers a good time before we face the foe?" The question was followed by disgusting drunken winks.

"Sorry," I lied glibly, "but my fiancée, Captain Iain Montgomery of the 1st Regiment of His Majesty's Footguards, would be upset about that."

The two soldiers looked at each other. "Oh, err…sorry, miss. We didn't realize," one said. "You won't say anything to the Captain? We really are sorry, miss."

I looked at them, men that Wellington called "scum." Yet, they would go and lay down their lives in droves on these battlefields. Within a day, these two men could be dead. On the French side there would be men in different-colored uniforms fighting for their ideals, or maybe just to put food on the table for their families. I took a guinea, pretending it was something that had fallen out of his pocket. I stooped down and handed it to him and his friend.

"Good, now you can eat and get some for your friends." *Oh,* a little voice said in my head, *they will only spend it on drink.* Then I shrugged. If I had to face a regiment of armored cuirassier French cavalry with sabers that could take your head off in one stroke, I probably wouldn't want to be sober, either.

"Corporal Carpenter and Private Johnston thank you, ma'am. *Confusion to Napoleon,*" they added, clinking their empty glasses together in a toast. "We must defend the ladies." They left after voicing additional thanks.

We finished our meal in peace and none of the other soldiers sat near us. Sebastian joined us. I asked him to sit with us so that if anyone noticed him, it would be evident that he was not annoying us, but was there by our invitation.

"What do you think, Seb?" I asked in a voice loud enough to be heard and not loud enough to allow others to grasp what we were saying. Conversation about a plot to kill Wellington could get the wrong people's attention.

"If'n I was gonna shoot someone heading to the battlefield, reckon I'd go for the church tower if'n I had me a way of gettin' away and not gettin' lynched by some of Wellington's upset soldier boys."

"What about back up?" Jayne asked. "Ankles get twisted. A horse could stand on a toe. An alert sentry could see him. You need someone to stand in if the first one gets caught. If the second guy fires first, then it means the one in the church tower doesn't have to do anything and can just get away."

Hera suggested, "Sebastian and I can take the church tower. You two watch the street. If I was organizing this, I would have a woman assassin at street level with what you call an airgun and dart." I had to agree with her.

"What we gonna do?" Sebastian asked, "Until the morning of June 18? We had to get here early to get y'all gals to that ball. Now we're done here in Waterloo on June 17, but the battle don't start until tomorrow. Reckon we should jump forward in time to June 18?"

I smiled at Sebastian. "That's a good idea on the surface. If we hang around here for the extra day, it could get complicated." I tried to hide the fact that I was really thinking about Iain. Why is 'love' never straight forward? Just dumping Iain would turn me into the kind of woman I have always hated. "But," I added, "what if something went wrong with the time machine? What if we didn't get back in time for the battle? I think, perhaps, that it is safest and easiest just to stay here and chill out. Sort of hide in the crowd." The enemy of time travel was *what if*.

"I need to rest," Jayne sighed. "It will be a long day tomorrow. Do you realize that soon there will be more wounded men out there that could fill any hospital we know about ten times over?"

Sebastian shook his head glumly, "Yeah, Jaguar, hon. Whoever said that war was hell didn't half describe it. Well, if y'all think it's best to stay here, I'm gonna sleep in the coach. You girls chill. Don't forget to eat and keep your strength up for whatever happens. Expect the unexpected."

Jayne and I, and even Hera, decided that catching a few more hours of sleep would help fill up what we hoped would be an uneventful day. When we awoke, we were all cold even though it was warm outside. We knew that Sebastian probably would be where the food was. We followed the scent of cooking food. We were all thirsty, too, but we knew it wasn't safe to drink the water. Time travel is dangerous and not always romantic. We sat on a bench and ordered vegetable stew again, a tart, and beer. Iain came into the inn. When he saw us, he smiled. "Tilly, you came to look for me!"

The two officers with him said, "Not good form to play gooseberry. If I had a lady like that, I wouldn't want to be interrupted." They left and found their own table.

Iain took my hand and, seemingly of their own accord, my fingers curled around his. "May I join you ladies? I haven't eaten for ages."

I looked up at Iain. I knew I should get up and leave or move further away…but motion seemed to have died somewhere inside my body and I was strangely paralyzed.

"Yes, of course, you may. It's only vegetable stew and some beer." He still held me with his eyes as well as his hands. I was powerless to break the grip of either.

"The food will be getting cold," I murmured, hearing a thump in my ears and realizing it was my heart. "The food…" I tried to repeat, but my voice faded away… "is… getting… hot."

"My beloved Tilly." The words fell from his mouth like a blessing.

"Just kiss me," I heard a voice say and was shocked to suspect it had been my own. Had I really said that? The voice had sounded strange…and strangely far away. Iain bent down and kissed me. I tingled from top to toe. When he kissed me again, his tongue knocked on the door of my lips like a polite suitor. My mouth opened to receive it. I was glad we were standing in the middle of the inn dining room, because if we had been elsewhere I could not have accounted for my actions. Worse yet, the kiss clearly shocked everyone else in the room. It had probably labeled me as a town prostitute. Kissing in public so openly simply wasn't acceptable.

The censuring looks from the others at the table brought me back to reality. I had forgotten that Hera and Sebastian knew Kitchi. I was trying to convince myself that my actions were for the good of the mission, but I was only kidding myself.

Unaware of the hostility leveled against us, Iain sat at our table and I ladled him out some vegetable stew and passed him the bread. He gave thanks and said, "This time we will stop Bonaparte for good. The fighting at Quatre Bras did not turn out as well as it should, but we are going to stop him about three miles from here."

I was glad Iain was talking. It saved me from embarrassing questions.

An ensign came to our table and saluted Iain. "If I may be permitted a word, sir, I have a message for you."

"Of course," Iain said, excusing himself. He and the ensign walked out of earshot. A written paper passed between them and then they both looked at Jayne.

Tears banded together in her eyes and trailed each other down her cheeks. "It's James," she whispered. "I know it is. He's dead." She cried with all the fire and intensity of youth.

"Miss Monroe," Iain said returning to the table. "I have some bad news…" His voice faded away at the sight of Jayne's anguish.

"It's James," she wailed. "He's been killed, hasn't he?" The color had drained from her face, leaving it so pale that her auburn hair took on a deeper shade of red.

"Yes, I'm so sorry," Iain said, his voice echoing the truth of his regret. "If it's any comfort, it was quick. He never knew what hit him."

"I can still hear his voice at the ball," Jayne whispered hoarsely, vainly attempting to clear her eyes of tears. "What we were going to do and all the things he was going to show me. We were to ride the hills together. I'll never forget the look on his face when he said, 'now I have something—someone to come back for. Oh, Jayne, I have so much to show you and tell you'." She bit off a sob. "Excuse me. I need fresh air."

"I will go with you," Hera said, rising gracefully from the table, "you should not be alone." They left.

Iain said, "Darling, I have to go. We might not meet again until after the battle that is surely coming." He kissed me and left.

That left Sebastian and I alone at the table

"Sebastian, I don't need a lecture."

"No, Tilly. You are a professional. You are here to do a difficult job. I just want to say, Kitchi has saved your hide a couple of times. Now you be lettin' your heart rule your head."

"I was trying to encourage Iain. He will likely get killed and…"

"Supposin' he don't get killed and you disappear on him back to your time. What's that gonna do to him? He's gonna wish he had been killed. And supposin' he don't get killed and you stay here with him. How you going to tell

Kitchi? Send him a *Dear John Letter* through the time machine? That come out at his end instead of you?" Sebastian turned a stern, unfriendly look in my direction that quelled me. "Your call, sister."

"Seb, help me! What can I do?" I implored.

"Look, forget just now about Kitchi and about soldier boy and focus on what the general sent you to do. You're in charge of a mission that will keep Reynolds from changing history. Fix the mission. Just do it. Once the mission is completed, go back and ask the general for permission to go and be with the guy you want. If Iain doesn't find you, it will hurt him. But these are troubled times and anything could happen. Our job is to stop the person in the tower— if that's where the assassin is—and anyone else backing him up."

"Poor Jayne…." I sighed, shaking my head.

"Jaguar is a mite tougher than you think. Every mission she goes on, she learns. She'll come through this one."

I had to keep Iain from seeing me again until Wellington was safe. *Focus and concentrate*, I told myself. *Sebastian is right. You have a job to do. And above all else, you must ensure the safety of the others.*

I found Jayne and she seemed to have recovered from the news about James, but who can tell how people deal with grief? Hera had consoled her by telling her of some of the friends she had lost in the arena. Not a great bedtime story for most people, perhaps, but it seemed to have calmed Jayne.

After a tense and fitful night of sleep, we headed for the church at 4:30 a.m., after stopping for a quick cup of coffee. I was amazed coffee was ready at this time in the morning, but I suppose they had to be prepared for all occasions. They probably thought we were crazy *anglais*, however, to be up and about so early when we were not soldiers.

Sebastian and Hera went one way and Jayne and I circled around the other way. Jayne asked, "Would you not have to be at fairly close range for an airgun or dart?"

"Yes. For now, let's keep to the shadows. We don't want to be taken as assassins. By the time Wellington comes out, the street will be busy." We gradually eased out into the street as it became busier. While looking for a possible suspect, we waved to the passing soldiers. So many colored uniforms: I could only remember a few of them from the paintings and reenactment photos we had seen at HQ. The Highlanders started to march out. Even in the dawn, they looked *braw chiels*. Cheers rose along with the sound of bagpipes. Musical bands seemed almost to mock the grim reason for which these brave lads were going to fight. There were bushes on the opposite side of the road to where Wellington would come out. They were not large, but someone could hide in them.

Crowds started to form on the roadside opposite the inn. You had to have eyes everywhere. I wondered how Hera and Sebastian were doing on their patrol. The clock inched toward 6 a.m. We had to catch Wellington coming out as he turned to the left to head for the battlefield. That's when he would be the most vulnerable.

There were spaces between some of the cottages, three especially, where an assassin could hide in the shadows. And because the road on the opposite side of the inn was slightly higher, these were likely places. The duke appeared with what looked like his second in command, the Earl of Uxbridge. Someone waving a Union Jack tried to block the street. The procession halted. Jayne looked behind us and saw a woman pointing what looked like an airgun at the duke. We couldn't get there in time, even though Jayne put on a burst of speed. A cavalry officer passed into the trajectory of the projectile. It hit him in the neck. He reached up, pulled it out, and threw it was onto the ground before crumpling to the ground himself. The assassin had vanished. So had Jayne. I rushed to where I had last seen them. There was Jayne facing a man with a knife who was making cuts at her. He had not counted on back up. I slammed him with a rock and he fell, not even knowing what had hit him. We pulled him into some bushes near an empty building and summoned the time car, citing it as Emergency One. When it arrived, I penned a quick note: *Question him...Reynolds operative.* We banged him and the air rifle into the car, slipped the note in with them, and set the control for automatic.

"Thanks," Jayne said. "I thought he was a woman. I wasn't expecting to tackle someone so strong. I was fooled by his disguise."

"C'mon," I said, giving her a quick hug. "Let's get back to the party and make sure Wellington is okay."

The now rider-less horse of the fallen cavalryman was being led away and the duke had resumed his journey. Amid cheering and ever-increasing numbers of British, Dutch, Hanoverian, and all the other nationalities that made up Wellington's force, the Duke himself rode off into the annals of history to win a battle still talked about more than 200 years after the event. The poor officer who took a dart for the duke would not be recorded in that history: the idea that the victory was brought about by the unintentional actions of an unknown cavalry officer who was in the wrong place at the right time would have been thought by many to be too incredulous.

Nothing had come from the church tower. We thought we should check it out. Jayne looked a touch embarrassed.

"I should have gone to the loo before we left the inn."

I had gone before we left. I had learned you go at every opportunity, but that was experience. Jayne's experience had so far been limited.

"Let's get to the church. How desperate are you?" I asked

"Err…seven out of ten."

There seemed to be no place for doing the needful, so we got into the church. Two elderly ladies in black were just on their way out. We exchanged, "*Bonjours*" with each of them in turn. People in Jayne's and my regular world wouldn't think about it, but churches in 1815 did not have bathrooms. There was, however, an alcove halfway up the isle with two large brass flower vases into which no flowers had yet been put. I pointed them out to Jayne and she was desperate enough to get the idea. She started to hitch up her skirt and I turned my back to watch in case anyone else entered the building. A girl's got to do what a girl's got to do, but she sure likes some privacy in which to do it.

While Jayne was relieving herself, I noticed a small flight of stairs leading up to the rotunda. We were armed, but gunshots going off in the church would echo around the dome. If shooting became necessary, we could hope the music from outside would mask the sound.

There was only one double door that we could see. It led into the dome. I stood in front of the door and signaled with my fingers: 5,4,3,2,1. Then we charged up the steps, dropped to the floor and rolled to make us smaller targets. All this and only to find two bodies on the floor. Hera sat with Sebastian's head in her lap. He was bleeding from his abdomen.

The two bodies on the floor wore the uniforms of French Chasseurs, a cheval with their green uniforms. Yet, they had beside them a British Baker rifle which could easily have taken Wellington out from that distance. I leaped to my feet and raced to Sebastian and Hera. Jayne guarded the door.

"We've got to get you back to HQ fast," I told Sebastian breathlessly, remembering when I had been stabbed at Foo-Chow. Prayer and Drew got me back safely. I prayed for Sebastian.

"I'm okay," Sebastian said through gritted teeth. "Tiger Lily here is lookin' after me real good."

"If you die on me, you big, stubborn ox, I'll never speak to you again!"

"We should all go back," Hera said after I told her what had happened outside. "There is nothing more to do here."

I signaled Jayne to join us after she bolted the door.

"I'm staying," I told them. "I have to find out what happened to Iain."

They looked at me as if I had taken leave of my wits. I probably had.

"If you stay, I stay," Hera said. I shook my head. "Thanks, Hera. But I think Sebastian needs his Tiger Lily right now more than I need you to watch my back."

Jayne sighed and shook her head. "I lost James. You can't even imagine what that feels like. Okay. I'm young and will get over it even though it doesn't feel like I will right now. I know how Meryl feels. If James were still alive, I would be staying to see what happened to him."

Sebastian coughed weakly. "Is this a private marriage bureau or can anyone match make? Y'all are gonna see things once the wounded come back that will rob you of sleep for months. Meryl, you and Jayne are known in the regiment. If you find them, then it might not be that long before you find your senses and return. We need to move. Because if the English Provost Marshall catches us, we may have some explaining to do. Or they may just hang us to save asking questions."

The time car arrived. Hera waved Jayne and me out of her way and lifted Sebastian into it, in spite of his muttering. "I ain't never gonna live this down. Oh, don't forget that Drew, Anton, Angus, and Professor Savant are out there on the other side. If you meet them, you've done gone too far."

The last thing we heard before the time car door closed was Hera saying, "Shut up, you big oaf. You're bleeding all over me."

"Where do we start?" Jayne asked.

"Let's see if any of the regiment is still at the Inn." We sped down the steps and then discovered the need to tiptoe the rest of the way out because mass had started. I wondered what the priest would say when he found the two dead Frenchmen. I was worried about Anton, Drew, Angus, and Professor Savant, but they would be fulfilling their mission just now. Jayne and I only had one-time car panel between us to summon help. If we lost it, we were stuck in 1815.

There was an air of expectation as we went back to the inn. At the side door, there were scores of injured soldiers who could still walk. There was a mass of wounded from Quatre Bras in carts trying to get to Brussels. Judging by the severity of their wounds, many would die before they got there.

We saw two injured soldiers on their feet. Their injuries appeared slight and they looked to be from Iain's regiment. I slipped the ring Iain gave me into the third finger of my left hand. It would carry more weight to be a fiancée instead of a friend.

"Do you know Captain Iain Montgomery of the 2nd Battalion of the Foot Guards?" I asked. "I'm his fiancée, Tilly Monroe, and this is my sister, Jayne. Sirs, please tell me where he is. I beg you."

"I am Sergeant Ebenezer Grant. Bless you, miss. Your fiancé is in Hougoumont with orders to hold at all costs. Miss, it's going to be a main attacking point by the French, or so the duke reckoned before he left."

"Is there no way of getting there?" I asked.

"Oh, miss! That's asking a lot! We know you want to be with your sweetheart, but it's bloody dangerous—well near impossible. None of the officers in command would ever hear of such a thing." There was a brief silence and then he added, "My word, miss, he chose well with you. You are as pretty as a picture and have the heart of a lion. Sometimes with them in command, what they don't know don't hurt them."

He held a quick conversation with his friend, then returned to us. "It's bloody dangerous, Miss, for both of you. The only thing getting to Hoggymont is the men from the Royal Wagon Train that takes the ammunition and powder. But if any of the officers try to stop you, you can say you are going to help the wounded. They will need tending. It be best if you take some bandages, some lint, and a couple of flasks of water."

"And one of gin," his friend said, "for medical purposes only, miss."

"There's much danger," Ebenezer Grant said. "If you are caught by the French, we might not be able to protect you."

I remembered that ammunition for muskets of that time consisted of paper cartridges, the tops of which had to be bitten off. There would be no barrels of gunpowder, but what was there was bad enough.

"The job is, miss, that whoever drives that ammunition to Hoggymont stands a big risk of getting shot. Miss, are you really sure?" he asked again.

"The wounded need tending to," Jayne inserted, "and we can help. If your regiment is forced out of Hougoumont we can leave with them."

"Come on," I urged the reluctant men. "What about Joan of Arc? She helped others."

"She was French," Ebenezer's friend said.

"Okay," I sighed, "bad example."

We hadn't seen the officer approaching. "What seems to be the trouble here?" he asked. Then he said, "Miss Monroe! I didn't recognize you for a second."

I realized that the new arrival was Lieutenant Meldrum, whom we had met at the ball. I smiled at him and explained, "We would like to go to Hougoumont to help the wounded. I must see how Iain is. We're engaged. But Jayne and I also will help nurse the wounded. Please, Lieutenant. I'm so worried about Iain. If I'm there and if the worst has happened, at least I can be with him. Jayne and I are both trained nurses. We are more than willing to help."

Jayne added breathlessly, "And maybe I can find out what happened to James. It would be a comfort to know the truth, the whole truth—even if it's not a comfortable truth."

Lieutenant Meldrum inclined his head and addressed me. "I have no doubt it will help Iain to have you there, even given the fact that he will worry about you." There was a pause in the conversation. Another wagon creaked by outside bearing its load of wounded and now-deformed brave soldiers. Despite their muddy clothes and countenances, how young they looked. These were the sights that movie-makers refused to project. The wounded did not make good box office.

"We are heading out with a wagon to Hougoumont," Meldrum informed us. "If we take you with us, you would have to lie flat in the wagon amongst the cartridges. We can't risk you on horses."

Jayne and I got to the muster point and were introduced to Private Brewer, the driver. He was red-haired with a cheery grin.

"Brewer," Meldrum ordered, "Get these ladies—and the ammunition—to Hougoumont South Gate as quickly as possible. I realize it's dangerous, but they need our help." Private Brewer saluted and replied, "Yes, sir."

"Well, miss," Brewer said to me, "We're off soon, so we need to get you on the wagon. It's a cartway. It will be bumpy. Just keep your heads down. You will hear musket balls bouncing off the woodwork just like when you have an argument with your old man at 'ome." He grinned.

"What artillery danger?" I asked. "Cannon balls?"

"Lord luv you, miss," he replied. "We're heading for the south gate and the trees should protect us a good bit. The whole kit and caboodle only has one open side that artillery can see, the west side, and a lot of the boys are on that side tryin' to discourage the Frenchies from popping off at us with artillery, although sharpshooters are more difficult to stop."

We set off and as ordered, we kept our heads down in the back of the wagon. The noise was deafening as we got close to Hougoumont. Balls whined off the metal fittings of the wagon and I found myself praying that Private Brewer wouldn't get hit. Canon fire that had been distant seemed to draw closer. I thought Gettysburg had been bad, but here the gunfire was nearer to us.

There was an explosion not far from the wagon. "Sorry about that, miss. That must have been the one what got away. Right careless the Frenchies are with them cannon balls. If one hits us, we won't have to worry about getting' to Hougoumont. It will be Heaven we'll be headin' for."

When we looked up, Jayne and I could see trees passing above the wagon. We made it and rumbled through the gate only to discover that we were out of the frying pan and into the fire.

The men were not interested in us, but fell eagerly on the ammunition. It was distributed with a speed and efficiency that would have done credit to the United States Marine Corps.

There was a pile of dead bodies in the compound near the north gate. They were French and must have been what was left of party that got inside before Colonel Macdonell and his men had shut the gate behind them. They lay there with several redcoats scattered among them. I stopped one officer and asked if he knew where Capitan Montgomery was. He replied, "Near the south gate, ma'am. There is the least chance of those buildings catching fire—maybe the gardener's house." He pointed and Jayne and I headed where he pointed. We decided to try to find Iain and then see what we could do to help others. Jayne stopped along the way, giving water and straightening twisted limbs. One badly wounded man grabbed Jayne's arm.

"I ain't gonna make it home, miss. Read to me from the Book."

"What book, sir?"

"It's in me tunic pocket." Jayne pulled out a much-used copy of the New Testament. Then she gave him some water.

"Read to me now, miss, please. From John Chapter 11, verse 25," he requested hoarsely.

Ignoring the commotion around us, Jayne opened the Bible where he had requested. During a few precious second's lull in the shooting, Jayne's young voice broke the silence in the midst of that place of death. "*And Jesus said to her, I am the resurrection and the life. He who believes in Me, though he may die, yet shall he live.*" Her words went up like incense. A peaceful smile passed over the man's face. Then he was gone. That copy of his New Testament was the one object Jayne took back with her.

The sounds of battle returned and we headed for the gardener's house. Wounded men were everywhere, some walking, some unable to even move. I asked one of the walking wounded, "Captain Iain Montgomery? Is he here? Does anyone know where he is?" At first, here was no response other than heart-wrenching groans from the most severely wounded. Then one gasped, "He might be next door. They puts officers in there."

We hurried to the next building. Bullets whined off the wall like so many angry mosquitoes. It was smaller than the other house and less crowded. "Captain Montgomery?" I asked. "Please, where is he?"

A mustachioed figure replied in a German accent, "He is round the corner there, *fraulein*."

Iain lay on sacking. The poor lamb looked so white. Then I saw the blood on his chest. "Darling," I said. "I had to find you."

His eyes flickered open and he smiled. "I wish someone would put a painting of you on my heart." He reached out for my hand. I lay next to him on the rough sacking with my head on his chest, being careful not to hurt him.

"You came to find me," he marveled. "Tilly, would you have married me? Would I have made a good husband?"

"Of course you would. And we would have had lots of children."

He smiled and nodded, then he began to shake. His teeth chattered. I felt under the rough blanket covering him and discovered he was naked, still damp from fighting in the rain. I went under the blanket with him and pulled up my dress, wrapping myself around him. We were clothed on top and naked below and I gave him my warmth. He was dying. If I could have given him the comfort of sex, I would have, but wounds and fever drove that from his mind. Like a small child, all he wanted was to be held. His fingers caressed me, and then he was gone. The breath left his body and he grew still. I pulled my dress back down and crawled out from under the blankets.

I ran outside to find Jayne and found myself back in the cacophony of battle. One of the defenders fell from the wall dead. He had been shot between the eyes. They say curiosity killed the cat. I wanted to see what the enemy looked like. I grabbed the dead soldier's rifle and clambered onto the platform. I peered out cautiously, not wanting to present my head as a target. I nearly froze when my eyes adjusted to the sea of blue uniforms. Cries of *en avant* rose into the air as officers waved their men forward. One seemed to be dressed in a slightly different uniform. When I looked again, I gasped. It was Drew!

Suddenly the old greeting, *Hello, I didn't expect to find you here*, took on a new meaning. What was Drew doing fighting with the enemy? Surely he had been forced? As Drew stood up, the soldier behind him stabbed him with a bayonet. Drew turned and the bayonet hit his shoulder. That man was trying to kill Drew! I crammed the rifle through the narrow opening, praying to God that it was loaded. It was. I shot the French soldier who had for some insane reason been intent on killing Drew. It had to be one of Reynolds' goons. Nothing else made sense. But how did he get here and why had he waited until now to show his hand? I wanted to rush out to Drew and see if he was okay. But before I could put those foolish thoughts into action, Angus reached Drew, who was wobbling on his feet and nearly fell. Angus grabbed him and held him steady. I was worried sick, but I couldn't afford to panic. Drew wouldn't die, would he? I mean, Drew couldn't die. He was always there. From the time when Drew started working for Vanguard, he was always there for me. We had backed up one another. *Oh, God*, I prayed, *don't let Drew die! Jesus, please! Help!* Drew and Angus disappeared into the melee of soldiers. I felt as if someone had taken the foundation of my life out of my sight and hidden it. Drew had been my friend, my brother, my fellow fighter and my lover. Gradually, I returned to the present enough to realize that Jayne was shouting up to me. "Tilly, come down! Don't be stupid! You'll get yourself killed!" The wisdom of her brief words hit home. I was responsible as team leader for getting Jayne back in one piece.

"I've just seen Drew and Angus out there," I stammered, slowly climbing back down the wall to stand beside Jayne.

"Calm down," Jayne urged. "Deep breath."

"Drew was bayoneted in the shoulder. I shot the man who did it. But the last I saw, Angus was trying to get Drew to fall back. Oh, Jayne," I gasped. "They could both be killed!"

Jayne grabbed my shoulders and shook me impatiently. "Meryl, think! Drew's uniform is thick wool and covered with straps; he has equipment straps over his shoulders. The bayonet may have not gone in that far. As for Angus, he seems well able to take care of himself and any number of other people along the way."

I tried not to think about the picture seared into my mind; that bayonet coming down on Drew's shoulder. It played over and over in my mind like a stuck track on an obsolete record. The endless reel in my mind transformed that bayonet into biggest, most vicious killing instrument ever created.

"Listen, Meryl," Jayne said, her reasonable voice finally getting through to me. "I've used up all the bandages and given out all water. There's nothing else we can do here. We must get back to HQ. We can't try to find Drew and the others. Plancenoit is about two miles from here and packed full of French troops. We would either get killed or raped."

I stared at Jayne. "Are you forgetting Drew's wife, Marie, is over there?"

She countered, "And are you forgetting that Drew already has help there to get Marie back? Angus, Anton, and Professor Savant are all still there somewhere. They will get Drew and Marie back."

Until that moment, I had never resented Marie. After all, I was the one who had left Drew for Kitchi. I had even been happy for Drew. But having just seen him wounded and realizing his life was in grave danger—everything in my well-ordered life tilted and my heart went bonkers. While I stood there exchanging glares with Jayne and attempting to wrap my mind around sorting out my domestic life, a Frenchman suddenly appeared on the firing platform. He hadn't expected to see two girls standing in front of him, one of them— me—clutching a rifle. The pause caused by his confusion cost him his life. He was shot and two redcoats replaced him.

"Miss, for pity's sake...get to some shelter," one of the men said. "This is not the place for either of you. You're just getting in our way and costing us time—and maybe our lives—while we try to protect you. We've got enough to protect already. When we try to get the next batch of wounded out, go with them."

I nodded at Jayne, which somewhat deflected her glare. "Thank you, Jayne. You are right, and wise beyond your years. You make an excellent Vanguard operative. We need to go, but we need some empty space so we can summon the time car."

Jayne and I sprinted for one of the buildings that looked empty, but it was on fire. "Come on," I urged Jayne, "this seems to be the only possible open space big enough for the time car. And because it's on fire, no one else should come running in here to interfere. We'll be safe once we're inside the time car. It's fireproof, I hope."

The fire advanced quickly, leaping across boundaries that offered it new fuel. The crackling turned to a roar and we were starting to get hot. "Is this really a good idea?" Jayne asked.

"I'm open to suggestions," I replied, gazing at the growing inferno.

Fortunately, the car arrived. I realized that I was still holding the discharged rifle. I dropped it and we ran for the car, leaped inside, and hit the timer just as the roof collapsed around us.

We came to a stop and looked outside. The place was a battlefield, but cut up and muddy and artillery. Shells landed close to us. Jayne pulled me back into the car and hit the button again and we were away.

"How did you know we weren't home?" I asked her curiously.

"One of my favorite books is *Goodbye to all That* by Robert Graves, set in World War I. He describes a rolling artillery barrage. You didn't want to be under that, and guess what? We were. It must have been 1915. We had only moved forward a hundred years." She smiled at me and said with the optimism of the young. "It was a jolly good thing the time car started again."

The artillery at Gettysburg and Waterloo was nothing compared to what would have landed on us in 1915. Well, I thought, at least time travel is not boring.

Arriving back at HQ, we must have looked a sight. I ran to the general's office and met him coming out the door. "How's Sebastian?" I asked. "Did they get back? There is something I need to tell you."

"I daresay there is," the general replied. "Canteen. Now."

Jayne found us. The general said to her, "Well done! Good! You're back safely. Go and get changed. I daresay you could use some rest and a shower."

"Yes, sir." Jayne replied. "It was quite a trip." Jayne left with steps that could only become wearier.

After she left, the general turned to me. "Meryl, you are an experienced officer and were in charge of the team. What in the name of heaven were you doing sending Sebastian and Hera back on their own while you went off to look for some man you had met at the ball?"

I had rarely seen him so angry, but I knew he was right.

"Your first responsibility," General Carlisle said, "was to carry out the mission. From what Hera tells me, that was achieved. But your next responsibility as team leader was the safety of your team. Personal concerns do not enter into it. What were you doing? You went to Waterloo, but where else?"

"Hougoumont, sir."

"Hougoumont! What in the blazes were you doing there? You put Jayne at an unauthorized and unnecessary risk. Meryl, what were you thinking? She could have been killed...and for what?"

"There's something else that may be put in in as extenuating circumstances."

"What?" the general asked, still holding tightly to his anger. I explained about Hougoumont and having shot the man who bayonetted Drew.

"What was Drew doing in front of Hougoumont? He was supposed to be at Plancenoit! Are you are sure you saw Angus trying to get him away?"

"Yes, sir," I replied. "There was nothing I could do. That's when Jayne and I realized we needed to get back to here and let you know. Actually, Jayne gets the credit for that. She convinced me."

The general leaned back in his chair and groaned. Then he sat up and scratched his chin. "In that, you did right. And if you had not been there, Drew would have most certainly been killed. God must have sent you there. What time was that at by Waterloo time?"

"About 3:30 p.m., sir. Do we try to rescue him?"

"No, we leave it to the others. Now go and get a shower and some rest."

"You sound like my Father."

"Yes, I suppose I do. And I am proud of you except when you behave like an idiot. If it hadn't been for you saving Drew, you might be up on a charge. Now, go on. Get out of here before I change my mind."

* * *

The following morning, after varying degrees of sleep, I found Sebastian and Hera. Much to my relief, Sebastian seemed completely recovered, although he was still in bed. Hera had installed herself in a chair next to him. I told them what had happened at Hougoumont, especially with Drew.

Sebastian seemed cheerful. *When was he not?* I wondered.

"The general will make the right decision," Sebastian assured me. "He has the responsibility."

"Just like I had on our trip. But I blew it."

"Oh, come on. I hate it when you're miserable. Don't go slippin' into one of them puppy parties."

It took me a second or two to think what he meant, then I laughed. "Pity parties?"

"Yeah, well them, too. Just that puppies is a site more cute than pities."

I threw my hands up. "Okay, I give in. You win."

"See, I knowed I could make you feel better. Now you done owe me a coffee and cake, at least, with lashings of chocolate. I do love that chocolate."

Hera said quietly, "You had to decide what was right, but in a fight you can't let your heart rule your head. I remember one fight I was in. My opponent was the best-looking man I had ever seen. It took all my effort to concentrate on staying alive."

"What happened?" I asked

"I killed him." She paused. "I survived, only because he let me." When I looked at her, tears pooled up in her eyes and rolled down her face. It was the first time I had ever seen her cry.

"Hera, you had to survive no matter how good looking he was."

She shook her head. "He was my husband. They threatened to kill us both. He told me to kill him so they would let me live and deny these..." she swore in Greek. I didn't ask for a translation.

"They killed my heart that day, but I had to go on or else he would have died for nothing. They said they would free the one who survived, but they lied. May they rot in Hades. Only Mikey has touched my heart since then."

I was going to go to her, but Sebastian swung himself out of bed, grunting slightly from pain. He dropped a muscular arm over her shoulders. Then he knelt beside Hera, grunting again, and pulled her head down, cradling it against his chest. "There, there, Tiger Lily, let it all out." And in the loving arms of a friend, with tears washing down her face, I could sense Hera beginning to heal.

I left them alone. I had so much to learn. I couldn't stop worrying and thinking about Drew. Was he alive? Was he dead? Unable to be moved? What about Angus and the others? And what about Marie, whose kidnapping had started all this insanity? Had she been rescued? We couldn't afford to put any more people at risk. Only time would tell. One thing I knew: God was in control.

CHAPTER SIX

Vive L'Empereur

Plancenoit, Evening of June 17, 1815;
Drew's Narrative

"Oh great," I said. "Just what we didn't need! The boss showing up when he wasn't supposed to."

Vive L'Empereur, sounded the cries, cheers, and joy despite the rain. We were shunted further up the street. I noticed out of the corner of my eye that Anton and Savant had joined the cheering before ducking into a doorway and turning their backs to the crowd.

Somebody jostled them roughly. "The emperor awaits. Come on, gendarmes, you can piss later." With loud guffaws of laughter, they added, "Now these glorified policemen will see a real battle!"

Then we lost track of what transpired. Napoleon and his entourage stood around a fire under a canvas shelter. When the wind blew in the right direction, heat came close behind. Firelight shone in their faces. Napoleon stood with his grey coat and boots, and the famous black hat, despite no longer being the handsome young general of Arcola and Lodi, and the battles of 1795, he had a presence about him. When he looked at you, his eyes held you as if he knew all about you. Just a little behind him were the Marshalls of France.

You couldn't get a history lesson like this on a computer. Despite the rain, here they were. Napoleon, who had conquered half the world. I recognized Marshall Soult, Napoleon's Chief of Staff. The other figure who was instantly recognizable was red-haired Marshall Ney, the 'bravest of the brave,' who had fought in the rearguard as the French Army retreated from Moscow in 1812. In spite of the entreaty by Duke of Wellington to save his life, Ney was killed by a firing squad in December 1815. Pleas for mercy fell on the bitter deaf ears of a bitter King Louis XVIII, whose ungrateful hide Wellington and Blucher had saved.

Ney stood in front of the men and said, "Soldiers this is the last order I will give you—shoot straight." There he was–one of my childhood heroes as large as life and a lion of immense courage. What stories he could have told!

Napoleon, as far as I could translate, said, "Soldiers of France, we have come far and seen many victories. Now, one last fight, one last battle, then peace. France calls on you, her sons, to stand with her in this hour. For the liberty of France and of her people!"

Silence reigned and for a few seconds, all you could hear was the crackling of the wood on the fire.

Then a voice shouted, "*Vive L'Empereur, vive La France.*" To my astonishment—the voice was mine. I was in the front row. I took off my hat and cheered. As I looked at Napoleon, he was impassive. It was Marshall Ney who looked directly at me. His face broke into a smile and his head nodded slowly up and down. I had been approved by the bravest of the brave. I believe if he had asked me, I would have followed Ney into hell itself.

Some infantry passed us and one of the soldiers said out of the blue, "Watch your back, old boy." Then he was swallowed up in the crowd.

I turned to Angus and asked, "Did you hear that he spoke in English with an English accent? He must be one of Reynolds' cronies. Oh, blast! I didn't see him and he…"

Angus replied, "He was trying to scare you. But how did he know we would be here? Drew, we need to get back to Savant, Anton, and Marie. That's why we came—to rescue Marie. To get your wife back for you."

"Right, let's find them." We headed down the lane to the inn where we had last seen Anton and Savant. We had to act calm and assured. This was supposed to be a joyous occasion; we were going to beat the Allies. Anton and Savant were gone. We hung around in the shadows, but there was no sign of them. Where were they? I had to check and see if Marie was still in the hotel. I wondered what my French accent would sound like to native speakers. What if the two goons at the door were not native speakers but two of Reynolds' henchmen? No use chucking stones at Marie's window; it might not be her who came to look. Reynolds, if he was here, knew history as well as we did.

"Fortune favors the brave," Angus said. "We go in and find out if she's still here. If she is, Anton and Savant might be with her. If it's Reynolds, we fight him, and if necessary, get rid of him. If she is here, we get her back to HQ and come back for Anton and Savant. We can use the passes from Chief of Police

Fouché put the fear of God into them."

We made sure our pistols were loose. The two men at the door were too taken aback to stop us. They ended up around the corner of the building, unconscious. Time was pressing and we had to act quickly.

The clerk obviously was nervous.

"What room is Miss Waleska in?" I demanded, showing him the authorization from Fouché. He started to hum and haw.

"There will be a battle soon and this place will be on fire. If I were you, I would take what money I have while I still have it and get my sorry ass on the road to Brussels," I snapped at him.

"She is not here, *Capitaine*. Two soldiers came and took her out the back way," he stammered.

"Describe them!" I challenged. "Now!" He gave a description of Anton, so there was no point in going to look upstairs. The longer we remained here, the more chance there was of Reynolds coming back. He would notice the absence of the sleeping beauties around the back.

"Good," I said with approval. "Now get your family out of here fast. The Prussians are not as nice as we are." (Actually, what I said was the Prussians, unlike us, are not gentlemen.)

We got outside. Angus and I said together, "If they are not here, then where in the name of heaven are they?"

Angus speculated. "If we go wandering off in the dark and meet some Prussian hussars, we won't have a hope in hades. We need to mingle with a group—a squad. The larger, the better."

I nodded my agreement. "The battle starts at about 11.00 a.m. tomorrow with an attack on Hougoumont. We can volunteer to be in that."

Angus objected. "But the squad of Gendarme Cavalry are not far from here."

"If we try to join them, we'll be spotted as phonies. I don't even know what the commanding officer looks like. The trouble is, we know what the emperor will do before he has even thought of it. He must have had it in his mind to attack Hougoumont for some time despite this blasted rain. Which units attack Hougoumont to start with?"

Angus thought for a moment. "We don't want to be in the attack at the start. We want them to use up their ammo, but not on us. There was a supply of ammo pushed through at about 3:30 p.m. That means the fire will lessen until the ammo gets distributed."

"If, and it's a big if," I mused, "Anton and Savant have Marie, they should have already taken her back to HQ. But we can't be sure they did. Let's see if we can find Ney and ask to join one of the infantry regiments. We'll tell him we're tired of being gendarmes. We want to be real soldiers and get a taste of battle while there is still a war to fight. I know it is a bit gung ho, but they could probably use more volunteers. There's no reason why they shouldn't believe us."

Angus reasoned, "How do we know if we go off that something hasn't happened to Marie or the others? Suppose they come looking for us?"

"I don't want to be here when the Prussians come storming through. Let's go get our horses and see if Savant and Anton's horses are gone."

We reached the horses to find two of them indeed gone. The next step was to locate Ney. We returned to the Emperor's gathering place. We were in luck. A tired-looking Ney was still there, handing out orders.

We saluted and he looked at us for a moment, then said, "The elite gendarme with the brave words. What can I do for you?"

"Your Grace, our battle experience is limited. We would like to fight at Hougoumont."

"Hougoumont? Why Hougoumont?"

"There is talk that the battle will start there later today. Any way we can help or encourage, we should be glad to assist."

"Even if it means taking our gallant infantry over the walls?" he questioned.

I thought, *any trace of hesitation now and we've had it.* "For France and for the emperor, we would climb the Alps."

Ney shook his head. "Capitaine, the walls of Hougoumont will be sufficiently high to satisfy the emperor." He smiled.

Angus spoke up. "With all due respect, your grace, the same courage that took you to the snows of Russia and back again will get us through."

Ney nodded. "And many a gallant son of France lies buried along that road. Why should I commend you to Prince Jerome? For he is in command."

I smiled, "Your grace, we both speak English without an accent. Should there be prisoners, we may be able to assist in getting information from them. After all, we are gendarmes. Some of the people we have dealt with have proved reluctant. Also, I hate Hanover."

"Your master Fouché is no soldier."

I took a deep breath and said, "Your grace, my master is the emperor Napoleon. Now my master needs us here."

Angus nodded in agreement. The result of our conversation was that we walked away with written orders to join Prince Jerome's staff. When the battle opened later on, assuming we did not float away on the river of rain that was coming down, we would be fairly safe barring the erring cannon ball, piece of shrapnel, musket ball, or squad of marauding British cavalry—or so we thought. My mother used to say: "*You know what thought did; planted a brick and thought a house would grow.*"

Napoleon's youngest brother, Jerome, King of Westphalia, was perhaps the least militarily talented of the Bonaparte family, and that was a wide gap. After a terrible struggle through the mud and several dead ends, we found Jerome's headquarters. We managed to stop our orders from Marshall Ney from getting soaked.

We were left kicking our heels by a sentry who departed to summon an officer. Angus wisely said to me, "If they ask you to speak English, make sure you do it with a trace of a French accent. The last thing you want is your English to be so good that they think you actually are English."

An officer came behind the returning sentry. We came to attention and saluted. He returned the salute, then introduced himself. "I'm Colonel Hortode, Prince Jerome's Chief of Staff. We don't get recommendations and requests about individuals from Marshal Ney every day. So you want to join in the battle tomorrow?"

"Yes, Colonel. We want to fight for the emperor. We speak English. We were sent on a mission here to look for a woman, but she is gone. We have these papers from Fouché, the Chief of Police."

Colonel Hortode looked at me, knitting his eyebrows together. "I am all too aware of who the Duc d'Otranto is," he said, using a derogatory term for the little-liked Fouché. "If you come through this, when we win tomorrow, you need to get yourself in better company. There is always a call for good soldiers and faithful followers of the emperor. I will put you on the staff tomorrow. We lost a good few men at Quatre Bras. Prince Jerome may want to see you, but he is very busy. Get yourselves as comfortable and dry as you can and get some sleep. You will need all your wits about you tomorrow." He pointed to a tent. "Bread and wine in there. Shelter, too, if you can stand the snoring."

We saluted and said, "Yes, sir. Thank you. *Vive L'Empereur.*"

When we were out of earshot, Angus said to me, "Listen, Drew. It's going to be one hellish long day tomorrow. We need to try and get some food and kip."

I grinned at him. "Sleep through all this noise?"

He ignored my attempt at humor and continued, "We have clean water in our canteens, but that won't last the day. We have wine, so top up your canteen. You really don't want to top up with the local water. Don't forget the water sterilization tablets in the survival kit. If you forget and get hit with bad diarroeha tomorrow, they won't thank you for having to crap every five minutes in the middle of a battle. If one of us gets hurt—and we still don't know about Marie and the others—then it's back to HQ. If it's a flesh wound, the wounded one might be able to come back to the time before they were wounded. So if we do get hit and have to go back, then it is important that we know the exact time so we can return to the same point and place in time."

"Suppose the other is killed?" I asked.

Angus shook his head. "You are a bundle of cheer! You were more positive the night before you went on your first time travel to Foo-Chow, but perhaps young Meryl had something to do with that in spite of my best efforts to keep you apart. A lot of water has flowed under the bridge since then. I hope we find Marie and the two of you can actually complete your honeymoon...complete with the fun part—sex, and lots of it."

We found a place to rest after our bread and wine. Sleep proved too strong to resist in spite of the surrounding snores. I felt that I had lived a lifetime in one day. Modern soldiers, I realized, must feel like this day after day. But at least Angus and I could tell our enemy by the color of their red uniforms—except they were not really our enemies. Confusion and tiredness warped my thinking. I wondered where Marie was. I hoped Anton and Professor Savant had managed to rescue her before Reynolds found out. Reynolds didn't and couldn't know everything, after all. He was not God—he just thought he was.

I fell asleep staring out of the door of the tent at the flames of fire flashing off the sentries' bayonets. At least he had some shelter, unlike the thousands of poor guys laying out there in the mud and rain, waiting for a day to come that many would never see end.

Hougoumont

I was wakened a few hours later as dawn forced its way into my eyes and Angus shook my shoulder.

"Come on, sleeping beauty. Napoleon is here. We need to shift."

I needed to pee and looked around for a suitable place, only to find that a large number of other men had the same idea. "There is a camaraderie in urination," one said.

"Yes," another agreed. "We will sweep over their walls like a veritable blue flood."

Another commented, "I wish the emperor had given us some rifles. Then we could have picked their sharpshooters off the wall before charging."

"Rather see some artillery hammering their walls and gates and then we could charge in," responded a corporal.

His fellow replied, "Trouble with them artillery boys is they start fighting duels with British cannon 'stead of protecting us."

Another sergeant who had joined us said, "Them artillery boys don't know what real fighting is; them and those poncey gendarmes."

The guy next to him indicated me with his head. "Sorry, sir, who are you?"

"One of the poncey gendarmes who has come here to learn what it is like in a real fight," I replied.

"Yes, sir, of course. No offence. We are all here for the emperor, *Vive La France*."

I nodded. "We are here to fight for the emperor."

"Yes, sir. Exactly, sir."

I smiled. "Good. That's what we like to hear. See you at the barricades."

I got back to Angus. He had found some bread and a K-ration breakfast bar, part of our kit, along with what was left of the water. Any additional water would need to be sterilized before consumption.

We checked our horses. They were fine. We caught our first sight of the French commander, Prince Jerome. The emperor was with him, but we were too far away to hear what was being said. We did see Colonel Hortode.

It seemed, watching this blue mass of soldiers and odd units of cavalry trotting around, that the defenders at Hougoumont wouldn't stand a chance. The British Commander Lt. Colonel Macdonell was there, along with some Dutch forces. But what I knew that neither Jerome nor Napoleon knew was that the back door to Hougoumont, the south gate, was wide open. The garrison wanted it left open so that ammunition and supplies could get in, but they would have to run the gauntlet of the French sharpshooters and what artillery was not trying to take out their enemy counterparts. A stupid thought passed through my mind; I could be an instant hero by telling the French commander that the gate was open. I could say we had done a late-night reconnaissance. The trouble was, that would have tipped the balance of being a time traveler to being a traitor. Suppose I were responsible for causing Wellington's main stronghold to fall?

Napoleon took off his famous black hat that Wellington said was worth 40,000 men on the field of battle and held it aloft. Cheers and cries of *"Vive L'Empereur, vive L'Empereur,"* hung in the air. Then the first artillery was fired, passing over the top wall and landing harmlessly in the distance. The Battle of Waterloo had begun.

Behind the first wave of soldiers pushing forward, there was a band playing *La Victoire est a Nous*. Some carried ladders. All were brave. Many would not return.

British cannon opened up from a ridge behind the farm. To me, that brought back memories of Pickett's Charge at Gettysburg. Thankfully, the mud was soft and cannon balls did not bounce, but with shrapnel there was no such reluctance.

French soldiers marched to the wall and tried to scramble over. Gaps formed as men literally were blown away. Limbs and heads spewed everywhere. Officers waved their swords and their headgear, just as Confederate General Armistead, who had led at Pickett's Charge at Gettysburg, had done.

I let my guard down. When you're in with those who seem to be friends, you can get careless. Carelessness often can have fatal results. I was near a rock at the back and a bullet whined off the rock. Even with a rifle, it could not have come from Hougoumont. It was way too far away. It was either a French squaddie who didn't like gendarmes, or it was one of Reynolds' thugs who had decided to take me out. A few of the other officers laughed, but when Angus and I looked at the scar on the rock caused by the bullet, it looked as if it had come from our right. My guess was the would-be assassin did not have a modern rifle. If he had a modern rifle, my narrative would have come to an abrupt end.

The officers were given watered-down wine. As for the men, it must have been hell for them because it was becoming unbearably hot. It was as if the other part of the battle was going on, but it didn't seem to matter. There was only this debacle that Prince Jerome didn't know how to sort out. The French had captured a lot of the ground and had chased the enemy from the orchard and bushes around the house, but they couldn't get into the chateau.

As the day wore on, it was the incessant noise that made one fear insanity—

the canon fire and jarring bands. The day grew hotter and the ground dried out, changing the effect of the cannon fire; the once harmless balls began to bounce. When there were men in front of them, the cannon balls mowed right through them. Even when the ball came to the end of the bounce, it still had enough power to take off a foot.

Angus knocked me off my horse. One of the balls had a fuse in it that spluttered. We could do nothing but hit the dirt, waiting for the explosion. The explosion never came. *Thank You, Jesus*, I thought. I had expected to be blown into three different parts of the battlefield.

As afternoon approached and word of the failure of Lt. Legros' men to survive inside Hougoumont leaked out, enthusiasm waned. The fire from the chateau had diminished. We wondered if they were running low on ammunition.

A cannon ball exploded, killing some men and a party of officers. Colonel Hortode rode up to us. "On my recommendation, Prince Jerome wishes you to join that unit and take them to the wall. You wanted a chance for glory and victory—destiny awaits, my friends."

My first thought was; *I wish people would stop recommending me: being recommended can get you killed.* We had no choice. I tried to make the best of it, endeavoring not to sound terrified even though my stomach was churning. It is possible to sound terrified in French. I even tried the old, *Eh bien mes braves lets go, tonight we dine in Brussels.*

The men began to draw level with the officers at the front. We were about 500 yards from the wall and Angus had fallen slightly behind. Unexpectedly, I felt a red-hot flame in my shoulder. I knew I had been either stabbed or shot, but I didn't know which, and I couldn't understand why the attack came from behind. Then a raspy voice mocked, "Professor's compliments. You die a hero."

I dropped and rolled over on my back to see a great brute with a musket and bayonet raised, ready to plunge. There was nothing I could do except die. Then a big gouge suddenly was taken out of the man's face and he fell back dead.

Angus caught up to me. He grabbed my shoulder and gave me a firemen's lift. We hid as well as we could hide in the middle of the battle.

"Listen, Drew, you've been bayoneted. We're getting you back to HQ. I've pressed for the small car. It will get you back quicker. I can hide. Try to come back for me. The time is 3:35 p.m." The smaller car swooshed into a space in the trees. Ignoring my protests, Angus shoved me inside and gave me the control.

"I am not leaving you here," I gabbled.

Angus sounded exasperated. "If that wound turns septic, you'll die. You know where I am. If you can't get back, I understand. Go with God, son. See you soon. Now press the button and get out of here."

My shoulder hurt like anything, but somebody on the wall had shot the killer before he could finish me off. I must have passed out, for when I awoke, I was being lifted onto a stretcher back at HQ. After enduring a day of battle noise it was so quiet that it actually hurt my body and echoed in my ears. I had never realized before that silence had an echo.

General Carlisle and Anton were talking to me. "Come on, you need the medic."

"I don't have time! I must go back and get Angus and Marie and...wait a minute," I exclaimed to Anton. "You are in Waterloo and Professor Savant is with you." I must have passed out again.

I was alternating between fainting and waking. No matter how hard I tried, I couldn't seem to open my eyes or keep them open, if in fact I managed to bully them up slightly. I felt the sweet brush of lips against mine. The accompanying voice woke my ears and my heart.

"My big, brave, major husband." The figure wavering ghost-like before me wore a white gown.

"Marie! Is it really you?" I couldn't stop the tears.

I awoke in a bed. Marie was next to me, holding my hand. It was as if I was dreaming the kind of dream from which you never want to awaken.

"You came back for me," she said. "Why did you come back for me?"

Then I heard Angus' voice in my conscience, though he may have been half-joking. "You will come back for me."

God, what was I doing lying here? I had left the man I owed my life to many times over back at Waterloo.

I tried to move and managed to force myself up. "I have to go back, Marie. Angus is in grave danger."

Marie took a deep breath, "Drew, you can't!"

"I'm not leaving my best friend to die at Waterloo. When the French break, they run everywhere. Angus is in danger." I struggled to get up and get dressed.

"Drew, we have only just found each other again. Anton and Savant rescued me. We have a honeymoon to catch up on."

"Marie, my best friend's life is in danger! I'm the only one who knows

Alan T. McKean

where he is. What kind of a honeymoon do you think we could have if I'm
burdened down with guilt and worry?" Why could I sense a *Dear John* letter on
the horizon? Something about Marie's demands and the way she was looking at
me seemed all wrong. The Marie I thought I knew well enough to marry would
have been filled with compassion and understanding for me, and genuine
concern for Angus. Or was it just my fevered mind playing ugly tricks on me?

General Carlisle strided into the room. "Drew! Why are you up and
getting dressed? Where do you think you're going? You must rest."

"I'm going back for Angus, sir."

He frowned and shook his head. "You stay here."

"With all due respect, sir, I must go." I finished dressing.

"Drew I'm sorry, but …"

I took a deep breath, ignoring the stabbing pain in my shoulder. "Sir, if I'm
not allowed to go, my resignation from Vanguard will be on your desk
immediately."

There was a long pause as General Carlisle and I traded glare for glare. This
probably meant my job and my future with Vanguard, but how could I leave
Angus to die? The simple answer was, I couldn't.

"General Carlisle, sir. You know our motto: *In time travel no one gets left
behind*. You organized the show that got Mike out of Beit She'an and Mi-Ling
off Bryant's ship." I looked at Marie, and prayed inside that she would not give
me an ultimatum to choose between her and Angus. "Your buddies rely on
you." Marie remained silent.

"The doc will give you a pain-killing injection," the general said, noting the
wince I tried to hide. "But you will not be going on your own, Drew. With that
injury to your shoulder, if Angus has been hurt, you won't be able to get him
into the time car by yourself even after you find him. So forget about turning
in your resignation—but, for heaven's sake, Drew—no heroics. Just get Angus
and get back."

"Thank you, sir, but no injection. I'll need my wits about me. May I suggest
Professor Savant if he will come? If anything were to happen, his knowledge
and bluff would be useful. We may need finesse."

At the start of the mission, Savant had committed himself to helping until
everybody was back. When the general asked him now, he responded, "I
wanted firsthand experience and it doesn't get much more firsthand than at the
front of Hougoumont."

Then General Carlisle told me, "Meryl saved your life by shooting that

Frenchman with the bayonet. She was on the wall at Hougoumont and saw you in the crowd."

"I'll have to thank her…but why was she there?" I asked puzzled. "And where is she now?"

General Carlisle shook his head. "As to your first question, I can't answer it. Confidential. As for your second question, she and Jayne have gone to some place called Sava Java in Aberdeen. She thought you would want to be with Marie. She doesn't know about Angus yet."

"Sava Java is a coffee place, sir." I decided to spare everybody the romantic associations the place held for Meryl and me. After we left Sava Java, I had taken Meryl to a jeweler on the pretense of getting something for my mother. What I had really purchased was a ring. Then I had asked her to marry me. As far as I knew, she still had the ring. She hadn't returned it when she broke off our engagement and left with Kitchi.

"I want you to take Savant and Hera with you," Carlisle said. "With her build, Hera could pass for a man providing they don't look too closely. If you get into scrap and you need someone to watch your back, she's about the best there is."

I had to agree with that. When I asked about Sebastian, the general told me what had happened to him. I went to see him.

"Shucks, I'm missin' all the fun. What way did I have to get stabbed for?"

I smiled at him. "The bad guy came off worse than you did. You stopped a real nasty problem from happening. Thank you."

"You're welcome. History sure is a funny thing. They were fighting each other back then, and it looks like nothing's changed. When folks gonna stop hating each other and live the way the good Lord intended? We've done got a whole passel of kids growing up being taught to hate each other. I need to get back to work. Mi-Ling and Libby promised to come by and see me later. They's getting' big and busy with schoolin'."

"Do me a favor, old man," I said, punching Sebastian's arm playfully. "Don't tell the girls I've been here and you've seen me. I think it's easier on them to assume I'm still gone than to know that I've had to make another trip so quickly."

Sebastian nodded. "You got it, old boy. I ain't gonna tell them a thing."

My shoulder was so sore that it throbbed with every step. I hoped the wound wouldn't open up again. Fast in and fast out, that's what we planned. Yet our timing really depended how quickly we could find Angus.

General Carlisle said to Hera, "Lieutenant, you are there to protect Major Faulkner and Professor Savant until they get Angus out. Don't go looking for fights. It's really important for all of you to stay together as much as possible."

Hera took a deep breath and said, "I know my duty, sir. We used to try to protect wounded friends in the arena." Her face fell into a deeply sorrowful expression as she added quietly, "We couldn't always do it."

The three of us, Savant, Hera, and I, examined several plans of Hougoumont. We located the south gate and the spot where I thought I had left Angus in reference to the location of the wall. Obviously, the majority of the trees had been shattered and would make poor landmarks. Strong apple trees in the orchard had looked like weeping willows. To avoid suspicion as to who we were, we had to be prepared to lead in battle. I reckoned that by now it was a wild stramash in front of the walls of Hougoumont.

We set off for Hougoumont, setting the targeting scanners in as narrow a frame as possible, and also where there would be as few people as possible. Savant had suggested that we try to avoid the Allied force called The King's German Legion. They were top-class troops and were on their way to Hougoumont. I thought we had better get there before we heard any more good news.

CHAPTER SEVEN

Hougoumont Revisited

"You two stick close by me when we get there and watch for Angus." We landed near bushes and trees. The scanner was programmed to look for a place with the least signs of life. We were armed with rifles of the time, which were shorter and could be used in trees. When a cannon ball explodes, you know it. Musket balls zipped past like so many angry wasps. Where was Angus? He was either okay or wounded. If you had no interest in getting over the wall and getting killed, and you knew someone was coming to take you out…what would you do? Hide…hide under bodies, perhaps? But how would you know when your rescuers arrived?

"Come on, you cowardly gendarme scum, get over the wall and fight." Some lower-ranking infantrymen passed us and then pressed on, too occupied to even be disgusted with us.

"Angus has to be hiding, I told Savant and Hera. "He's not going to risk his life."

Hera missed her footing and fell into some brush. We went after her and were shot at almost immediately. We saw the figures ahead and Savant said grimly, "Kings German Legion sharpshooters." Even from where we were, we could hear the harsh commands. "Keep moving. Keep low. Present as little a target as possible."

We fired back, hitting one. He fell and did not move again.

"Back through the bushes," I said urgently. Savant flagged down some French infantry and told them, "Those German Legion sharpshooters are heading your way."

At that point, a figure on the wall above us raised his rifle. It was pointed in our direction. Hera shot first. He fell back.

"I think I only wounded him," Hera grumbled. "I must be slipping."

Some of the infantry disappeared in the direction where the time car had deposited us. "They must be General Foy's division," Savant said. "It's going to get busy here."

Savant and I began shouting in French, "McTurk, where are you? McTurk!"

Hera said nothing, just watched our backs. We took an occasional shot at the wall trying not to hit anyone. I passed a thick thorny bush.

"McTurk, where are you?" I yelled again.

A hand and arm shot out of the bushes.

"For the Lord's sake, Major, shut up! You'll waken the dead and there are enough of them already."

Angus was cut, but his thick woolen uniform was not just for show. It had given him some protection from the thorns. His face was bleeding, but thankfully, his eyes and the rest of him seemed uninjured.

"I'm not wanting to appear ungrateful, laddie, but can we get the heck out of here? As quickly and quietly as possible?"

"Great to see you, too, Angus."

"Cut the chit chat, sir, and summon the blasted time car. It doesn't matter who sees us once it comes. Who would believe them anyway?"

I reached into my tunic pocket to get the control unit. It was gone.

"It's not here," I said, panicked. "I must have dropped it! Perhaps when Hera fell through the brush and we had a run-in with those Kings German Legion Riflemen."

"Is there no spare?" asked Angus in an exasperated, *haven't you learned anything* voice. My silence gave him his answer. If the gilt ever came off the gingerbread about time travel, it was naked now. Time travel might send adrenalin rushing through your veins—but it was purchased through extreme danger and any error, however small, could prove deadly.

"Exciting things like this never happen in academia or in the movies," Savant said. "And to think that this is real life!"

Angus looked and sounded exasperated. "What do you think these bullets whining around our ears and those English cannon balls exploding above our heads are made of—Scotch mist?"

"You two stay here," I said to Angus and Hera, attempting to grit my teeth and ignore the pounding pain in my shoulder. "Keep your backs to these thorn bushes. Nobody is going to voluntarily come through them. If you get a chance, scan the area with your devices and see if you can locate the control. Savant and I will retrace our steps and look for the control unit. If anyone has picked it up out of curiosity, we will negotiate. Gold seems to be good currency in all the times we've visited so far."

Carefully watching our surroundings for hidden dangers, we started off. "I suppose," Savant said, "if the watch doesn't work, we can always take it to the manufacturers and ask for our money back."

I looked at him.

"French sense of humor," he said.

With bullets whizzing around us and cannon balls exploding, he injects humor? No wonder his lectures at University were so popular.

French sharpshooters and infantry were firing at the King's German Legion and seemed to have checked their advance, but it could only be temporary. Sharpshooters worked in pairs, no matter what nationality. One sighted and the other fired, then reloaded, all while protected by his buddy.

We heard the noise coming from one pair who had stopped firing. Savant could move quickly. He came up behind them as they were shaking the box.

"You have it," Savant accused.

"Lieutenant, this box …"

"*Non mes amis*. It is the box given to me by my grand mere. She says you must guard it."

"Why is it making that noise? My ears feel as if they explode."

"That is not the box." A stray canon ball bounced past.

"That is the spirit of my grand mere. She guards the box. If you let me buy it back from you, the noise will stop and the spirit of my grandmother will be at peace. Six Napoleons for the box?"

A voice rose above the noise.

"What is up with you two? You are supposed to be killing Germans, not having a picnic."

"Six Napoleons?" Savant offered again. They nodded. With amazing sleight of hand, the gold was at Savant's fingertips. While they were distracted by the sight of gold, I pressed the button on the unit and the noise stopped.

"Look," Savant said, with awe in his voice. "Grand mere is happy." Both of the soldiers crossed themselves and went back to the simpler task of fighting an enemy you could see. The poor guys were more frightened of grand mere's spirit than of the Germans.

We quickly retraced our steps to Hera and Angus. We found a circle of trees further back and summoned the car. Just before getting in, I took a gold-hilted sword and a scabbard from a dead French Infantry officer. It would be my present to the lady who had saved my life from the walls of Hougoumont.

How we had all got back safely and unhurt, apart from Sebastian and me, was nothing short of a miracle. My uncle, Professor Adrian Conroy, was delighted to know that the gadget he had invented to find errant time control car units had worked. We were just delighted to have made it back in one piece. That night, I thought, Marie and I would at long last get our first taste of love, but she was not interested. She explained that she was bleeding because it was her period, and that sex would have to wait.

Disappointment is not a strong enough word for how I felt. I tried to hide my frustration. I reminded myself that sex would have been difficult for me to enjoy with the romping pain staging its playtime in my shoulder. It wasn't the lack of sex that worried and hurt me the most, however. It was the fact that for some reason, Marie didn't want me to touch her. We climbed into bed together, but each time I tried to put my arm around her, she moved away.

Somehow, the next day, things started to sour...perhaps ferment would be a better description. General Carlisle called all of us in for a debriefing, including Meryl, Jayne, and Marie.

The general smiled at us. "Well done," he said. "It was tough going, but everything turned out alright in the end, people. We got Marie back home."

There was a smile on Marie's face, but the smile failed to touch her eyes. Nor was there a single word of thanks from her in spite of the fact that we had risked our lives to rescue her. I was embarrassed by Marie's coldness. It was okay that she had turned away from me in bed last night. Perhaps she just wasn't ready to give herself in love yet. But it was wrong for her to freeze out the others who had given so much and suffered so much to save her.

I presented the sword to Meryl. "To the girl who saved my life at Hougoumont, a token of my thanks."

Everyone crowded around to admire the sword. Then Marie's petulant voice demanded, "And what did you bring back from Hougoumont for me? After all, I'm your wife."

It was the second time in my life I had heard silence echo. No one moved. In fact, everyone seemed to have forgotten how to breathe.

"If you will excuse me, General," Marie said. "I'm not an operative. I don't need to be debriefed. Drew, you know where I will be when you're finished." She left, swirling out the door.

I had never been so embarrassed in my life. I could feel the heat from my face and knew it must be flaming. "I'm sorry, sir. She's still overwrought from the kidnapping," I apologized.

General Carlisle asked, "Anton, Professor Savant. What happened when you got Marie out of the inn at Plancenoit?"

Guilt was written all over their faces. There was obviously something I didn't know.

"You go first, Anton," Savant said.

Anton looked down at the floor and around the room before he finally looked at me. "Drew, she didn't want to come with us. Or, should I say, she wanted out of the inn, but she didn't want to come back here. She had heard what Guy Leppard and his men had done against the Prussians in the forest. She knew that Napoleon was going to lose the battle…but she liked Guy. She kept asking for him and if he was okay."

General Carlisle interrupted. "Did she not ask about Major Faulkner? Her husband?"

Looking more miserable than I had ever seen him, Anton slowly shook his head. "No, although she did say she was glad he wasn't hurt."

"But I saw her at the window of the inn!" I protested. "She smiled at me and looked so joyful. She didn't stay at the window for very long, but I put that down to there being a guard in the room."

Meryl sat with her head in her hands. She said nothing. I saw tears rolling down her cheeks. She quickly brushed them away. "Drew, please take the sword back. It was lovely of you to think of me, but I can't accept it if it causes you problems with your wife. I'm sorry."

Reluctantly, I took the sword from Meryl. General Carlisle said, "Major, give it to me and I will take charge of it. By rights, it's a war treasure anyway."

Young Jayne, who had an amazing capacity for understatement, said, "Sir, Marie has done in five minutes what Reynolds failed to do in five years. She has put Vanguard in an uproar."

"People," General Carlisle said. "We must focus on the fact that once again we have stopped Reynolds, but not caught him. We can take it for granted that he will try again. The last thing we need is a loose cannon. I remember what happened with Dr. Lucy. I think I need to talk to Marie."

Hera coughed. "I can go get her. She owes her life to me. She may have forgotten Joshua Bryant's attempt on her life, but I haven't. She owes me a favor. It's repayment time."

Joshua Bryant had grabbed Marie on St. Cyrus beach after the operation that had restored her sight and was about to knock her blind again, trying to make me beg. Hera had come up behind him, cut Joshua's throat, and saved both Marie's sight and her life.

I was installed in a side room with a two-way mirror supplying access to the conversation when Marie arrived back. General Carlisle sat behind his desk. Escorted by Hera, Marie shuffled into the office. "I will not be treated in this way," Marie spat, glaring at the general. "If you want my cooperation, there's a price."

I had married this arrogant woman? Thank God we had not NOT consummated the marriage, I thought in horror.

"I demand to be taken back in your machine to the man I love."

Whatever the general was expecting, it was not that. He was clearly as shocked as I was. "The man you love? You just married Major Drew Faulkner. Isn't he the man you love? Your husband?"

"Perhaps once. But not now. Take me back now and I won't cause you any more trouble. If you don't take me back…you will pay for it."

"May I remind you, Madame Faulkner, that if hadn't been for Hera stopping Joshua Bryan's attack, you would be blind again now…or perhaps even dead."

"Yes, I remember that. I also remember Drew standing by while I was getting hit."

Her words were unfair. They hurt. I had only stood by to keep Joshua from carrying out his threat to kill Marie if I intervened. I dropped my head on the desk in the hidden room and let tears wash my eyes even though my hurt was too deep to flow away with mere tears. Why, oh why, had what I thought was love turned to hate, disrespect, and indifference?

The general seemed at a loss for words. Finally, he ventured, "May I remind you that you would still be blind without our help?"

"God healed me. Not you."

The general folded his hands. "Yes, God probably did heal you, but Vanguard paid for the surgery. Have you forgotten that?"

I couldn't take any more. Oh, for pity's sake! What did I have to do to win a girl's heart? Win her and keep her? I left the room with the mirror and entered the room with Carlisle, Hera and Marie. Marie was surprised. "What are you doing here, Drew?"

"I work here," I said. "My friends and I risk our lives to save other people. Marie, I was on the other side of that mirror. I heard what you said." She squirmed uncomfortably. "Marie, what did I do wrong? I thought you loved me."

Instead of answering, she looked vacantly at the table in front of her. "Is Guy Leppard so different from me?" I stupidly asked.

"I met him after I got kidnapped. They said you were dead. I…I fell in love with Guy. I needed someone to tell me I'm beautiful and smart for who I am and not just how well I play the piano. Someone who would find a way to bring the moon down out of the sky and give it to me if I asked him to. Guy is like that. I need him I want to be with him. I trust him. He has no one else in his life. I could never trust you and that Meryl woman."

Unfortunately, someone else had heard a lot of the conversation. Mi-Ling had come looking for me when she heard I was back. She had been listening outside the door. None of us had realized she was there.

Now Mi-Ling crossed the room to Marie. Her face was chalk white. I had never seen her young face register such pain since we had left Foo-Chow.

"Why?" she asked. "Why are you doing this to us, Mummy Marie?"

"You are too young to understand."

"You forget that my heart is older than my years," Mi-Ling stated. "Why do you hate Papa so much?"

"I suppose you hate me now?" Marie asked.

Mi-Ling shrugged slender shoulders and brushed silky, long, black wings of hair back from her face. "Does it matter to you what I think?" Mi-Ling asked. There was a brief silence. Mi-Ling continued, "Mi-Ling feels sorry that you carry so much hate. Take it to Father God. He will help you."

Marie snorted. "God can't help in this."

"Yet, only a few minutes ago Mi-Ling heard you say that God healed you of your blindness when you could see only darkness. Mi-Ling prays to Father God that He will heal you of your new blindness. It is worse than the old blindness."

Mi-Ling flung herself into my arms and hugged me so tightly that I gasped for air and my shoulder began throbbing again. I could feel the wetness of tears on her face. I held her gently for a moment, then she slipped out of my arms and left, giving me such a look of love and compassion as she left that a lump thrust itself into my throat, nearly choking me.

Casting a malevolent look at Marie, Hera followed Mi-Ling out of the room. My heart filled with gratitude. Hera was both lion and lamb. She would enfold Mi-Ling in soft, comforting lamb's wool.

"I will give you my decision in the morning," Marie informed me haughtily. "Although I don't expect to change my mind and agree to stay. Meanwhile, Drew, you can stay with Victoria and Adrian and the girls." Almost as an afterthought, she added, "Thank you, General. I'm sorry it has to be this way." She left like an ice-laden breeze on a winter's day.

"I feel like going for a drink—and not just coffee—but I know that's not the answer," I said.

"Major, I am so sorry," General Carlisle said. "I'm actually speechless."

"So am I. Does Meryl have to know about this? At least she and Kitchi have found happiness. I want happiness for her almost more than I want it for myself. Where is she anyway, if I can ask."

"She has gone back to 1759, to see Kitchi."

"That's good. She couldn't do better than Kitchi. We owe him so much. I owe him the life of my daughter. Meryl made a choice between me and Kitchi and got it right. I made a choice between her and Marie and got it wrong. Funny, I can fight battles and rescue people, but when it comes to women...I lose every time." My words reminded me of Lucy. Meryl had given me up because she thought I should marry Lucy and she wanted what was best for me. I sighed so deeply that I sank down into my chair until a stabbing pain in my shoulder made me sit bolt upright again.

General Carlisle looked at me and shook his head. "There is one heart who never stopped loving you loving you and who loved you enough to let you go."

"Who?" I asked, although I suspected he was talking about Meryl. I smiled and said sadly, "She has Kitchi. He's a great guy. He'll make her a good husband. Sir, maybe it's time I got out of time travel and went back to boredom and the Finlander Lounge and my friends at the weekend." I got up and walked around the room. "Sir, I can't do this anymore."

"I would consider it a favor if you stayed," he replied.

I shook my head. "Nobody is indispensable, sir."

"In this case, that's not quite true. I'm not talking to you as your boss, but as a father. Meryl Scott is my daughter. Her real second name is Carlisle."

"I know, sir. Your wife told me. But I can't see where I come into that. I nearly married Meryl. Perhaps I didn't try hard enough. She has been a good friend and..." I felt my face turning red. Meryl had been so much more to me than just a good friend. But I wasn't comfortable admitting that to her father!

"Anyway, sir, that's all in the past. She has Kitchi now and he will make her happy. I would rather die than see her hurt again. At least if I gave my life for Meryl's happiness it would be for something good. She's always been there for me. I was so young and stupid once that I expected perfection in others that I didn't have in myself. That unreal expectation hurt Meryl, and I'm sorry. We are all human and we all have flaws and make mistakes. There are no heroes, just those who try to be. Does Meryl know you're her real father?" I asked.

He took a deep breath. "No, Drew, she doesn't. It's something my ex-wife hid from her at the same time she hid Meryl from me. By the time I found Meryl, well...I couldn't bear to barge in and upset her happy adoptive home and parents." He sighed and shook his head. "Was I right? Was I wrong? That's something I may never know. But...Drew...there's something else I need to tell you. Kitchi...Kitchi is dead."

"What? No, that can't be! General Carlisle, you said Meryl had gone to see Kitchi..."

"Yes, to attend his funeral, or the Native American equivalent. He was ambushed by the French and their Huron allies. He fought them single-handedly to let the others in his party escape. The others got help, but it was too late for him. Meryl is heartbroken. You just said you would rather die than see Meryl hurt again. Major...Drew...take care of my little girl. I'm tired. It's been a long day for us all. The doc will give you something if you can't sleep. Please, think over what I said. Goodnight, Drew."

I got up. "I will think of nothing else. Poor Meryl. She must be hurting so much, and she's so far away."

Mentally and physically, I was zonked. My shoulder burned like fire and my pain knowing Meryl's grief was no less intense. I decided to get help to sleep from our small pharmacy.

"Yep, this will do the trick. Make sure you go to the loo before you take it. You might not get warnings. In fact, better take a couple of these." The doctor tossed out what looked like an adult version of a child's diaper.

"Put that on and it won't matter if you wake up or not. Cup it in the middle and do the tapes up and Bob is your uncle. If I didn't make the offer, the housekeeper would nark at me if the bed got wet because of something I had given you."

Well, I thought with a shrug. *Astronauts wear them to spacewalk, why not time travelers?*

Even with the aid of the sleeping pill, my mind fought hard against forgetfulness. The what-could-have beens. Sadly, I thought of Marie's angel touch on the piano keys. I remembered the concerts, and Queen Victoria, a mish mash of all that had happened. I knew I had to take Marie back myself if she still wanted to go in the morning, which I knew in my heart was inevitable. I would not ask any of the others to take that risk, and going back to Plancenoit was a huge risk. I couldn't just let Marie go and point her in Guy's direction. Then it began to dawn on me: suppose Reynolds showed up? Did he know of Marie's feelings and that they had changed? It had seemed almost too easy for Anton and Professor Savant to rescue Marie from the inn at Plancenoit.

Angus had gone with Meryl back to 1759. So, in the general's office, that left Jayne, Anton, Sebastian, and Hera. Hera's husband, Mike Argo, had been sent on a brief mission to the Middle East. Professor Savant was still with us. That was good. We needed his expertise.

The next morning, we all met in the briefing room. I was glad to see Sebastian there and looking a lot more chipper.

The General told us, "We have to return Marie to Waterloo so she can link up with her lover. Drew has volunteered to go back with her so she gets there safely."

"I don't want anyone else to put their life at risk," I explained.

"We never go alone," Anton objected. "General Carlisle, sir, I volunteer to go back with Drew. Having helped rescue Marie in the first place, I know the lay of the land."

Savant piped in, "Never let it be said that I turned down a chance to get back to Waterloo. I, too, know the area. When we let Leppard and her meet and talk…my, he must have been a fast worker."

"There was no love in the first place, apparently," I sighed. "Not on her part. Just my stupid mistake."

"I do not understand women," Savant said.

Anton coughed. "Allow me, dear professor, to send you my copy of my book, *How to Understand Women*. The introduction alone runs to 2,000 pages." Then the familiar impish grin stole over his face. "I jest! The introduction is only 1,000 pages. I had to simplify things."

"Yes, Anton," General Carlisle said. "I love my Clarissa, but at times I feel that I need to read one of those long, educational books on how to understand women." He cleared his throat. "But for now, thank you, Anton and Professor Savant, for volunteering to go back with Drew."

"When we were there," Anton continued, "I think we got out the back door as Reynolds was coming in the front. Marie had no further desire to meet him than we did. The point is, where do we target the scanner to land? I think I can recall the path we took from the inn to where Guy Leppard was. I'm sure I can find it.

"When Reynolds realized that Marie was gone, he probably guessed she had been rescued. No woman would have gone wandering off on her own at that time. Not even you, Lieutenant Hera."

Hera shrugged her shoulders. "You do not risk your life without a purpose," she agreed.

"Hera, you and Jayne stay here," the general said. "I can't risk more operatives on what is an unofficial mission. Drew, you've got backup. So take Marie back. All of you know what Guy Leppard looks like and approximately where to find him. It shouldn't be hard, yet I confess...I can't shake the feeling that this will somehow end in grief."

We called in Adrian Conroy. He reckoned he could hit the right spot. "Just watch out for Reynolds and his tricks. He's about as straight as a rusty corkscrew."

Marie was briefed. She promised not give anyone away as long as she got to Guy. There was nothing else to do. As Marie got into the time car, my mind went back to that raven-haired girl who played Chopin with so much fire.

We shot through to 1815, the evening of June 17 near Plancenoit. Anton was as good as his word. He found the hussars and Guy Leppard.

"My thanks," Guy said to us, "for bringing the lady here."

"A touching scene," a voice said, "where the gendarme delivers up his wife to someone else. Oh, don't worry, captain. The emperor will be most grateful." Reynolds stepped out of the shadows.

I swear I could smell Reynolds before I could see him; he smelled like sour, clabbered milk. "Now, if you will just hand her over to me, I will return her to the emperor who thinks she is his Marie."

Leppard grew annoyed. "You insult a lady's honor sir, *my* lady's honor. I demand satisfaction, coward."

There was a hush and a sigh. "How boring and dull." Reynolds yawned mockingly. He was way too calm.

Pistols were produced. What an army—little food and water, but always a set of dueling pistols to hand.

Javel was Guy's second in command and Colonel Liegeard was Guy's superior officer. They attempted to reason with Reynolds.

"This duel does not have to take place. Good God! There's a whole melee of nationalities to kill off. Why try to kill each other?"

Reynolds could not be dissuaded. He got first choice because he had been challenged. Guy took the pistol that was left. One of Reynolds 'yes' men acted as his second. I remembered the last duel I was involved in and how I would have been killed except for Meryl.

The assailants each took fifteen paces, during which time Reynolds started singing, "*Tick tok, tick tok.*"

Oh, dear God, he's up to something, I thought.

Reynolds, stopped, turned, and sang, "*Tick tok, now you turn to see my Glock.*"

Then everything happened in a blur.

Reynolds had the dueling pistol in one hand, but pulled out a Glock with the other. It added seconds onto the sequence. He had made a mistake and had not taken the safety catch off. Marie knew what was happening. She ran toward Guy. Three or four shots rang out. Guy and Marie were both hit. Marie picked up Guy's pistol and fired back at Reynolds. The shot hit him in the shoulder. You could hear it as the ball entered. He lost his calm demeanor. The pain must have been awful, but he ran into the darkness.

Liegeard said to some of Guy's men. "After him! Ten Napoleons dead or alive." Then they put Guy on a stretcher and carried him away.

Marie lay on the ground coughing up blood. I dropped to the ground beside her and took her head in my lap. "God in Heaven, Marie, you didn't have to do that. You hit him."

She smiled wanly. "If I had not, the next shot would have been you. I have already brought you so much unhappiness and you don't deserve any of it. Drew, say you forgive me."

"Marie, my darling, of course I do."

She sighed. "I've been a stupid woman. I said a lot of things I shouldn't have said and didn't mean." She gasped as more blood trickled out of her mouth. "I think I was stupid because I spent so many years blind and believing that no one could love me. That I had nothing worthwhile to offer. When I got my sight back, it went to my head. Drew, promise me. Please tell Mi-Ling I'm sorry. Tell her I love her and would have been proud to have been her Mummy Marie. Tell Libby, too. Please, Drew. Promise me." I kissed her lips in spite of the blood.

"Marie," I whispered with tears charging down my face and dropping onto Marie's face. "Don't go. I love you. I really love you. God, Marie, don't die! Please, don't die."

"If you can forgive a foolish woman, I love you, my Major, my hero." Her words were weak and I felt her body relaxing in my arms.

"Marie! No! No, Marie! Please don't go! Don't leave me." The color drained from her face. I knew she was gone. I held her in my arms and kissed her again and again, rubbing my face against hers. I couldn't believe it. Not again. She was home. Nothing could hurt her again. But what about me? I sobbed over her, my tears mingling with her blood, sending pink froth spattering against the ground.

Javel put his hand on my shoulder. "I'm sorry, my friend. You must have loved her greatly."

"She was my wife, Javel. She saved Guy's life. She gave up her own to save his. And you know what, she played Chopin like an angel."

"Now she will play Chopin with the angels," he said softly. "But I am so sorry. Guy did not know…I did not know. We did not know she was your wife."

I stood up, gently sliding Marie off my lap and gave Javel the gold I had. "Please bury her in the most beautiful churchyard you can find. Ask Elouise. She will help."

Javel nodded. "I will do that. I promise you as one soldier to another."

"How badly is Guy hurt?"

"He will recover if the wound does not go bad. But what a strange shape the bullet was. You go now, Major. I will take care of Marie. She saved the Captain's life. To us she is a heroine. What was her favorite flower?"

"Violets," I replied.

CHAPTER EIGHT

God's Healing Touch

Lord Jesus, I prayed silently, *that didn't need to happen. What are you putting me through? What have I done that I have offended You so much?* The answer was immediate and startled me. I looked around to see if anyone else had heard the voice. *Peace, Drew The day is not over yet. Trust Me. All will be made clear. Don't let your faith die with Marie. She is safe now. I will take good care of her.*

Anton came over, wrapped his arms around me, and pounded my back. I nearly yelped as sudden pain shot through my shoulder. "My friend, I don't know what to say except how sorry I am. I hope Reynolds' wound turns bad and that he never sleeps except in death."

I could still taste Marie's lips. It is amazing how deep love goes. The story I would tell General Carlisle would be slightly altered. I could not let Marie be remembered as selfish and ungrateful. She had earned the right to be remembered as courageous. I could at least do that for her. I hoped Anton and Savant would back me up.

"Come on guys," I told them wearily. "I've had enough of Waterloo."

When we arrived back at HQ, the looks on our faces reaffirmed General Carlisle's premonition, even as he asked, "Did Marie find Leppard?"

"Sir," I said, "Marie is dead. She was shot in a duel with Reynolds. Reynolds had planned to kill Leppard and then me. Marie had planned all along not just to head back to Waterloo, but to take us with her. It wasn't about going back to Guy, but about stopping Reynolds. She had to sicken us enough that we'd be glad to get rid of her to achieve that aim. It almost worked."

General Carlisle drew in a deep breath. "It worked, but how wrong we were. How wrong I was."

Anton cast a brooding look in my direction, but remained silent.

"Guy got riled up and called Reynolds a coward."

"A somewhat excessive compliment, but appropriate," the general remarked.

"It led to the duel. In a straight fight, Leppard would have killed Reynolds even with one shot. But Reynolds is a coward. He had a Glock. Thankfully, he forgot to release the safety catch. Marie saw what was happening. She ran in front of Leppard. She realized that Reynolds would shoot me next. Reynolds hit Guy twice and Marie twice. Guy had turned to the side, but Marie faced him directly. She picked up Guy's pistol and fired back at Reynolds. The ball hit him in the shoulder and he dropped the dueling pistol. But he hung onto the Glock and ran off with his arm hanging by his side."

"He has my sympathy," the general remarked dryly, "but one has to say it's a pity it was not his neck he was hanging by. Still, half a loaf is better than none, but I do hope the injury causes an excessive amount of pain and that doctors are unable to save his arm."

"Sir, Marie died a heroine. She tried her best to get Reynolds to come far enough out of the woodwork that we could get him. Hopefully she crippled him and he will have to get to more modern medicine. Guy Leppard seems to have survived, thankfully."

Carlisle turned to Anton and Savant. "Would you gentlemen agree with the Major's account?"

Anton smiled, "What is it the English say? I agree; we agree with knobs on."

"Marie's name will go on the memorial plaque in Vanguard HQ along with Kitchi's," Carlisle said. "Courageous heroes who have fought the battle against evil with us."

Carlisle looked around at Hera, Jayne, Anton, and Sebastian. He asked Adrian to join us. Meryl and Angus were still away, but, meanwhile, we had a problem. Marie had smashed Reynolds' shoulder with her shot, but his head was still intact and he would not give up engineering malevolence.

"Right, people. Are we agreed Reynolds will try again?" the general asked.

Anton scratched his head. "Once he gets his shoulder sorted, if he gets it sorted."

Uncle Adrian said, "He can never quite manage to beat us. We are always one step ahead of him. I fear he takes that as an insult to what he considers his superior intellect. We need something that is so attractive to him that he lets his guard down. On his own, he can't yet defeat us. And conversely, as close as we have come, we have never been able to catch him. What the answer is…well, that's another matter." Adrian thumped his chin thoughtfully.

"Difficult or no, we have to come up with the right answer, and soon. While Reynolds is injured, he may look for a second in command. We can't afford another Caleb Bryant. Okay, people, thinking caps on and get back to me quickly. Meanwhile, John, can I have a word?"

"Of course," General Carlisle said, rising from his chair.

The rest of us left. Apart from condolences, there was not much anyone could say to me. I walked outside HQ. Suddenly the world seemed a very lonely place. I went along to see Mi-Ling and Libby. They were in Victoria's sitting room, reading. When they saw me, they dropped their books and ran to hug me.

Libby was angry, but not at me. "If it hadn't been for my father, none of this would have happened. I'm sorry!" Her tear-stained face broke my heart. Even her normally bouncy, curly hair looked sad. How, I wondered, had she found out about Marie before I could tell her?

We sat on the couch together. Mi-Ling went to the other side of the room and pretended to read a magazine. I knew she was only pretending because the magazine was upside down.

"Sweetheart," I said to Libby, taking her hand. "You are in no way responsible for what happened to Marie. Nobody blames you."

"My father did nothing good ever! He was mean! Everybody hated him," she announced through tears.

I tilted her head up and looked into her eyes. "Listen…one wonderful, fantastic and lovely gift came from your father."

"Really?" she asked with a hopeful voice. "What?"

I smiled at her. "God took a hand and you came into the world. Pretty, brave, tender and caring. I'm going to be the best father to you that I can be until someday when some handsome young man falls deeply in love with you—head over heels. Then the two of you can come back to visit this sad old man with four grandchildren, two large dogs, and a kitty cat for good measure."

Libby giggled at that vision. "You'll never be a sad old man. And I like small dogs, not big ones."

"Whatever. But no more tears. I love you, and Mi-ling loves you…in fact, everyone here loves you. How could they not? You are so special."

Libby looked suddenly grown up for her years. "I was thinking of you. I'm going to continue praying that you will meet a nice lady who will stay with you and love you." She gasped at the idea and added in delight, "Then Mi-Ling and

Libby will have lots of sisters and brothers."

Mi-Ling, who had finally turned her magazine around the right way, said, "Father God doesn't want Papa to be lonely. He will sort things like mending a broken toy. Papa puts things back together again. God fixes things even better than Papa does."

Victoria came and told the girls, "You two need rest if you don't want to get old and wrinkled like me. That's what happens if you don't get enough sleep."

Mi-Ling said, "Papa must get a lot of sleep. He has no wrinklies, except when he forgets how to smile."

"Goodnight, you two. How can someone stay sad with daughters like you?" Kisses and hugs were passed around, and then they were gone.

Victoria said, "You have still have your daughters. Cherish them. Love them. How's that shoulder holding up? Do you want to sleep on the couch?"

"Thanks, Mum, but I better go up to bed. The girls are settled in with you for the night, so I'll go on back to my flat. And pop around in time for breakfast with the family?"

She laughed at the hopeful note in my voice. "Yes, Drew, you better. The girls would never forgive me if I let their papa starve. And you need to spend some time with them now that you're back."

I meant to head for my flat immediately, but I was so deep in thought that I lost all track of time. I was walking down a corridor at Vanguard when I saw Meryl heading in my direction. I stopped and waited for her. "Meryl, I'm sorry about Kitchi. You must be devastated."

She nodded. "As are you. I am so sorry, Drew. I still can't believe it about Marie. I just don't know what to say."

"Get some rest, my friend. Mi -Ling has informed me if you don't get enough rest, you get wrinklies." Meryl smiled. "See you tomorrow," I said. I hugged her and started to walk away. She stopped me, reaching up to kiss my cheek. I had not wanted tomorrow to come, but now as my head hit the pillow...I was no longer sure.

* * *

After breakfast with Victoria and the girls, I met Angus and Sebastian. Mike had safely returned from his mission and he quickly joined us. We wandered around the compound checking security points. I asked, "Guys, say you wanted to attack our HQ. To raid with an aim to destroy. How would you do it?"

Angus replied without hesitation, "Create a diversion at the front gate, then fly in helicopters. Land people in different spots and try to knock out the command center. You would have to have a ground plan. Unless you knew the strength of the defense you couldn't risk a major firefight."

It took Mike longer to reply. From the look on his face, he was still reveling in the greeting Hera had given him when he returned. She had been a bit on the grumpy side and had excused it by telling us how much she missed her husband. "I agree, helicopter landing," Mike said cautiously, "but that makes you vulnerable to missiles and rocket-propelled grenades. You would need a gunship and troop carriers."

Sebastian shook his head. "Plan A would be to destroy the time car terminal. If that failed, I would try to kill General Carlisle."

Meryl walked out to join us. She wore a light blue suit that made her look like a summer sky. It was only the stress on her face that spoiled that vision. She had just lost the man she loved. Sorrow was untimely upon her. Remembering her loss, we fell silent out of respect. We all owed much to Kitchi.

"Penny for them, guys," she quipped. "Is this a private confab? Or can anyone join in?"

"We were just thinking about how Reynolds would attack this place should he come here for a show down. So far," I explained, "we have decided he would blow up the time car terminal and kill the general. After landing in helicopters."

"Cheerful thoughts," Meryl countered. She shook her head and a lock of blonde hair fell across her face. She pushed it behind her ear and sighed. "This place can be rebuilt or relocated, probably with American help. General Carlisle can be replaced. But the originality of Professor Conroy can't. He is the font of time travel ideas and research. Once you block him, we'd be finished."

We all nodded in agreement with Meryl's deduction.

"The other possibility," Angus mused, "is that you don't blow the place up. You make it uninhabitable for a long time."

"How?" I asked.

"By using a dirty bomb. Make the place so radioactive that nobody can come near, and like Valentenoi, that place in Russia where the reactor blew up HQ gets encased in concrete and the area all around is cut off. That puts time travel into the hands of a terrorist and his organization. It frees them to go back in history and right the wrongs as they see them."

It took a while for the picture to sink in. All the terrorist or nationalist groups paying PATCH to change history for them. They would have governments eating out of their hands.

Even so, Meryl was right. They had one piece missing before they could get total control. They had to get what my uncle knew about time travel. I shuddered to think of what they would do to get that information from him. I really wished Marie's bullet had hit Reynolds between the eyes instead of in the shoulder. We had to get Reynolds to make a move. This called for a meeting: if Reynolds were going to attack, especially if he had a professional terrorist as an "advisor," the attack would be at night. That much we could guess with fair certainty.

At the heart of Vanguard Headquarters is a special room packed with security devices that can be shut off from the outside. I hadn't known about this room. It was only when the general mentioned it that I realized it was there. So we trooped into the secure room to discuss options. The general, Adrian, Anton, Angus, Meryl, Jayne, Sebastian, and Mike and Hera... in fact, the whole team. The room was decorated in green and beige and looked quite normal. When we got inside and sat down, Adrian addressed us.

"I'm going to change sides. Going to join PATCH. It really is very heady if we're right. I could have a great deal of power working with Reynolds and his terrorist buddies. I'm going to go to the newspapers and expose Vanguard. If I do it right, there will be such a ruckus raised that Reynolds will think I'm open to offers. Then I'll have to do something to betray Vanguard. I'm telling you this because I have no desire to be killed by any of you who think I am really supporting Reynolds or PATCH."

We must have looked like a collection of goldfish that had just seen a cat staring at us from the other side of the bowl. "What I'm going to do." he continued, "you will have to wait and see. Meanwhile...this is of utmost importance! All you have to do is act normally. We will install one or two little surprises to welcome helicopters. The people at the gate have been told to dress down so they look more like banana republic guards than highly trained soldiers. There will also be some SAS boys about. Don't worry. You won't see them until you need them. We're also getting help from Craig Carter of the USMC. They, too, will keep a low profile. Craig Carter himself is coming over to help us."

Craig was a USMC special operative who had come to help us when we went back to 1868, to save the life of Queen Victoria after PATCH operatives had tried to kill her and put someone else in her place. Craig had been a big help. He also would be acting as a liaison with the White House and the new President—Galbraith—who understood what PATCH was and hated them as much as we did. When Galbraith was mentioned, General Carlisle always said, "Now, that's a man you can work with."

The meeting in the secure room gave us confidence in the face of everything else that was going on in the world. Craig would come along with Hank Goodburn. Hank had been with us when Caleb Bryant, Reynolds' then second in command, had been cornered and had fallen from the castle walls at Dunnottar. Hank had shown even more abilities since then and was now in Special Forces.

We suspected a night attack, so lighting had been increased. Over the years, bushes had been encouraged to grow around the house and on the roof, providing cover from aerial observation. We had to be ready. We decided to keep Mi-ling and Libby with us at Vanguard HQ. If Reynolds found them somewhere else, they would be more open to kidnapping. Poor Mi-Ling had had enough of that.

It took a couple more days to finish our precautions. After that, Adrian would drop his bombshell. Time travel would seem so unlikely, so way out, that high-ranking scientists would scorn talks about it and dismiss his claim that he could no longer hide his secret and had decided to go public. Adrian would become the brunt of public ridicule, but that should get Reynolds' attention. Our plan was that Reynolds would approach Adrian with an offer for a change of employment. Those who knew that time travel was true would take Adrian seriously. That included Reynolds and his terrorist sidekick.

CHAPTER NINE

Showdown at Last

Adrian Conroy proceeded to pen statements that would shred his scientific credulity. He claimed that time travel was true. More ludicrous to many was his claim that he and the people who worked with him had met various historical figures, and that Napoleon I of France was really a jolly decent chap. Of course, he explained the caution needed to refrain from upsetting history. He warned that there were many who wanted to change events, but stated that doing so was quite impossible. He didn't want to start a panic.

Adrian sent out statements to the major universities in the United States, United Kingdom, Russia, Peoples Republic of China, and a selection of universities in Europe, Asia, and South America. "E-mail is a great thing" he observed enthusiastically. "One can achieve so much in such a short time. This is bound to get Reynolds' attention, for like us, he knows that time travel is factual…and worse yet…that events can be changed."

The good and the famous of the world's scientific communities lined up to distance themselves from what Adrian said. The papers loved it. It made front page news: *Mad Scientist Claims Time Travel Possible.*

Contests sprung up overnight. "We are running a special contest and the winner gets to go back to whatever time they feel they belong in. Collect our special coupons over the coming week; the winner gets to spend a week in time of your choice. See the War between the States firsthand. Get a grandstand seat at Vicksburg. What were WWI trenches really like?" So it continued: "Did Cleopatra look anything like Elizabeth Taylor? See for yourself! Instant return home in face of danger."

Major insurance companies began offering insurance rates for time travel depending, of course, on how dangerous the brokers considered the ultimate time travel destination. Eminent men appeared on television, over the internet, and on Youtube conjecturing the reasons behind why one of the greatest scientific minds had become unhinged. Some speculated on possible treatment options for Adrian Conroy.

President Galbraith of the United States delivered a statement: "The scientific community of the United States of America wishes to distance itself from such fanciful flights of scientific fantasy. We have always put as our priority the serious issues that face America and the rest of the world today. Congress holds that our attention has been, and will continue to be, focused on the real needs of the American people and our allies. We are a government of the present and of the future. The past is gone. It cannot be changed. God bless America."

Actually, President Galbraith was worried. He foresaw the significance of time travel and recognized the danger of it falling into the wrong hands. If the U.S., or any other government, put out an all-points bulletin on Reynolds, he would simply move to another time. We had to keep Reynolds off guard.

"Keep me informed," President Galbraith had requested when he spoke to General Carlisle.

What stuck with me was the response given by Professor Levoranta of Turku University, in Finland. Levoranta said, "We would love to think that time travel was real. Just think of the good that could be done and the evil that could be undone. Think of the lives that could be saved by the changing of one decision. Suppose men of peace who were cut down in their prime by an assassination had been able to escape death. What a difference it would have made if Martin Luther King had been allowed to continue; if Lincoln had not been assassinated; if Kennedy had not been shot in Dallas. The list of good men and women cut short in their prime is long. The danger is that were we to possess such a power, we would live in fear that time travel would fall into the wrong hands. That it would present to an enemy such a weapon that the nuclear bomb would fade to insignificance. I suspend my judgment, as at one time it was thought that flight or traveling to the moon was impossible. All we can do is wait and see if this truth or hoax. The world is in God's hands."

We spent as much time as possible combing through the papers and broadcasts in case Reynolds had left us a clue as to his plans. Professor Levoranta had got it right. He had spoken sense.

I was with Meryl in the canteen. We had just finished cups of extremely strong coffee. She had read what I had read. "Drew," she said. "All the people who are here are it. We're the last defense. I'm starting to realize how the folks at the Alamo must have felt."

"We've got to stop Reynolds or die in the attempt. Meryl, I'm glad you're here."

She smiled and said, "Remember the phrase we used at one time? '*Amigos para siempre.*' Friends always."

"Friends always." I squeezed her shoulder, then turned and started to walk away. Turning back, I said half in jest, "and when we are grey haired, we can tell our time travel stories to our grandchildren."

She replied instantly, "And they will be bored stiff, saying, 'Oh, Gramps and Gran, you tell some funny stories. Can we go and now and get ice cream at Sava Java?'" I saw a look in her eyes that I had not seen for a long time and found that my own eyes began to blur. I waved and forced myself to turn away. I had just made the door when her voice stopped me. "Drew, hold me."

I stopped, suddenly paralyzed. I turned slowly around. Meryl stood holding her arms out to me. I had heard words that my heart longed to hear and thought it would never hear again. I ran across the room took her in my arms and held her. Then, somehow, like two long-parted lovers—our lips found each other again. I could smell the scent of coconut from her hair. All the good memories flooded back. We didn't speak. Words would be superfluous, but there was much sighing.

There was a cough at the canteen door and General Carlisle's voice remarked, "Well, there's a sight to gladden the eyes. What a perfect way to end the day. If you could see your faces…you both look about ten years younger."

Waving aside our objections that we had just finished coffee, the general brought us two new cups. "Strong. Just like both of you like it. Strong, just like the both of you. I know it's not that coffee you like…what is it you call it? *Saint Java?* but it's all we have here. I hate to remind you, but we are all in imminent danger. As if you two have not already had enough things happen you to last two lifetimes. When you get your fill of strong coffee to keep you awake, get back to checking the world's press for any clues about Reynolds. It's about time he contacted us again on the sly. Mocked us."

Carlisle excused himself. Alone now, we sat across the table from one another and held hands. Words did not seem important until three words rang through both our hearts.

"I love you," I told Meryl.

"And I love you," she replied. Words as old as tea, but when you are on the receiving end, how wonderful they are.

We were reluctant to speak in case speech broke the spell. We had both left each other behind for new loves, yet somehow, that which could have died had not died.

"Drew, you are going to find it hard to believe, but in my heart I've never stopped loving you. I tried to keep busy. I was powerfully attracted to Kitchi and I loved him, too, in a way, but a different way from how I've always loved you. I owed Kitchi so much—my life even. It was owing him that, and infatuation, and a school girl crush." She sighed and the silver of her tears shone under the light.

She shook her head. "When I heard news about you, or saw you, I could feel my heart race in my chest as if he were trapped—a prisoner. He wanted to be where you were. I didn't think it would ever be possible again. When I hugged you just now, I felt peace as if my heart had found his other half again. And, yes, I'm sure. I love you. My love for you has never died. It's been hidden away like buried treasure deep in the dungeon of my spirit, crying to be found again."

I pulled Meryl close. I closed my eyes and kissed her. Now I knew the long journey of the boat of my life had found a home at long last.

Meryl gently pushed herself out of my arms. "I have something for you. Something I should have given back to you, only it reminded me of our love and I didn't want to let go of it." She produced the sapphire engagement ring I had brought her and placed it in my hand.

"It is beautiful," she said, looking at the blue ring of fire dancing around the ring, "but not as beautiful as the heart that gave it to me."

"Meryl, I love you. Marry me. Let's make a forever home for us and Mi-Ling and Libby." Meryl nodded. Her rogue lock of blond hair fell across her face. She pushed it back behind her ear with her left hand. I grabbed her hand and slipped the ring on the third finger of her left hand.

I was sure I could hear a sigh as it slipped into place. She smiled, not a smile of triumph, but a smile like summer sunshine. "Till death us do part. *Amigos para siempre.*"

We shared another kiss before Anton's voice broke into the cold reality of our situation. Yet, with Meryl's hand in mine, it didn't seem so bad.

"Join me in the briefing room, both of you," Anton said. "I think I've found something."

The general, Anton, and Adrian were already there when Meryl and I slipped quietly into the room. Anton held up a copy of the Russian Newspaper PRAVDA and said, "I was running through the responses to Professor Conroy's statement. There's one from the Sorbonne in Paris…ah, the Sorbonne. What champagne! What singing! What beautiful women…"

He realized we were fidgeting in our chairs. "Ah…I get a deep impression that you would like me to recount my Sorbonne experiences at another time. Still, my reading was not nostalgia. This is supposedly from a Professor Reynard of the Sorbonne …*The existence or nonexistence of time travel and its discovery and development is in the hands of Kismet, or Fate. If Professor Conroy is correct, then time travel will be developed and let us hope it falls into the right hands. With time travel, one could change the world and history to make the world a better place and put the right people in control.*" Anton paused to let the quote sink in with everyone. I've checked. There is no Professor Reynolds on the staff of the Sorbonne."

I reached out for Meryl's hand, for the place had become cold, suffused by the veiled and evil malice of what Professor Reynard had stated.

"It's got to be him," General Carlisle said. "I can smell him from here. Well done, Anton. Thank you. Adrian, can you get your boys on the computer to run a check on all known terrorist groups? Check for any link with Kismet or fate. I have a feeling this is his teasing warning—but with deadly implications."

Adrian nodded. "I'll get on it right away. I think you're right, so let's try and discover what we might be up against."

Adrian left with Anton on his heels. I smiled. Anton had, with due diligence, found the clue. He wasn't about to be left out of the next stage of our campaign to stop Reynolds!

General Carlisle noticed the ring on Meryl's finger and smiled. "It really does become you, Meryl. I'm happy for you both. Just stay alive when Reynolds turns up. The only death I want to see is his. He's earned it. Repeatedly.

"I expect we will be attacked at night. Even if Reynolds wants to be foolhardy and show contempt, he won't willingly risk defeat. Besides, I have a feeling that the leader of Kismet—if we're not barking up the wrong tree there—will know the value of a night raid." He spun the pen in his hand around quickly several times. "I would estimate about 3 a.m. They will know that's when people are at their sleepiest and least alert. Let's hope it isn't a moonlit night they choose. Remember, their primary target will Professor Adrian Conroy. Drew, I want you to make the dispositions. You're responsible for the arrangements of the troops. If anything happens to me, you are in command and that is an order."

We looked startled.

"Well, after all," the general told us. "I'm not immortal. I'm not going to go on forever. Actually…" he grew pensive. "I would like to retire someday soon. Go and build up my model railway."

* * *

We held planning meetings with the SAS, Marines, and Special Services and decided on a division of the area in the grounds and around the house into quadrants. There were two obvious weak spots, so the Marines and SAS covered them. Each group worked on the assumption that it would be the focus of the attack.

Kismet turned out to be a terrorist group from the Russian border. They were not religiously motivated. Their motive was power. How they would be of help to other terrorist groups who were religiously motivated in using time travel was all too obvious. It was a fearful contemplation.

Waiting. Waiting. Waiting. Days turning into nights and nights turning into mornings. Professor Savant left. He had done his bit and this was not his fight. There he was, the only living Napoleonic historian who had been to Waterloo. We hoped we would live long enough to see the book he planned to write be published.

Finally, there was a sharp rap on my door one morning at 2 a.m. I awoke from a light sleep, leaped out of bed, and admitted Sgt. Cathcart. He saluted. "Beg your pardon, Major, but this just came through from RAF Kilcreggan."

I returned the salute "Thank you, sergeant. You boys okay?"

"Fine, sir, thank you. I've never drunk so much coffee in my life."

"Remember, anyone who needs wakey, wakey tablets…for want of a better description…can get them from the pharmacy."

"Thank you, sir, but we'll stick to caffeine. That's strong enough."

He left and I read the message: "*3 unauthorized helicopters heading your way. Just appeared out of nowhere on screen. Profile would suggest a military nature. They have filed no flight plan nor have stated destination. Hailed on intercom but refuse to answer. We have been instructed not to intercept. End of message. By the time you get this should make contact with them in 20 minutes.*"

We had a code word to pass to everyone to galvanize them into action: "Spinners." Code word sent and received…then we waited. Our plan involved allowing any group that could be identified as being with Reynolds to gain entry after a token resistance. Any other group would be strongly and powerfully opposed. We thought that Kismet leader Ammal Guryanov would be with Reynolds because he was the one funding the terrorists. Guryanov would not like to lose his meal ticket. We knew from news broadcasts that Kismet had been responsible for several attacks and bank heists.

Sure enough, in twenty minutes, we picked up the sound of rotor blades. We cut the lights to blanket the building in darkness, save one light at the back. Next thing we knew, machine gun fire raked the house, followed by the explosion of rocket grenades. The SAS boys were able to camouflage themselves and outsmart heat-seeking cameras. At about 80 feet, a couple of rocket grenades hit one of the descending helicopters and it burst into flame. Then we slammed on the lights as the figures from the second helicopter started to jump down. They headed for the house and were quickly met with fire from out of what appeared to be darkness. That forced them into a ditch that ran around the house where, hopefully, they would be killed or pinned down and arrested. There must have been at least 60 of them and soon they would get their ordinance set up. What heavy weaponry they had we could only guess. As they fired on us, concentrated fire was returned against them.

The third helicopter was the smallest and probably contained Reynolds and Guryanov. Craig Carter joined me. He looked up at the approaching chopper and said, "I reckon there's about 20 inside. I agree with you, Major. Reynolds and Guryanov must be in that one. We'll let them get in the back door and to the control room before we stop them. Guryanov is a nasty parcel of goods. Let's hope we stomp both rattlesnakes with one boot."

The two guards at the back door split in the face of such fire and joined the SAS in a preplanned position. Some of our boys had been hit and were not moving. We headed for an emergency entrance that took us up to the control room. We had deactivated the security. We came in one door and Reynolds and Guryanov, and four of Guryanov's followers came through the other door. Professor Conroy and General Carlisle were studying a map. Meryl and Hera were already there ahead of the rest of us. I suspected Angus and Sebastian were hiding somewhere. Sebastian was good at hiding. I wondered where Angus was. He was the best one in a fight.

"Before you pull that trigger, dear boy," Reynolds taunted when he saw me, "I should warn you. I have a little surprise for you." Before any of us could react, he produced a round metal object from his briefcase. I had seen one before. It was a bomb.

"I take it you are the piece of trash that has been causing us all the problems?" the general asked calmly.

Reynolds bowed. "I always like to be of service. We aim never to disappoint. You will like what I have in mind for you. This is a uranium bomb and soon this place is going to bear a great similarity to Valentenoi, where the reactor exploded with a little help from Kismet. The foolish government would not pay the trifling ransom that was suggested."

We heard continued fighting outside. General Carlisle turned to Professor Conroy and glared at him. "Adrian, so you did it. You finally gave in. You traitorous rat. You're the one who gave away our position and brought them here. Why? Why did you do this to us? I thought we were friends...family even."

Adrian drew himself up to his full height. "Why? I'll tell you why. I'm tired of playing second fiddle. I have secrets that in the right hands could make me the richest man anywhere."

"Adrian! Think of what Vanguard stands for! Look at the good we've done! You know PATCH is evil! You know the things they've planned. You can't do this!"

"You've botched things, General, old boy. So I'm taking over. To make sure they succeed."

"Very touching," Reynolds said, nodding his approval mockingly, "but we seem to have the upper hand already, Conroy."

"You came for me," Adrian countered. "You need me. You need my secrets. I'm willing to help you...for the right price."

Reynolds laughed. "You help PATCH? That's a laugh! I don't believe it, Conroy. We used to work together in the Vanguard lab. Remember? You were always the goody-goody two shoes. I don't believe you've suddenly changed, not for any amount of money or prestige."

"Agree to my price and I'll show you how much I've changed."

"Okay, good buddy. Let's do it this way. Let's see what you're made of. What is your price?" Reynolds motioned to the rest of us. "And if the rest of you want to stay alive, drop your guns and kick them over here to me. You know how tricky bombs can be." Gun clattered as they were dropped on the floor and kicked. Reynolds had such a sickly evil smile on his face that it was all I could do to keep from flinging myself at him and attacking him with my bare hands, which would have been both stupid and ineffective. "Good!" he said, nodding his head as if rendering approval to unusually bright pupils. "Good indeed. Now, Conroy…back to you. Name your price."

"When the new world government is set up, I want to rule in Scandinavia. Especially Sweden and Finland."

Reynolds looked surprised. "Adrian, I thought you would have suggested something more academic."

Guryanov, who looked edgy, said in broken English, "Let's take him and get the hell out of here."

"Patience, Ammal. Everything comes to him who waits. But, first, we must give a little test to Professor Conroy. A simple little test that will prove his loyalty." Reynolds bent down and picked up one of the guns and tossed it to Adrian. He pointed to General Carlisle. "Kill him. Kill your General John Carlisle to prove your loyalty to the new order."

Adrian fumbled as he picked up the pistol. He turned it around in his hands experimentally as if he were unsure of what to do with it. Then he looked directly at General Carlisle. "Sorry, John, but this is business…and I'll get a stream of lovely Scandinavian beauties to do my bidding."

Carlisle gawked at him. "Adrian! Are you crazy? Have you lost your mind? What about Victoria? You're married. For heaven's sake, man, think of your wife! You brought her here to this time to be with you. And what about Mi-Ling and Libby? You and Victoria love them like your own children. And Drew is your own nephew!"

Conroy shook his head. "*Victoria* loves them like her own children. Replacements for Lucy, or so I would imagine. But as for me…I'm rather tired of child minding and the domestic scene…and Victoria. I want a change. An upgrade, one might say. But enough blethering, John. *Professor* Reynolds wants to get out of here. And I want to start my new life…Sorry, John. Really I am."

Adrian pulled the trigger three times. General Carlisle fell to the floor. Blood flowed out of the bullet holes, painting the floor in crimson.

Meryl, Hera and I stood in stunned silence.

"Now can we get on," Adrian said cheerfully, turning his back on the dead general. I noticed the thug who had been set to guard the door had vanished, but I was too traumatized by the sight of General Carlisle's dead body and the spreading pool of blood around him to even attempt thought or action.

"I rather enjoyed that," Adrian said in a chipper voice, waving the pistol. "Who do you want me to kill next?"

I've heard of Victorian ladies swooning, but if Hera hadn't caught my arm, I would have crashed to the floor. Meryl's face was so white that her blonde hair burned like sunshine around her face.

Reynolds laughed. "Dear boy, take your choice, but let's keep the women for a bit of entertainment back at the helicopter." He gestured with both hands, including the one with the Uzzi in it. While the weapon was raised in the air, Adrian spun and shot Reynolds in the head.

Guryanov was taken aback. His hesitation proved deadly. As he raised his gun, Hera shot over the desk and plunged a knife into the back of his neck. He dropped his gun, coughed up blood, and fell. She could move and if Hera put you down, you stayed down.

We had made the mistake of assuming Reynolds was dead. While our attention was diverted by Hera, Reynolds activated the bomb. With a mixture of slobber and blood oozing out of his mouth, he gasped, "See you in HADES..." I snatched my gun from the floor and shot him again just to be sure he died this time. I planned to take Adrian out with the next shot. He was no longer my uncle, but rather a stranger who had shot General Carlisle, the man who had been more like a father to me than my own dad ever had.

Meryl raced over to General Carlisle and threw herself down beside him in the sea of blood. She lovingly cradled his head in her lap. "Sir, please don't die! Please don't die!"

I had just trained my gun on Adrian when General Carlisle's eyes popped open. "What? Die and miss my daughter's wedding? Dear me, that would never do. I get to give the bride away."

"Drew," my uncle said in his familiar voice. "Put the gun down, son. The general and I never thought about telling anyone else about the arrangements for our little trap in case someone...like you, Drew, dear boy...would take things too seriously. The general is fine. It's fake blood. We knew Reynolds would demand some kind of test. As for Victoria, I would never in all the time travel years possible leave my beloved wife. And as for Mi-Ling and Libby...I do love them, Drew. It's no act."

My face and lips felt white and tightly stretched as I lowered the gun. But, dear God in Heaven, the bomb had been activated. *Lord, what do we do?* my soul asked. Strangely enough, a picture of Libby flashed into my mind. "Libby!" I exclaimed to the others. "I've got to get Libby!"

I raced down the hall to the room Libby shared with Mi-Ling and shook her awake. For a moment, she was startled. Then she realized it was me. "Libby come to the control room fast, very fast, sweetheart," I said, "we need your help." If the bomb went off, we would all be killed.

"What's wrong, Daddy?" Libby asked as we raced back down the hall. We entered the control room and I pointed to the bomb. "Libby, sweetheart, this bomb will kill us all unless we can stop it. You helped stop a bomb once before. Can you remember the sequence of the four buttons on the top that deactivate it?'

Libby looked up at me fearfully and licked her lips. "There was a nursery rhyme. That man," she said pointing to the dead Reynolds, "he had cases of bombs like that and he practiced starting them and stopping them by pressing the buttons. I know! It was to the tune of *Twinkle, Twinkle Little Star*."

"Right," the fully recovered General Carlisle said, "Please help us, Libby."

Libby's expression turned fearful again. "This bomb is bigger than the others," she whispered. "I don't know. I just don't know…but there are still four buttons even if it is bigger…so maybe…"

Libby knelt beside the bomb and said, "Dear God, help me get this right."

She pressed the first button and said, "Twinkle." Then the second, and said "twinkle" again. Then the third button and said, "little." Then the fourth button and said, "star."

We were all watching Libby, not daring to move, forgetting to breathe. She had pushed the last button and there was no change. Dear Heaven, the bomb was going to explode. Then a light of sudden recognition washed over Libby's face.

"The second half of the rhyme! How I wonder what you are!" Starting at the fourth button, she went backwards, four, three, two, one…

Her fingers flew across the four buttons flawlessly as if suddenly trained by memory. I think the rest of us in the room were holding our breath. I know I was. Libby hit the third button for a second time and there was a click. The lights went out. The bomb was deactivated.

We cheered and gathered around Libby. Everyone hugged her, but when it came to Craig Carter's turn—it was Libby who had to be persuaded to let go.

I don't think any of us could speak. We stood and looked around at the shattered control room with both real blood and fake blood spilled across the tiles. The fighting outside had stopped. We were informed that all the terrorists were either dead or captured. We had lost two men and another four were wounded. Angus had been outside where most of the action was and he returned, thankfully, unharmed. Hera was usually jealous when someone else went to battle and left her 'home,' so to speak, but enough had happened in the control room that she didn't seem peeved this time.

I looked at Reynolds' inert body. Dead. He had finally been stopped. I tried to hate him for what he had done to Marie and for all the other evil he had masterminded through PATCH. But when I looked at his splintered body soaking in its own blood, I couldn't find hate. His relentless ego–his proud, godless boasting–had attracted death to him just as surely as bloody water attracts sharks. Through Reynolds' evil plots, we had suffered injury, loss, death, and unnerving close calls. In the end, Reynolds had been so sure of his success that he had let his guard down and the scheme that Adrian and General Carlisle engineered had worked.

"We cremate his body immediately," General Carlisle said. "We don't want any of his friends getting hold of it."

"Major, you can go call President Galbraith and give him the good news. Don't forget to thank him for his co-operation. Tell him we'll get his military staff back home just as soon as we finish celebrating. You can also tell him that the Kismet leader Ammal Guryanov is dead, killed by a woman. A woman with a sword. I'm sure that will make his day."

Meryl followed General Carlisle into his office. I signaled to the others that they needed time alone. I knew, as they probably did not, that Meryl was his daughter. If she didn't know it yet—and I didn't think she did—she was in for a pleasant surprise. Our job…this one, anyway, was finished. It was time for all of us to get back to bed and try to snatch at least a short rest before bouncing out of bed again. The last image I had in my mind was of Meryl throwing her arms around the general's neck.

Libby was the real hero of the night. She had kept her cool and worked through the process logically to deactivate the bomb. One mistake and we would have all been blown up brighter than a Christmas tree.

Angus remarked somewhat sadly, "At last, Major. Reynolds is gone, killed by his own pride in a way." I nodded. His words echoed my thoughts.

Anton shook his head. "We've got rid of the two big chickens. Let us be wise and watch in case more hatch."

Libby waited for me to take her back to her room. She was shivering. I took off my combat jacket and slid it over her shoulders. She drew it round herself thankfully. "I was frightened, Daddy, but I couldn't show it."

"You did great, Libby. I love you and I'm so very proud of you! Let's go tell Mi-Ling how her brave sister saved the day."

"But, Daddy…won't Mi-Ling be asleep? It's early still."

I laughed. "With all the noise from outside? I don't think we'll find anyone sleeping!"

Mi-Ling was sitting with Victoria. She squealed when she saw me and ran over to throw her arms around me. "Sweetheart," I told her, "it's not Papa you should thank tonight, but rather your 'bravest of the brave' sister."

Victoria made all of us cups of hot chocolate. Then she and Mi-Ling listened to details of what had happened. Mi-Ling looked up to the ceiling. "Thank You, Father God, for hearing Mi-Ling's prayer and for my brave sister and daddy, and nearly Mummy Meryl." She was wise beyond her years, my first daughter. How had she figured out about Meryl? Meryl and I had only just now figured it out ourselves!

Victoria promised to put Mi-Ling and Libby back to bed. That would be easy, I thought. They were both yawning and sagging down into the couch. I went outside to see the others for debriefing. I thanked them and asked about the casualties and fatalities. The PATCH helicopter was still burning where it had been shot down. That over, I headed back to the flat to catch a bit more sleep myself.

Victoria was waiting up for me. Uncle Adrian hadn't returned yet, so I figured he and the general were taking care of official business before they called it a night.

"How did Reynolds die?" Victoria asked. I had skimmed over those details when relating the story to Mi-Ling.

"Adrian shot him."

"Adrian! My Adrian? I didn't know my husband could even use a gun."

"He was brilliant with it," I told Victoria. "I imagine we were all surprised. After Adrian shot Reynolds, we forgot to watch. We thought he was dead. But he wasn't. He managed to activate the bomb, so I shot him again. His plan was to set off a dirty bomb and make this place radioactive so it could not be used or even rebuilt. You heard the rest. Libby deactivated the bomb."

She nodded. "I also heard what Mi-Ling said. Do you love Meryl?"

Her question caught me off guard. How had she found out about Meryl? Just from what Mi-Ling had guessed, or was there more? "Yes," I told her gently. "I loved Lucy with all my heart, and I'm so sorry you lost your daughter. I would do anything to bring her back for you, but after having been in Heaven with Jesus, I don't think she would want to come back—even for you, even as much as she loved you. Lucy can't come back for us, Victoria. She's not coming back. As for Meryl, well, I need a wife who will stick. I think Meryl is the one, and yes, I do love her."

After a short night of sleep for all of us, I met with our defenders again. "Thank you," I told them, "all of you for your bravery and sacrifice. There will be medals handed out. If that second lot from the other helicopter had got inside the house—even if half of them had got in—we would have lost. Well done! And thanks also to our American friends. I hope and pray that there will always be a strong relationship between the forces of U.S and the U.K. President Galbraith has been informed of the victory and your crucial part in it."

The damage to Bellefield could be repaired. We made sure that everyone who needed medical treatment received it. We also made sure everyone was well fed and rested. We all had the one and same question: with the death of Reynolds, had PATCH been destroyed? Somehow, I had trouble believing that could be true.

CHAPTER TEN

Back from the Dead?

We met in the general's office the following day. "Well, people," he said, "it's good news and bad news."

I didn't mean to groan out loud.

General Carlisle directed a look of rebuke in my direction and continued, "The powers that be are happy that Reynolds is gone. So it's pats on the back all round."

Anton said, "I like the kind of pat on the back that crinkles when you touch it and helps make you wealthy."

"And sir," I said, "I suspect we're all waiting for the bad news part. I suspect there's something coming we won't like."

Angus nodded and laced his fingers together. "My guess is that what happens to us now is the same thing that happens to soldiers when the threat to the country is over and they're not seen as not needed anymore. We'll be demobilized, stood down, or put out on the street."

Meryl nodded thoughtfully. "Admittedly, this is a high cost department. The cost was accepted as worthwhile while the PATCH danger existed. Now that the danger is past, priorities are bound to change. That doesn't bode well for us in our careers."

"But what we don't know," I pointed out, "is whether Reynolds' organization has vanished, or whether PATCH's resources and equipment have been squirreled away to another time."

Anton added thoughtfully, "Old Russian saying: *If you want to catch the wolf, you must make him believe the hunter is not there.* While we are up and running, PATCH won't show themselves. They've had a kick in the teeth. They will need time to regroup under another leader,"

"True, Anton," the general said with a nod. "But President Galbraith is not convinced the threat is over. He has booth boots on the ground even if they stomp the odd rattlesnake or two."

"Sir," Jayne suggested, "is there some way to pretend the closure of Vanguard and fool PATCH into thinking we are no longer a threat?"

"Yes," I agreed. "I think Jayne has a brilliant idea. We could use the phrase decommissioned and keep the surveillance time contacts in place watching for anything where they are that is trying to change history. We have an idea of what forces showed up during various key historical times. We would be alerted of any efforts to change things that were stopped. If anything out of the ordinary shows up that has not been recorded in history, then we would have definite proof, not only of our necessity here at Vanguard, but of immediate action."

The general nodded in agreement. "I like the decommissioning idea. We can pass that onto President Galbraith. Then we'll wait to see if PATCH takes the bait."

"This going to seem awful dumb," Sebastian apologized, "but..."

"Sebastian, we are into any idea—no matter how dumb it may sound at the first reading."

"Well, sir...y'all don't suppose Caleb Bryant is still alive, do you? We done never did find his body."

I shook my head. "No, Seb. I saw him pitch off the cliff into the darkness. It was a long fall and no one was going to get up after that."

Sebastian continued, "But, what if somehow Reynolds managed to time shift Caleb Bryant's body while he was still alive? If'n he was shifted so fast he was totally uninjured? Or, if'n he was injured, what if Reynolds resuscitated him? Even if Bryant was hurt bad, and it took time to get him back up to speed, he might have been worth the effort to Reynolds."

Cold clutched at my body like dragon claws and froze me from inside out. Bryant alive? Evil personified—alive? He had shot and killed my Lucy in cold blood. He had kidnapped Mi-Ling, he had...no! He simply couldn't be alive! I wouldn't allow him to be!

Adrian seemed distracted, lost to the rest of us as he jotted down calculations and studied them. "Hmm...it is possible. Yes, quite possible. Bryant might have had time during the fall to be caught up into another time. And even if he fell and were badly injured, he could have been put in stasis while his wounds were healing. If that had happened, he could have been subliminally programmed with all the details of time travel that Reynolds knew."

I dropped my head into my hands and groaned.

"Does that seem likely?" Anton asked.

Jayne chucked. "Hasn't everyone warned me since I got into time travel to expect the unexpected?"

Adrian explained, "There are certain functions the brain controls that are common to everyone. The autonomic system: breathing, blinking, even sex to a certain extent. Certain responses that everyone makes. But what makes us individuals? Outward appearances can change, but what does not change are the experiences, the knowledge, the memories and personality. Yes, as we get older, we can fail to remember things, and we look back on our high school yearbooks of experiences and forget bits. That aside, if we add these things together and put all that into a living brain in a body—that body and brain become that person"

"Hang on Adrian," General Carlisle said. "Are you trying to say that in the future we could encounter Bryant again? But that this time, it would be his body infused with the mind and academic ability of Reynolds?"

"Yes, John. It is possible. Quite possible and workable."

I felt like throwing up.

Jayne acknowledged, "There are many groups who would like to see the head of a beloved leader put on a younger body. Imagine a Hitler aged 25, and Trotsky aged 20, a Napoleon aged 30, a Lenin at 35…"

"Please, Jayne!" I stopped her. I was shivering and my teeth were chattering. "Can you not be so blasted cheerful about this! Killing Bryant once was more than enough for me! If he hadn't slipped trying to shove me over the wall at Dunnottar Castle, I would be dead and he would be alive."

Angus reflected, "It's a good thing our voices don't carry. Anyone outside this room who heard us talking about this would think we were crazy."

General Carlisle stated, "If you really, and truly long for something to happen, it's amazing how extreme both in attempt and imagination you will become. Bryant alive would mean PATCH alive. It would mean that Vanguard—and all of us—are still relevant."

"It's only an idea," Sebastian said. "We ain't got no proof."

"Okay," I said taking a big gulp of air. "So perhaps instead of me panicking and flying to bits over the possibility that Bryant survived…perhaps I should embrace it. Perhaps we all should. It could mean our jobs. Could we not make a statement to the effect that the government-backed security group known as Vanguard has been decommissioned because the threat that brought about its existence is no longer a threat to national security? Some of our publicity people can rephrase it so it doesn't arouse too much interest. Perhaps we could get it published in some of the American newspapers. The main thing is to put a test out there…troll the waters for PATCH operatives. Hope they read it and act accordingly so we can finish this."

"Good idea, Major Faulkner," General Carlisle approved. Then he looked around the room at all of us and cleared his throat. "It's time that all of you knew the truth about one of your fellow operatives, Meryl Scott. Meryl's last name isn't really Scott. That's the name of her adoptive father. Her real last name is Carlisle. She's my daughter. Furthermore, she and Drew are engaged. Hopefully, this time the wedding will go through." He paused and smiled at Meryl and me. "We can't hold the celebration yet because that would make you both a target for PATCH. Once we know for certain that they have been stopped, we can…I believe the expression is…party."

Meryl smiled, her blue eyes sparkling with joy as she looked first at General Carlisle, then at me. "I'm still trying to wrap my head around the wonderful news. Both parts of the wonderful news."

Anton jumped up from his seat and announced, "On behalf of the team, we offer our hearty congratulations. We look forward to the celebration—whenever it is. This time, may I suggest that you go on honeymoon to a place where you can both walk through the hotel door together." He paused, then added, "I have a relative who has a hotel in St Petersburg and can…"

A cough from the general stemmed the tide of Anton's words. "If we can just concentrate on the matter at hand …."

Hera stated, "There is an old Greek saying, *The rat catcher never kills all the rats or else he would not be needed.*"

"What do you mean, Lieutenant?" I asked, afraid I already knew.

"If we remove all the PATCH people, what is the purpose for us? Besides, how will we know they are all gone? PATCH, too, must be recruiting. It is amazing what lies people will believe."

Sebastian put in thoughtfully, "I'm gonna guess that they have seen that one group and one leader won't work. What do you do if the leader gets killed? I would reckon they have split up—maybe five or six groups each with its head and its own command structure. Intelligent vermin trying to make others' lives a misery."

"If these conjectures are right," Angus remarked, "then we will need American help and they will need all the technology and information we have.

They have the resources. Thank God it's Galbraith who is Commander-in-Chief. Had it been Monaghan, he would have sold all the technology to PATCH and used the excuse of a level playing field. Then he would have looked out some kind of an agreement with them."

"Well," the general said, "let's leave American politics to them. We have our own problems. Our first concern is getting PATCH—if it still exists—to come out of the woodwork. And if nothing comes crawling out...we may have to find a way to prove that Vanguard still exists for a valid reason. Dismissed, people. I'll get on to our publicity squad and see what they can come up with."

Meryl and I got the general's permission to head into Aberdeen. We needed time to be together by ourselves. Mi-Ling and Libby were content to stay behind with Victoria, who had organized a small party for them with some of their friends. Meryl and I had our Sava Java coffee and a snowball each. Then we laughed at each other for being showered with coconut crumbs.

Meryl told me about Kitchi—the full details I had never heard from anyone else. I told her about Marie and Waterloo, and thanked her again for saving my life at Hougoumont. This time we didn't have to keep chattering away as if we were trying to convince each other of our sincerity. We headed for Duthie Park. The sun shone down, alleviating the fear, which we would not admit to each other that was in the back of our minds. What if Bryant were still alive? I held out my hand and Meryl wrapped her fingers around mine. Oh, that magic touch.

The words from the Carpenters' song drifted into my mind *Love, look at the two of us...strangers in many ways. It will take a lifetime to tell I knew you well, but love will grow for all we know.* Meryl looked gorgeous, as if summer had come alive. I felt my heart entwine itself around hers.

"Meryl?"

She smiled and replied "That's me." And I kissed her, writing the moment on my heart.

"I just wanted to say your name, Meryl. You are so beautiful. I keep thinking I am going to wake up and you won't be there. I have no life without you. Mi-Ling is happy about us. She needs a role model, as does Libby. Shoot! That came out all wrong."

Meryl ran a strand of hair through her lips and quipped with a Texas accent, "Why, sugarplum, I declare but what you don't say the cutest things. I think you are cuter than a bug's ear." Then she smiled that smile that melted my heart and knocked my pulse up several dozen beats.

Our brief moment of sunshine and strolling in the park ended with the ever-eager rain. Within a few minutes, our hair was plastered flat against our heads and our wet clothes drew cold cords around our bodies. "Darling," Meryl said, "We better get back. This looks like it's going to last a while."

We walked quickly. Hearing a wet squishing noise behind us, I turned round just in time to catch a glimpse of a figure darting into the trees. Not wanting Meryl to worry, I kept the information to myself. We got to the car park and slipped into our Volvo. Four cars back, a guy got into a Renault. When we turned out of the car park and headed back in the direction of Bellefield, he followed us. There was no point in hiding it from Meryl any longer. It could portend danger.

"Looks like we've got company," I told her.

Meryl looked in the side mirror. "The Renault?"

"Yup."

"I bet we checked our guns in back at the ranch."

The driver of the Renault moved up on us. He was now three cars behind.

"Let's hope he's a good bad guy and has left his gun at home," Meryl said.

"Well, maybe he's a part time bad guy and wants to be law abiding. How do you stop terrorists without a gun, anyway?" I asked. "Of course, terrorists wouldn't bring a gun to Aberdeen. It's a gun-free zone, right?"

Meryl smiled at my sarcasm, but we were both more than a bit uptight. We communicated our position to HQ.

We were on a quiet stretch of road. All at once our tail accelerated. Realizing that the Renault was leaping toward us, I gunned the Volvo, keeping the edge on the Renault.

Meryl gasped, "If anything comes out of these side roads, we're going to make a big impression on it. And they will be totally innocent, unsuspecting folk."

The first spurt of bullets hit the back window of the car, which was thankfully bullet-proof.

I weaved from side to side. A combine harvester started out of a side road which was nearly hidden by dense brush and vegetation. There was only one option. I cut sharply around the harvester. There couldn't have been more than a coat of paint between us and the blades.

Meryl yelped, "Thank You, Jesus!"

The Renault hit the combine's side doing about 50 miles an hour. Awed, we looked back at the pall of smoke. The combine driver was unhurt. The same could not be said for the occupant of the burning Renault.

"It looks as if we might be back in business," I told Meryl. "Looks like the note about the decommissioning of Vanguard worked."

"So fast?" Meryl questioned. "It was only published two days ago!"

"General Carlisle needs to hear this, but first, we better check on the combine driver to make sure he's okay. And we better stick around until the police come. We don't want him to get blamed for what happened. People who shoot machine guns at cars in front of them tend not to notice what's coming out of side roads."

My heart was already thumping from our narrow escape, but when Meryl leaned over to kiss me, the thump resonated at an alarming rate.

* * *

At a meeting in General Carlisle's office in the secure room, the general said, "Right people. What happened to Major Faulkner and Lieutenant Scott indicates to me that we are dealing with the settling of a grudge."

Adrian queried, "If you were they and you believed that the organization that opposed you—Vanguard in this case—had been discontinued, would you risk showing yourself so soon in a direct attack on two of that operation's operatives? Especially when they could do much more damage to Vanguard by remaining silent and working undercover."

"Call it what you want," Meryl said, "but it looks like a grudge. A failed attempt at revenge."

The General looked at Sebastian and said, "I'm inclined to go with your theory, Sebastian. I think we are dealing with Caleb Bryant, or someone operating as Bryant. Now, what motivates him at this point with his boss dead? Bryant wants to prove himself smarter than Reynolds by being able to do what Reynolds could not do: in other words—destroy Vanguard and get even with their operatives. He is smart in one way, but stupid in another."

"Revenge may be sweet," Angus said, "but it's also dumb."

I sighed loudly and added, "If Sebastian is right, then both Libby and Mi-Ling are in danger. Libby is Bryant's daughter. He might take her back by force whether she wants to go with him or not. As for Mi-Ling, Bryant hates her even more than he hates us."

"I should have shot Bryant in Foo-Chow," Anton lamented.

"Let's think, people," Meryl said. I hid my grin. Having just found out that she was really his daughter, Meryl seemed to already be picking up some of General Carlisle's mannerisms—or at least his way of speaking. "Bryant is a good sailor. He's an American, and his real time is the 1860's. When we stopped the plot to try to persuade General Lee to get British help the aim of PATCH was to weaken the union and to divide America into two countries. Think of the effect on history that would have had. With Reynolds gone and Bryant attempting to supplant him…where will he strike next? Besides at Drew. I don't think he will ever forgive Drew for being the one Lucy loved when he wanted her for himself."

Sebastian scratched his head. "Just because you fail once, it don't mean that you don't try again. If you stomp on a rattlesnake and he's not dead—just a mite dazed, you don't go on about your business and give him time to recover."

Angus asked, "Do you really think Bryant would try to do the same thing again?"

Sebastian shrugged his shoulders. "Maybe not with General Lee."

"Then who, Sebastian?" Meryl asked. "Whose death would be a game changer?"

Jayne quietly interjected, "What about President Lincoln?"

"No Jayne," Sebastian said, "he done got himself killed in 1865, and what a sad day that was. Mighty sad."

Jayne put her hands together thoughtfully. "But suppose Lincoln was killed earlier? Say 1863? His death would make a difference and those who wanted peace in Washington might have come to the fore so that a treaty was made with the South."

"But what happened in 1863 that would cause that?" Anton asked. "Apart from Mr. Lincoln being a war leader?"

Sebastian said, "Mr. Lincoln's Emancipation Proclamation, signed on January 1, 1863. When we heard about it, even though the planters tried to hide the news from us, I mean to tell you there was joy and celebration and howdy. Truth has a habit of coming out on top. I was looking at the news today, and there is still slavery going on all over the world—jest a change of peoples and the exploitation of those peoples. Don't man ever learn nothin'? Sorry, I get carried away by sad, ugly memories once in a while."

I looked at the big guy and realized that although he was so cheerful and optimistic and always seemed to find something good even in dangerous situations—like the rest of us—he carried hidden baggage through life. He had helped us all of us keep going at times when we would have given up. Mi-Ling, especially, loved Sebastian. Both of them were close to God. Both of them were quick to praise the Lord and give Him credit for every victory. Another reason they were such good friends might be because they both had experienced the pain of having been judged by outward appearances. Their self-appointed judges had been blind to the treasures inside.

"Did Lincoln make a speech?" General Carlisle asked. "Like he would do at Gettysburg? What was the weather like on January 1, 1863, in Washington?"

"No speech is recorded," Sebastian replied. "But that don't mean that he didn't make an appearance. Gettysburg was in the middle of July of that year. As y'all who were there remember, it was hot. The Emancipation Proclamation was signed in the middle of winter in Washington. Perhaps he put in an appearance to test the waters—see what folks would say. Not everyone was happy, but there again…they weren't all slaves either."

"Let's go see," I suggested. "At least with Reynolds, he gave us clues to see if we could work out what he was going to do. What kind of clue could Bryant send us?"

"How about an iron chain?" Sebastian asked.

"Right, people, we would be working purely on a surmise," General Carlisle said.

Adrian added, "My guess would be that if Mr. Lincoln were going to put in an appearance it would be in the lightest and warmest part of the day—about noon."

Jayne was working on her phone and responded, "It was a good day on January 1, 1863, in Washington."

Adrian said, "Take Kairon detectors with you. It might be the only chance you have of finding one determined individual."

"What do we do when, or if, we find him?" I asked. Reynolds died because he tried to destroy us, but we are not assassins. To kill someone in cold blood because of what he might have been going to do is wrong."

"Right," General Carlisle said. "Try to bring him back in one piece. If we interrogate him, he might lead us to Bryant in whatever form he has taken. It's Bryant we need to stop. If we can't destroy PATCH, we can at least weaken it. Bryant has a lot to answer for." We nodded. All of us agreed with that statement.

"Now we come to the risk, and to one of the differences between Bryant and Reynolds. It's time to plan a wedding." He looked at Meryl and me. "I hope that you two are going to get married?"

Meryl and I nodded, not sure where this was going.

"Good! I want you to choose a date for your wedding; the place, the time, your names, and most importantly—the names of the bridesmaids. I assume that will be Mi-Ling and Libby?

"Right, people. Once the wedding is announced in print—in the newspapers—we'll get invitations printed. So, if you find an assassin moving in on President Lincoln, get him, and get him back here. We'll promise to let him go in exchange for the info we need. We'll remind him of how we could make him disappear if he fails to cooperate. In exchange for saving his hide, all he will be required is to drop in at his HQ and leave the invitation so that Bryant finds it."

Won't Bryant think it's strange that a wedding invitation just happens to be lying around? "I asked

"Not if it's in a wallet along with other things…perhaps a picture of Meryl and of the girls. He could say it was on a desk and he took it to help PATCH. Bryant will know that we would have been bound to try to stop him once we figured out what he was planning. Though the Emancipation Proclamation is a longshot, Bryant probably guessed we would find out." General Carlisle added, "and when your wedding takes place, we will be waiting for him. We also have to assume that he has the same technology that Reynolds had so he could appear anywhere."

Adrian added, "With the help of a couple of new developments, we may be able to tell where he's going to appear just before he does. I can give you the physics of that achievement if you want?"

"No, Professor, thank you!" the general replied. "I'm sure you would lose us in the first three minutes. Right, people. We've got a hook to bait and a wedding to plan."

"Should I choose my wedding dress?" Meryl asked.

"Of course, sweetheart…err…Lieutenant." Carlisle said.

"Maybe Victoria will help me," Meryl suggested.

Anton coughed and remarked, "If the assassin resists, he may get killed."

"Let's hope that good sense prevails over passion and misplaced loyalty," Carlisle said. "Meanwhile, I hand the planning of the wedding over to the ladies."

Meryl and I chose June 12 as our date because it was the anniversary of the day we had met. She had never forgotten that date. It's amazing what a woman carries in her heart. Thoughts of Marie passed through my mind and I wondered where Javel had buried her. I hoped he had acted honorably and spent the gold I had given him on her burial.

I knew the next thing I had to do was talk to Mi-Ling and Libby.

"My Father is not dead?" Libby asked in horror. "But, Daddy, he has hurt so many people. He even tried to kill you." Mi-Ling hugged Libby and held her close.

"Libby, we need to stop your father. He may be running a very evil organization. We need your help. He hates Mi-Ling because she loves Jesus and Jesus has protected her and kept her safe when evil has come against her."

Libby sighed, and said with the deep seriousness of her years, "Daddy, Mr. Bryant may be my biological father—but you are the father of my heart. I love you and Mi-Ling. And Meryl."

Mi-ling smiled and looked at her sister with such love and compassion that no words were needed.

I said to Mi-Ling, "You could be in danger, sweetheart."

She shook her head. "Father God will take care of me. Jesus has looked after me until now and He will not stop now. Especially after healing me and talking to me." I knew Mi-Ling was talking about the travel back in time that I thought of in my mind as *The Scent of Eternity*. Mi-Ling had been dying and doctors couldn't heal her or save her. So we had traveled back to see Jesus. Jesus had healed Mi-Ling, I had found Lucy and been assured of how joyous she was in Heaven, and Mike Argo had brought back his Greek gladiator wife, Hera. With all that Mi-Ling had been through, the Lord had never been lacking in His care and love. She was right. He wouldn't stop now.

At the final meeting we had before setting off, Adrian said, "We have knockout darts and compounds that if they get into the system will render someone compliant without causing them to collapse. They just need to break the surface of the skin to work. We're working on one or two that can be absorbed through the skin."

General Carlisle nodded. "I suggest Major Faulkner, Lieutenant Scott, and Lieutenant McTurk undertake a quick extraction operation. Then get back here as fast as you can. It is possible—although perhaps not likely—that he knows the location of the PATCH nerve center."

"Oh, well," Meryl said, "back to the corsets. At least they are bullet proof."

"Quite so," The general agreed with a smile.

"Well, blessings to y'all," Sebastian said. "Now go take care of the President."

Once again, I became aware of the things and people I had seen. Perhaps someday I could write a memoir.

I was glad Meryl was coming with us. Apart from the fact she was a darn good operative and had taught me a lot, I didn't want to lose sight of her. I was determined that anyone trying to harm her would have to come through me first. I suddenly realized that I had been focusing on me and self-preservation instead of the woman I loved and my two children, both of whom were precious gifts from God. I would never forget that Mi-Ling had saved my life when that thug Lancaster went after me with a knife. He had tried to rape Mi-Ling and I had stopped him. During the resulting knife fight, I had slipped on the deck of the *Night Arrow*, the ship that won the China to London Tea Race of 1867. Mi-Ling, even after her narrow escape from rape, had the presence of mind to shoot Lancaster and save my life. For that, Caleb Bryant hated her. Lancaster had been one of Bryant's goons.

"Right people, let's go see Mr. Lincoln," I said with more confidence than I felt.

CHAPTER 11

Washington – The Capitol, January 1, 1863

There was a crowd and a sense of expectation in the air when we come out at a clump of trees nearby. Trees are a gift to time travelers; you can arrive without being seen and it gives you a visual point for your return.

The Capitol was crowded. We decided to choose a focus point, then go west, east and south from the Capitol steps. We couldn't get any closer to the Capitol, as it was well guarded. The guards indicated the possibility that Mr. Lincoln would put in an appearance.

"Right," I said. "Walk twenty minutes in each direction, then rendezvous back here. Meryl, you and Angus go together. Angus, I don't want anyone getting the wrong idea about Meryl, and they might if she's on her own.

"Meryl, I know you can take care of yourself, but if you get hit with admirers and perhaps even get propositioned—well, it just eats up valuable time. We can't afford to get this wrong."

I went south from the Capitol steps. It was growing a bit colder; though still a passable day for January. There were more blue uniforms than anything else, but with a sprinkling of green from the uniforms of Berdan's Sharpshooters. Some of the soldiers wore coats. All of them wore hats or caps.

The ladies wore shawls or capes around their shoulders. All of them wore bonnets. Interspersed, there were those wounded warriors who had not been so fortunate in battle and had lost limbs. Some hobbled about on crude crutches. These men had given their all for their country. They had been on the winning side, yet they had come out as losers. I tried to picture the streets of Richmond and the grey uniformed figures that would be there; men who had marched off to Manassas or Bull Run with a dream in their hearts and then came back as a casualty—or not at all. Yet, there were still homeless veterans and men who had given their all sleeping on park benches 150 years later.

There was no indication of Kairon as I checked my detector. I wondered if Angus and Meryl had had more success.

I got back to the rendezvous point to find Angus and Meryl waiting.

"We got a reading," Meryl whispered excitedly. She indicated a tall soldier, a Union officer in a cloak who stared intently at the Capitol steps, seemingly oblivious to the crowd around him. He seemed to be alone. We needed to check him out. Reynolds worked his assassins in pairs. Would Bryant do the same thing?

We sidled up to him. Being in uniform would have been handy, but it also could have got us shot as Confederate agents. We had no choice other than to approach him and hope he would comply. If we had to shoot, we would have no hope of getting out of there alive. We also had to hope the drug we used to inject him would work quickly, yet allow him to walk, because he was a big, tall guy. Fortunately, we also had whiskey to "spill" over him so that any faltering steps would be put down to being tipsy.

Meryl took my arm as we stood by him.

"Were you at Fredericksburg, Captain?" Meryl asked, guessing at his rank since we couldn't see his epaulettes. No matter how reluctant men were to talk, there was something about Meryl's looks that encouraged them.

"Yes, ma'am. Glad to live through it. A lot of good boys didn't," he said, taking off a glove and wiping his brow.

"Well," Angus said, sticking a gun against his ribs, "you won't live through this unless you are nice and quiet."

With those words spoken, Meryl quickly injected the hypo spray in the back of his gloveless hand. I splashed some whiskey over him as he began to sway.

"Are y'all going to kill me?" he asked, with obvious bewilderment. Meryl straightened the hat on his head. "We're from the Pinkerton Detective agency, sweetheart," she replied, "and you're coming with us."

Angus gave our now-confused assassin the international language of a continued poke in the ribs with a gun, which he understood. He nodded, then shook his head, then looked at Meryl. "I'm going to sleep with you, is that what I have to do?" he asked in a stronger Southern accent.

I thought, *Jings! He can't be that far gone!*

"Shhh...keep your voice down. Just come with us. Otherwise, you won't be seeing Dixie again." We headed for the trees where the time car was. We couldn't search him for weapons without drawing attention to ourselves. We had to assume that the hypo spray would keep all such thoughts of escape out of his mind.

"Ma'am," he said to Meryl, "you sure are cute. You got to be the cutest jailer a feller ever had."

We couldn't rush. We were still about 1000 yards from the trees where it would be safe to order the time car. We tried to look as if we were helping our friend find somewhere to sleep it off.

I looked behind me. There were a couple of soldiers who had been circulating through the crowd. They noticed that a person who looked like an officer was leaving the vicinity of the Capitol when President Lincoln was expected at any moment. We kept walking while they worked their way through the crowd toward us.

"Keep going," I hissed. "They won't fire their rifles in case they hit an innocent bystander."

The sergeant caught up with us. "Are you, alright sir?" he asked our prisoner.

"Thank you kindly, sergeant, ma health has never been in a better condition."

Angus and I produced our Pinkerton agency documents. Meryl threw them completely off balance by saying, "The Captain and I are just going to those trees so I can show my gratitude to this brave soldier boy. He was at Fredericksburg and bravery gets a reward. I can do the same for you. I could give you more fun than what you'll get listening to 'ole Mr. Lincoln…but officers first, boys. You're going to feel a whole lot better when you leave those trees than when you went in."

The guys either decided that we didn't present any danger, or they were too embarrassed by Meryl's performance to stick around. Although I could tell that the private, at least, longed to follow Meryl into the trees to see what happened. Sometimes, I wished Meryl wasn't such a good actress.

"Come on, let's get back on patrol," the sergeant said. "She's only a whore, no matter how pretty."

As they walked away, I heard the private saying, "But, sergeant, it wouldn't take me that long and I ain't ever been with a woman before and I sure could use the practice."

Meryl shuddered and said, "I've heard of contributing towards the war effort, but a girl has her limits."

"We need to get out of here just in case the sergeant comes back with a few more of his friends," I told them. I saw a group of figures on the platform at the Capitol, but the distance was too great to for me to see clearly. I couldn't tell if one of the figures was Lincoln.

The assassination we stopped in 1863, John Wilkes Boothe would carry out in 1865, and in so doing ensure President Lincoln's immortality. "Government of the people, for the people, and by the people shall not pass from the face of the earth." How soon we forget.

"Is this where the fun starts?" our hopeful soldier boy asked.

We bundled him into the time car, scrambled in after him, and threw the switch.

Vanguard HQ: Modern Day

We decided that when the guy came around from his trip it might be better that we had a couple of guards just in case he believed in the old adage that it was a soldier's duty to escape. Meryl's guess at his rank of captain had been right, but he should have been wearing grey instead of blue. A take down rifle was found on him, but very little else with the exception of some US dollars to the value of $10,000.

General Carlisle dressed in uniform, as did we, and by the time he came fully around, even Meryl was in uniform. I didn't tell her then, but I thought she sure looked cute. When I saw her, thoughts of a future honeymoon with her made it nearly impossible for me to concentrate on anything else.

"My name is Lieutenant General John Carlisle of the British Army. You are our prisoner."

He looked startled…and more than a little disappointed.

"What do you want with me? Britain to my knowledge is not at war with the Union."

"You were sent to assassinate President Lincoln. You are no more from the North than I am. That rifle you have is only used for one thing."

"In war, sir, is it wrong to want to remove the Commander-in-Chief of the opposing army? Even if it means losing your life in such an objective?"

"Very commendable, but my interest is not in you, or even Lincoln. It's in the person who contacted you and arranged things. The one who had set you up and told us where you would be. How else do you think we found you?"

He frowned. "May I ask who is 'us' and where I am? And how did I get to England?"

"Before we reply," General Carlisle said pleasantly, "may I ask who you are?

You are no Union soldier, but are probably in the confederacy?"

"Captain Titus Contrell of the 5th Texas Infantry under the command of General John Bell Hood."

Then we took turns explaining to him about time travel and how he was sitting in the 21st century. We took Titus outside so he could see cars and modern buildings and conveniences. He was eventually convinced…well, as convinced as a Texan can be.

"I still do not profess to understand everything," Titus said with dignity, "but I accept what you say. If you know all this, then you know the result of the war."

"That," General Carlisle said, "we can't tell you, but we can tell you that President Lincoln is assassinated in 1865, by a man named John Wilkes Boothe."

"The actor? Lord above who would have thought!"

"The actor, and he does not get away with it. Now, Captain Contrell, we could take you back and hand you over to the federal authorities, in which case they would imprison you, unless they decided to hang you to save a trial. There is no glory in that."

"I will not betray my country, sir, so do not ask me to do that."

"I would never dream of that, Captain. What we want is the man who put you up to assassinating President Lincoln. We believe him to be using the name of Reynolds, or his New Englander name of Caleb Bryant. He's a sea captain." There had been no response to the name of Reynolds, but to Caleb Bryant— the expression on his face confirmed the surmise without words.

"The regiment knows nothing about my attempt to kill Lincoln," Titus said, "for I was given leave after Fredericksburg."

"We can get you back to where your regiment is," I told him.

"I can't go back in this uniform. They would shoot me. And it stinks of whiskey. I do so hate alcohol."

Sorry," Meryl apologized. "It was to divert suspicion in case we were stopped. Oh, by the way…Major Faulkner is my fiancé."

Angus added, "In exchange for your Union uniform, we can give you a Confederate one." He chuckled. "One that doesn't reek of whisky."

"I surely would appreciate that," Titus said. He turned to Meryl, "Ma'am, I wish to apologize if I said anything unbefitting to an officer in your hearing, but I was…err…under the weather."

Meryl smiled sweetly and said, "No offence taken, Captain."

"May I say, sir," he said to me, "you are a very fortunate man." I could no way disagree with that statement.

The general produced my wallet with various things in it, including a wedding invitation with all the details. "Can you make sure Bryant finds this? You can say that you thought that he might like some information on the group that stopped you from getting to the President. In the end, Captain Contrell, President Lincoln didn't even make an appearance on the Capitol steps that day, so your wait would have been wasted. Besides, I think you are a man of honor and would not want to be remembered as an assassin."

"I have a feeling the South is to be defeated," Titus said sadly, "but although you can defeat an army, you can't defeat a spirit."

For Vanguard's future, everything relied on this brave, young soldier passing on the information. We trusted him and he did not let us down. We were, however, saddened to learn later that he didn't survive the war. He was killed at Gettysburg later on in the same year to which we returned him, 1863. Over the time he spent with us while we were getting his uniform ready, Captain Titus Contrell made a deep impression on all of us. I guess you should never judge by outward appearances.

So all we could do was wait June 12th ...six weeks to go. I tried to blot out thoughts of Bryant. He didn't deserve the respect of either thought or fear. He had murdered Lucy because she refused to marry him. If he had operated out of even a part of Reynolds' memories he was also responsible for Marie's murder. Reynolds was physically dead, but if his evil mind lived on in Bryant— Bryant had to be stopped.

Meryl and I went to Aberdeen again, armed this time. It was decided that we should have the capacity to stop any future attempts on our lives before they had to scrape the assassin off the side of a combine harvester in a situation where an innocent bystander could have been killed.

I guess I wanted to hang onto Meryl's hand in hand even in the street. Her touch seemed to make everything okay. Our love had taken a long time to grow. Because we had laid the foundations, the building of our love was good. I was looking forward to the honeymoon when we could finally get to bed together.

"Darling," Meryl said, "I'm not going to let fear of what might happen ruin my life. I want to be with you. Even work with you. As long as we're together, it's good no matter what we're doing."

"Your father is so proud of you, and rightly so. I'm still getting to know him as a person and not just my boss."

Meryl laughed. "Just think of me!" She exclaimed. "I'm still getting used to knowing him as my father! Yet, I know I'm a blessed girl finding a father and a husband in a short space of time "

"I'm just glad you love me. My track record for marriage is dismal."

Meryl smiled at me. "Darling, none of that is your fault, but we need to leave the past behind us. I've left Kitchi in the past. He was a very courageous, unselfish, and practical man. He wouldn't want me moping over him. He used to say, *Life is for living; be thankful to God for each day. Enjoy the kiss of the breeze, and when you head to your loved ones, enjoy The Scent of Home. Listen to the birds sing for joy; for they do not worry about what might happen.* Lucy is in heaven. Marie died saving your life and is also in heaven. Darling, let's enjoy what life we have been given and what life we have left. Take a deep breath. What do you smell?"

We were alone. No one else was around. We both inhaled deeply. I smelled the most beautiful scent. Meryl looked at me and smiled. "I smell it too. It's like the *Scent of Freedom*. Now, at long last, we're free to love. Let's not waste an hour. Come help me choose my going away outfit." She laughed at my pained expression. "Well, darling, you're the one who's going to have to look at me. When we get back, I want to talk to Mi-Ling and Libby. They get to make some fun choices, too."

Meryl wanted yellow shoes. Yellow was her favorite color. We went to twelve shoe shops. We must have seen every yellow shoe in all of the Granite City. Green was my favorite color, so Meryl chose a yellow and green dress and a wide brimmed white hat. When she came out of the changing room, I could hardly believe that I was going to be blessed enough to marry someone so beautiful. She was just drop dead gorgeous. Then reality hit me. I prayed earnestly that Bryant would not turn what now preyed on my mind in the form of fear into a reality.

Meryl and I traveled back to 1867 to see if Mr. Thornton, the minister who had conducted my wedding with Lucy, would be willing to marry us. The date on our marriage certificate from 1867 would be changed to our modern times date and could be used for all legal purposes. Reverend Thornton had also married Marie and me, a wedding ceremony that I expected to be a window to a future of happiness and success—indeed, a perfect life.

"I have been in the ministry for 30-odd years," Mr. Thornton told me with great compassion, "and I've never come across such a tragedy as what you've been through, Drew. Two wives, both murdered. It's...shattering. Are you sure you're willing—and ready—to try this again?"

"Mr. Thornton, I must be completely honest with you. You have every right to refuse our request to conduct the marriage ceremony. It's possible that there will be danger in your church during the service. Unfortunately, we have no way to know ahead of time. When I married Lucy, you remember what happened after you pronounced us as man and wife and we were coming down the aisle?"

He scowled. "It was the most tragic, horrendous thing—the most evil and vile action I've ever witnessed in my life. I will never forget even if I live to be a hundred. I will never forget the shock and grief on your face and young Mi-Ling's. The sorrow of the funeral afterwards...a sea burial, I remember."

"The problem is, Mr. Thornton, that the same person who killed Lucy has threatened to turn up again and repeat the performance, this time bringing along some of his friends."

"Friends? He has friends? An evil pretend-to-be-man straight from the depth of hell? Can someone who has no knowledge of God and no love for God can never be a true friend to anyone?"

"I agree. And I also admire you for agreeing to conduct another marriage ceremony that involves me in it."

He shook his head and chuckled. "Retirement for me soon, I fear. Might as well squeeze every drop out of the ministry God gave me before I leave. Meryl, you must be a young lady of great courage and you must know how to trust God as well."

Meryl nodded. "I try, Reverend Thornton, but I confess I haven't always been successful. And even though often I haven't succeeded, God, in His mercy and goodness, has rescued me from some pretty tight places."

Mr. Thornton smiled and said, "Yes, He is good at that. With the Lord, it's best to expect the unexpected."

Meryl and I looked at each other. We realized and knew in our hearts that this time it was going to work.

"You are willing to trust God again," Reverend Thornton mused. "Perhaps this time God will have a surprise for the one who tries to spoil His plans."

"We can arm you if you wish, Mr. Thornton, for protection." I offered.

"Thank you, but no, Drew. Jesus has been protecting me all my life, and in all of my ministry. He has never let me down yet."

He looked at us rather sternly, like a father delivering a serious message. "I can tell by the amusement in the glances you gave one another. You wonder what protection someone would need in the Christian ministry? Believe me, Major Faulkner, the tongue and heart can cause just as much damage, if not more, than anything fired from a pistol. Sometimes the assassin can have the most religious of credentials. But enough about me and my daily battles. Where will you go on honeymoon?" Seriousness broke off his face and vanished like a bite of ice cream slipping off a cone and hitting hot pavement. He cleared his throat. "Ministers are not supposed to know things about sex, I suppose. At least, that's the impression I get from some of elderly lady widows in my church. But, all the same, Drew, I imagine you are rather eager to finally get a honeymoon out of a wedding ceremony."

Meryl and I both laughed. We hadn't thought ahead to our honeymoon. Meryl was still giggling when she announced—much to my amazement— "probably through to Waterloo, in Belgium. We both visited there separately, but it would be fun to tour around together…especially with no war going on and battle sights and sounds raging."

"Yes," Reverend Thornton said. "You will see a lot of Napoleonic battle sites and famous buildings, but it must have been terrible 52 years ago."

"Yes, it was terrible," Meryl said solemnly, but now honeymooners go there."

"As strange as it may seem," the minister commented, "if you were to tell me you had been on the walls of Hougoumont, I would believe you."

Traveling back to our time, I said to Meryl, "I didn't know you wanted to go back to Waterloo for our honeymoon. I had been thinking exactly the same thing. And, thanks, again, for saving my life."

"Drew, enough already! You keep thanking me. Let's just say that it's your turn to pick up the tab for coffees and chocolate cheesecake."

I looked into her eyes. "Just think. Soon, we can shower together."

"And?" she asked. "What's so important about that?"

Skipping the obvious, I said, "Well, you need someone to do your back. As wonderful and genius and gorgeous as you are, you still can't wash your own back. So I volunteer to stand in the firing line."

"And?" she asked again.

I kissed her and whispered a few original ideas into her ear. Her breathing suddenly sounded more like panting and her skin glowed.

"Only if I can return the favor and do your back…and anything else that takes my fancy."

It was getting warm. Thankfully, the wedding was soon—but soon was still too long away. My granny used to tell me that anticipation was better than realization. She had been wrong. With Meryl, it would be the other way around.

CHAPTER TWELVE

The Hitch on the Way to the Altar

Angus and Anton wanted to take me out on a stag night, but I didn't want that. First, I wanted to spend as much time with my girls as I could before I left them again for the honeymoon. They would have enough adjustments with a new mother suddenly thrust into their midst, no matter how much they thought they wanted a mother and how much they thought they loved Meryl.

And another important factor—I wanted to be in the best condition I could be for loving Meryl. Besides that, since finding a purpose in life—alcohol didn't hold the same appeal, or place in my life, that it once did. Life was too short to fill it with occasions of drunkenness—not being able to remember the details of what I had done and said. Also, both for my marriage and my job, I needed to be in good health.

Ten days before the wedding, I started to shake. I just couldn't get things together. Every time I closed my eyes, I saw Lucy lying in the church floor, her lovely face turning white and her lovely gown turning red as blood flowed out of her taking her life away with it. And I heard the mocking laughter of Bryant.

I told Meryl. "Drew, I understand, I think, but you're not changing your mind, are you?"

When I didn't answer immediately, she nodded. "Drew, it's only been a short time since the death of our last partners. Perhaps we are rushing things. Maybe we're not ready to get married again. We can't call the wedding off because of the plan to trap Bryant. But we could pretend like they do on TV. Bryant wouldn't notice any difference. We could catch him without actually getting married."

"But I do love you, Meryl. I have no doubts. It's just that I can't stop this shaking."

Meryl shook her head. "You either have to go see a therapist, or you need to do something to boost your confidence."

"But I am confident that I love you," I protested.

"Darling, the person you don't have confidence in is you. All the missions we've been on, you've had Angus or me to fall back on. Remember, we assessed you for all this. We've been there to help, but you need to be sure of yourself.

"Yes, you've been an important member of the team, and the leader even—but it's never been just you. Nothing beats the confidence of command. You can do it, Drew. You can lead, but you have to believe you can lead and lead others. Anton, Mike, Jayne, and Hera are good team members. They are there to follow your example. They have their own talents, but they're part of a team, and a team needs a leader. You can lead, but you have to believe that you can."

She sighed and pushed an errant blonde curl back behind her ear. "In the end, when you've sought everybody's opinion—it is the leader who makes the final decision. I What makes a good leader is the willingness to risk that which you love for a greater end. General Carlisle has another mission. He wasn't going to tell you until after the wedding and after we got back from our honeymoon. I'm going to suggest that he send you and leave Angus and me out of it."

I felt sick to my stomach.

"Drew, I know you hate the idea, but we both do a dangerous job. We work against ruthless people. Suppose I was killed and…"

"No! Meryl, don't talk like that," I stammered.

"Darling, you are a major and you have risked your life many times. What would you do if I was killed? Or Angus? If it was on a mission, it would mean there was a team looking to you to get them home, with or without us."

I knew in my heart Meryl was right. I was dependent on her and on Angus. Especially on her. I realized that being dependent on someone is okay if you are ill or injured, but it's not healthy in marriage. Loving someone, cherishing them, dying for them—yes. But being so dependent on them that it made you a captive of fear—no.

"What do you want me to do?" I finally asked.

"Darling, it's not what I want you to do. It's what do you want to do?"

"I want someone to love me and stand by me. Someone to whom I can give my heart and life to and trust. But one thing we have both learned is that our main dependence has to be on God—not on any person.

She nodded and smiled at me. "Good answer. My father will tell you about the mission. The team will go with you if you want, but not Angus or me. Pull it off, and I will marry you tomorrow and never look back."

I smiled—a bit grimly, and told Meryl, "It reminds me what the Spartan mothers used to say to their sons when they gave them their big round hoplon shield. Come back with your shield, or on it."

I could have chickened out and left Vanguard and Meryl. I could have gone back to counting the empty bottles on the table at the Finlander Bar. But I knew that I would never be able to live with myself if I did that. And what kind of life would that have been for Mi-Ling and Libby? They deserved more than that. They deserved the best I could give them.

Meryl kissed me so passionately that I wanted to forget everything else in my sphere of existence except her. She pulled away. "Drew, come back. I promise you a honeymoon that you will still be feeling the effects of when you are 80."

Reluctant to turn from love—or especially making love—to life, I sighed. "What's the mission? It sounds very mysterious."

"The general will tell you. I'm not trying to sound mysterious. There's a very good reason for me not to say more, as you will find out, darling."

I spoke to the other team members, Hera and Mike Argo, Anton, Jayne and Sebastian. They all said they didn't have a clue about a new mission. I had to believe them, as they were putting their lives at risk. If I had been a cat, I reckoned I would still have about six of my nine lives left. The second in command was Anton. He was to take over if anything happened to me. It felt like the line of the song. "all dressed up and nowhere to go."

* * *

We were summoned to General Carlisle's office. Once we entered, the door was shut and the security barrier activated. Two guards were stationed on the door.

When we looked at the General, we found he was with a Royal Air Force officer.

"Thank you for coming, people. The briefing, about which I have no doubt you are curious, will be given by the RAF gentleman on my left, Squadron Leader Mike Pender."

Squadron Leader Pender said, "I'm honored to meet members of this branch of our armed forces. I'm aware of your many nationalities, but you all have the highest security clearance. You are professional soldiers, but dealing with time travel, which as I understand involves stopping certain unscrupulous, power-hungry individuals who are attempting to change history. You are used to this. We call upon you for help because something has occurred that puts the present balance of power in grave danger."

Pender looked at us. Hopefully we all appeared suitably impressed.

Mike Pender nodded at us as if satisfied with our response. "You may be familiar with the name *Enola Gaye?*

"Isn't that the B29 that dropped the atomic bomb on Hiroshima?" Jayne asked.

Mike Pender nodded. "Exactly. On June 7, 1945. The newsreel film of the Manhattan Project showed a bomb being tested earlier in 1945 successfully. Nuclear weaponry did not involve the Soviet Union until the Rosenbergs gave America's secrets away to the Russians." He paused. "Sorry, Mr. Devranov," he said apologetically to Anton, "but it's true."

Anton laughed. "You forget Squadron Leader Mike Pender; I am a Czarist, and no supporter of communism. When I was born, the only things that flew were birds."

Pender nodded. "Forgive me. All the aspects of time travel confuse me. Going the speed of sound, I can cope with. But the speed of time...well, that's something else."

General Carlisle coughed and said, "Now the bomb?"

"Yes, of course," Pender responded. "The bomb did not suddenly appear in 1945. The Treaty of Quebec in 1943 was an agreement between Britain and America that the bomb would not be used against another country without mutual agreement."

Pender surveyed our group. "Any questions so far?" His question was met with silence.

"These events are public knowledge, at least now. What I'm going to pass along to you just now is not just top secret, but so to speak, top-top secret. You can't get more secret than that—at least not in Britain. Before Quebec in 1943, a fully functioning prototype of uranium bomb was developed and tested underground in the desert. It was one of the most successful operations ever." Again he gave us a chance to interject comments, but a picture was starting to form in our minds and we didn't like what was forming there.

"Well, someone high up decided that since we had this super weapon and allied forces were being killed, why not use it on the Germans under the guise of helping the Russians. Scientists had calculated that the bomb, when detonated, would destroy everything in an area of four square miles from the epicenter of the explosion. In 1945, this is what happened in Hiroshima when Fatboy was dropped and detonated. In 1943, the Wehrmacht was pouring more troops, German and their allies, into Russia. The Soviet Army, although it had the man and woman power, did not have quite the same equipment. The means of production in Russia had either been destroyed, or the factories were being dismantled and moved east into the snowy depth of Siberia. This left a lot of the Red Army dependent on captured German equipment and what local outlets could produce. The Germans and their allies wanted to hold onto their arms."

Coffee was brought in, for which we were all grateful.

Sebastian said, "If there was a big bomb in 1943, then we wouldn't be gettin' called in unless some bad guys had either gotten aholt of it or had access to it."

"Nearly," Pender replied. "The other factor is that although Stalin was tying up thousands of German troops, Stalin himself had his eyes on the bigger picture. He had plans for buffer states around Russia. He was perfectly prepared to get them. Poland, Romania, Czechoslovakia, and Hungry. Throw in Austria, if he could get it. He saw all these countries as being part of the Soviet Empire. There was even a possibility that Finland would be sucked in. He had part of it. He wanted the rest of what he had not taken from the brave Finns after the Winter War of 1940, when General Mannerhiem gave them a run for their money."

"So what you're saying," I ventured, "is that if that big bomb went off and killed a lot of Germans, but so happened to kill a few Russians, no tears would be shed and it would be seen as no big deal?"

"Let me expand further," Pender said, now warming to his subject. "The group in Charge, known as Committee XV, decided they could authorize its use as they were made up of Americans and British and had contact with Mr. Churchill, the British Prime Minister and war leader, and contact with President Roosevelt. They did authorize its use."

Pender's listeners whistled. The thought of a uranium bomb going off in Europe was fearful.

"The first choice was to drop the bomb in an area called Katmatchskoya, an area and town where it was hoped that the native population had scarpered off. The Russians were told that the area would be particularly heavily bombed. We couldn't tell the Russians the nature of the bombs, for although they didn't have it, they were familiar with the concept. The area was particularly heavy with German tanks and armor, so the emphasis for high explosive and incendiary qualities were needed."

"Where do we come in?" Anton asked, puzzled.

"Well, Committee XV decided that the two component parts of the bomb would be flown on separate aircraft from New York. The two parts of the bomb would then be united and flown—probably in a B29—with a Mosquito fighter cover to the target area. The plane would join a small bombing raid and then head for the target. Her fighter escort, being Mosquitoes, had the speed and low flying ability to fly under German radar. What we suspect was a B29 would drop the bomb, and then quick as you like, fly to nearby Sweden, which would be the closest safe landing spot. Hopefully the Mosquitoes, once the bomber had entered Swedish airspace, would fly back home. The Mosquito pilots were told to keep a certain distance from the bomber, but not the reason why. This was to take place on July 12, 1943. Well, the B29 taxied onto the runway and was about to take off when the mission was aborted—one might add thankfully. So, on a runway at an airbase on July 12, 1943, there was a bomber fueled up with a primed atomic bomb inside."

"Where was it going to take off from?" Jane asked sensibly.

Squadron Leader Pender looked sheepish. "Ah, well, that's the problem. You see, the documentation containing that information and the only copy of it—after 70 or so years—is missing. Stolen or otherwise purloined."

"So we have," General Carlisle said, "a bomber with an atomic bomb on board and we don't know the operational base from which it was supposed to go? On its sortie on the 12th July 1943…mmm. I see."

"Well, to be fair, sir, we did discover that it was in Scotland. You see, sir, top-top secret documents and any microfilm are not checked every week—especially after 70 years. The longer they lie somewhat like sleeping dogs, people don't bother about them."

"How was the misplacement discovered?" Anton asked.

"Well, sir, I was told that one of the locked safe boxes where these things are apparently stored was found open, and the key missing. When the documents that were left were examined, it was found that the details of "Operation Russian Fire" were missing."

Anton put on his philosophical expression and said, "In one of the Czars' courts, someone lost a secret. I think it was one of the Czars called Alexander."

"What happened to him?" Pender asked.

Anton smiled a wolfish smile and said, "They shot him. The pension fund was running short, so they had to take action."

Hera said, "I gather Operation Russian Fire was the name for what they were going to set off? It would have been better if it had been Operation Greek Fire."

I remembered Greek Fire was a substance that started a fire, and if you tried to put water on it, it exploded.

"Oh, jolly good, miss. Nothing like a classical education." Pender said approvingly.

General Carlisle thought aloud. "So, we have a bomber with an atomic bomb on board protected by Mosquitoes that could, if the wrong crew got on board, be heading for London. It could flatten four square miles of the city, make it radioactive, and infect people with radiation sickness. Once that was done, that would put new heart into the Germans and turn the war. So we find the bomber…and then what?"

"Well," Squadron Leader Pender said patiently, "then you stop it."

"Please define *stop* for us," the general said.

Pender rubbed his chin. "Well, blow it up, or otherwise make sure it can't fly."

"What about the air crew?" Jayne asked.

Pender seemed hesitant to answer. Finally, he said, "In the interests of national security, they have been deemed expendable."

Jayne gasped. Her horrified expression seemed to make Pender uncomfortable.

"By whom?" Carlisle demanded.

Sebastian guessed, "By Committee XV, or their grandchildren."

Pender nodded.

"Good to know your boss is rootin' for you," "Sebastian said sarcastically.

"I don't mind dealing with bad guys," Anton told Pender, "but to kill someone for doing his duty runs counter to the way the Vodka flows."

"Did the aircraft have a call sign?" the general asked.

"Oh, yes," Pender replied. "That we do know. *Papa Joe One*."

"One begins to wonder," General Carlisle remarked, "which one of the combatants was the original target? We have an aircraft with an atomic bomb on it with the capacity to destroy London. We know the date of the operation, and that it's in the north of Scotland. We don't know about the aircrew, but we have permission to destroy the aircraft."

"You will be given special SOE classification," Pender said, "for if you are not, you may be shot as spies."

General Carlisle told Pender, "You do realize that the one who stole the original documents is probably a PATCH agent, don't you? They're the only ones that have the ability to turn this information to profit. I suggest that you check all the people who have access to these files are who they are supposed to be. Another trick of PATCH is to put duplicates in place of originals. We've had to deal with duplicates before. Retina scanning hadn't been invented then. PATCH has the capability of putting in a substitute Churchill, or Eisenhower, or even Stalin. What about a substitute Hitler? One who would know to release the Panzer tanks and the Reserve Wehrmacht infantry divisions against the invading Allied forces in Normandy in 1944, much sooner. One who would know where the Allies would land and would be waiting."

Squadron Leader Mike Pender whistled.

"You need to inform Committee XV of the seriousness of the situation." General Carlisle emphasized.

"Of course, but we would have to introduce it as information received and play down the time travel aspect. The ability to travel in time would come as a surprise to them," Pender said.

"Not half as much of a shock if an atom bomb were dropped on London in 1943," the general responded. "I think that would be what our American friends would call a game changer.'"

"I will do my best," Pender said. "I'm here to help in any way I can."

"Oh, and as you have technical expertise, it would be well if you went with our team," General Carlisle added.

"Jolly good," Pender said. "I could be temporarily seconded to Vanguard."

"If you are squadron leader, the first thing you gotta do is leave your will with somebody you can trust," Sebastian warned.

General Carlisle coughed. "Thank you, Sebastian. I'm sure Squadron Leader Pender realizes the dangers. Now Squadron Leader Pender, if you will excuse us…the team has a lot to discuss."

Pender shook hands all around, and left. I noticed Jayne's hesitation to accept his hand.

We took a short break and headed to the café. We chatted and discussed other things, but made no mention of what we had been told inside the secure area. Nor did we mention Angus or Meryl. We didn't ask what they were doing, although I was dying to know what danger Meryl might be in. It was an additional security measure that we were not told what missions others were engaged in, unless we were directly involved.

Then we filed back to the secure area to find Adrian waiting for us. General Carlisle had apparently filled him in on the details because Adrian said almost immediately, "So the bomber would have to have enough fuel to go from wherever it was in Scotland, fly to the target, and have enough fuel to get to Orlanda Airforce Base outside of Stockholm, and turn themselves over to the Swedish authorities. Well, we can run that info through the computer and it should come up with a result. But how Pender's lot couldn't have done that on their own computers, that I don't understand."

General Carlisle said, "It would mean the curiosity of their computer bods getting fired up, one of whom just may be a PATCH operative. My money is on Lossiemouth as the station from which the bomber would fly."

"Anyway," Adrian replied, "we will give it our best shot."

"Do so," the General commanded, "or else history may turn out to be a lot different from what we imagined."

Then Carlisle turned to me. "Right, Major. You are the boots on the ground and will have to put the operation into place once the destination is known. A lot depends on this." He was thinking atom bomb. I was thinking wedding and honeymoon; *A honeymoon you will still remember when you are 80*. There was a lot hanging on this mission, and for me, not all of it was in saving London!

"Mike," Carlisle said, "you are on standby. The other team may need you, too, so by staying here—you can help where you're needed most. Jayne, I would like you to act as look out. You will have a short two-way radio connected to another set in case we have to go into the plane. You warn of any activity outside the plane and of any headlights coming toward the plane. You'll be picked up after the plane is immobilized and taken to the exit point where the time car can pick everyone up. If you're caught, you'll probably be treated rather roughly. You should be prepared. I don't want you inside the plane where you might get hit by a stray bullet should the crew put up a fight."

Jayne nodded. "I have good night vision, so I would be of most use outside the aircraft."

"Drew," John Carlisle said, "over to you. Since you're the boots on the ground leader, you know where your team needs to be."

"Right," I agreed. "That leaves myself, Hera, Anton, and Sebastian. Two teams. Pender will also be with us. Hopefully he will know how to defuse the bomb should it be activated.

Sebastian remarked, "Well, if anyone comes looking for us and it's dark, I ain't gonna be seen before I sees them."

"Okay, what about the crew?" I asked. "Can't we use some kind of knock out gas? If we knock them out, we'll have to pull them out if the plane goes on fire. But I think all of us here agree that we totally oppose murder. Fighting back, self-defense…but we've never killed anyone who wasn't trying to kill us."

"Even me," Hera agreed. "And I like to fight."

Mike Argo slipped an arm around his wife and kissed her. "I'm glad you like other things more than you like fighting, darling." They smiled at each other exchanging secrets that probably would have embarrassed the rest of us had they been spoken aloud.

"We can try to stun them," I suggested, "like we did Confederate Captain Titus Contrell in Washington in 1863. Pender talked about destroying the aircraft, but can we really let a plane with an A-bomb on board go on fire?"

"Drew…it might interest you and the others to know that there was only ever one uranium bomb," Adrian told us. "The others were plutonium, which is a manmade element which must be detonated by an ignition device. Fire alone wouldn't be enough, although fire might damage the case."

Jayne said with the insight of a good intelligence, "If the plane is on the runway, or even in trees where it can taxi out ready for takeoff…surely all you need to do is put a charge of explosive on each wheel strut. Blow the things. That will render the plane useless; belly down. And that should be that. Shortly after that's accomplished, if what Squadron Leader Pender said is true, the mission will be called off."

Sebastian nodded. "Good thinking, Jayne. Only thing is—if there are bad guys on board, they might just set the fuse out of cussedness.

"Adrian," General Carlisle asked, "how long would it take the bomb to explode after the trigger has been activated?"

"Well," Adrian answered without hesitation, "the bomb that left the Enola Gaye took 53 seconds to descend and explode."

Carlisle remarked, "That would be well within the possibility of setting the fuse and getting outside to a time door or whatever they have, and leaving the thing to explode and do whatever damage it could once they're out of the road."

Adrian nodded. "And suppose that's their Plan B and they can't get to

London. The next best thing is to set it off in Scotland. It would damage British-American relations for a long time. Perhaps well past June 1944, when the Germans may have their own nuclear weapon."

"Either way," Anton remarked bitterly, "they hold all the vodka."

"Sir what happens to the bomb if we stop them?" Jayne asked.

"I assume," General Carlisle replied, "that it gets taken back to America and used in 1945. I suspect committee XV, who seem to have thought this up, didn't think of what the Russian response would be if a whole lot of their troops got wiped out by something the Germans didn't have anything to do with. In fact, it could drive them into Hitler's arms again, as in 1940, when Poland was attacked and invaded. If you throw in a determined Japanese assault, then things would look bad for everyone."

"One has to hope that the aircraft is not fueled until nearer take off," Adrian remarked. "If it was newly filled, it would create quite a stir if it exploded."

Adrian's information caught up with him from our computer. He read it out to us: "Our guess is that it's a Lancaster bomber. Seven crew members; the aircraft had been adjusted to carry the tallboy bomb, or grandslam, bombs, which were used on selective targets. The Lancaster was also adapted to carry the bouncing bomb. Wing Commander Guy Gibson lead Squadron 617 in the Dam Busters raid on May 16 and 17, 1943, using bouncing bombs."

Adrian concluded, "The Lancaster was a night bomber, painted black except for below—which was dark blue. I take it you all know what a Lancaster looks like?"

Sebastian, Anton, and Hera didn't know, so they were told that a picture would be included in their briefing folders. Mike nuzzled his bride's neck. "It's okay, darling," he told Hera. "You know all the important things."

I was happy for Hera and Mike, but watching them together made me realize more than ever what I was missing with Meryl.

General Carlisle took over our briefing. "The crux of the matter is that if the crew are PATCH operatives, then we must stop them. We can't risk leaving them to ignite the bomb. I suspect that devoted PATCH members have a strain of Kamikaze in them. So we neutralize the bomb and the plane. If necessary, give the crew a chance to go back where they came from. Not much when you say it quickly. Major Faulkner, any more directions for your team?"

"Spend the rest of today and part of tomorrow familiarizing yourselves with the layout and details," I told them. "Then we go. We'll arrive on the evening of July 9, at about 10.30 p.m. Any questions?"

Anton, who had been lost in contemplation, asked, "Are they really going to leave this flying thing out in the open without guards? Isn't it the job of the RAF regiment to guard hangars and aircraft out on the runway?"

"I can't answer that question for you right now, Anton," I told him. "It's a good question. I suspect we'll just have to wait and see. But one thing we do know from past experience, if there's anyone there who tests positive for Kairon, we knock them out—as roughly as necessary—and if they don't test positive for Kairon, we use the dart. Try not to hurt anyone, people, unless it's absolutely necessary."

"Right," General Carlisle approved. "Major Faulkner seems to have covered every eventuality. I can't think of anything else. Drew, it's your show. Anton, you're second in command. The rest of you—you are all just as vital to Vanguard and to this mission. Okay, go study the briefing and the layouts. Get some good eats and some good sleep. Dismissed."

As they left the briefing room, Mike nuzzled Hera's ear again. She giggled, an incongruous sound coming from Hera. Jayne and Sebastian smiled tolerantly. As for me…I tried not to be jealous or to be bitter about that sweet intimacy that had been denied to me twice even after I had married.

CHAPTER THIRTEEN

Lossiemouth RAF station, July 9, 1943, at about 10.30 p.m.

We headed to the time car dressed in camouflage, including darkened faces, except for Hera and Jayne. Jayne wore a black beret, thick woolen coat, and 1940s woolly hose and slacks. She had objected to wearing a 1940s skirt in case there was any action, as she explained. Hera wore a dark green coat and slacks. Her slate-grey eyes looked somber and her raven-black hair was tucked under a beret.

Jayne said, "I look a right dork in this outfit. I hope none of my friends see me dressed like this"

Sebastian chuckled. "Honey, how many of your friends do you reckon are gonna to stop a bomber that could obliterate London and change the course of World War II...and that all before breakfast?"

Jayne smiled at him and giggled. "Not many that I can think of. They'd never leave their cellphones long enough."

"You got brains, Jayne. You're a whole lot smarter than them cell phones they call smart."

"Seb," Jayne said, reaching for his hand. "I'm glad you're here."

"Well, I'm glad that you're glad, and that's startin' this mission with a whole heep of gladness."

Hera elbowed Sebastian, "You've been needing someone to watch your back, you big ox, and looks like you've found her."

"Lordy, Lordy," Sebastian exclaimed, "if'n you didn't have you Mike, Miss Hera, I'd think that name callin' was out of jealously."

I wondered if I would ever get used to time travel. It seemed that we were barely in the car and had programmed it before it stopped again.

We put on night vision goggles, apart from Jayne, switched off the internal time car lights and exited. We didn't want some sharp-eyed sentry noticing lights flashing off and on and becoming trigger happy.

We crouched by a clump of trees and watched to make sure the coast was clear. Each of us attempted to memorize the position of the time car so we could find it again. We skirted the runway, keeping 50 yards between our two groups. We slowly worked our way forward until we saw a long, large mass of camouflage netting in the distance. As we ventured closer, we saw that the front half of the netting had been pulled back. The Browning machine guns from the front turret poked towards the sky in salute, and I hoped that a passing German night fighter did not think that he was in luck, for the Lancaster was a sitting target.

We examined what we could see through the night goggles. There were two guards by the Lancaster. One had a Lee-Enfield .303 rifle. The second had an American Garand rifle, which was an excellent weapon. Obviously, the Flight Sergeant was not around because Jayne spotted the glow of their cigarettes—a forbidden and foolhardy indulgence so close to the plane. They walked around the aircraft from opposite directions, meeting in the middle after 30 paces. Sebastian was the one able to get closer. He could move quickly. He ran the length of the plane in the darkness underneath. When one of the guards came around, Sebastian tested for Kairon and found none. He ran at the guard and slammed into him, the force of the impact knocking the guard out. Sebastian dragged him to one side of the plane and injected him to make sure he stayed asleep.

The second guard said with an unmistakable Glasgow accent, "Harry, Harry, where are ye maun? Stop piddling about." His question got him the same treatment as Sebastian had given "Harry," with a mere a grunt on the guard's part to mark the occasion.

We could see Jayne keeping an eye out then Anton and Jayne picked up the guard's weapons and began walking around the plane. It was dark enough that unless anyone got close, they wouldn't detect the change in uniforms. Pender, Hera, and I went up the crew access ladder and headed for the front of the plane. Hera slipped into the back of the plane and the sound of thumping brought three guys from the front of the plane racing toward the back to check on the commotion. Our Kairon detectors buzzed loudly in our ears.

"What the heck are you doing here, and who are you?" Aircrew were allowed to carry pistols in their uniforms, and one of them went for his. I had no choice but to shoot. I hit him in the arm.

"Don't be stupid," I told him, "the next time it will be your head, You're no more RAF officers than Hitler is. You work for PATCH. We're from Vanguard. Off the plane. Keep your hands where we can see them. We know what's on board, and you won't be taking off with that bomb."

"What are you talking about?" the highest ranking officer said. "What kind of crazy are you? I know what you are; you're German saboteurs. My name is Marshall, my rank is Flight Lieutenant, and you will all be shot for this."

"If you are RAF," Pendel said, "you will know what Tee-Emm is?"

"Tea is something you drink, you German swine."

"If you don't know what *Tee-Emm* is, you must be the only aircrew who doesn't know the RAF Aircrew magazine is called *Tee-Emm*. Now, we're going to make sure the plane can't take off."

Hera joined us. "The ones in the back will sleep for a while. They were uncooperative, both of them."

"Good," Hera," I told her. "Well done." Then I gestured to the two men from the front. "Right," I told them, "out! You can stay with the other guards who are taking a bit of a nap."

Anton and Sebastian entered the back of the plane and dragged out the two men who had experienced an encounter with Hera. We pulled them out and drugged everyone that seemed capable of moving in a relatively short time.

Jayne who had returned to watching for any trouble her voice then broke the stillness. "*Cat's eyes to momma, cat's eyes to momma, we've got company. It looks like a small armored car. Over.*"

"Cat's eyes return to momma," Anton said. "over."

"*Roger, wilco, momma,*" She replied.

"Set the charges on the wheel struts," I ordered. "When the plane comes down it should damage the propellers and stop it from moving." Then I realized with alarm that the armored car had caught up with Jayne. Two gunshots rang out into the night. Sebastian ran off into the trees.

I held the detonator in my hand and had stopped Pender and Anton from going after Sebastian. "Hera, go after Sebastian and back him up." She shot off with the lithesome grace of a leopard.

The armored car drew to a stop opposite us, and the leader said, "*Wir haben...*"

"We don't speak German" I said.

"The hell you don't, Nazi scum! We have the girl and will kill her unless you drop your weapons and whatever you have in your hand and walk towards us. There was a twenty second wait before the explosives detonated...twenty seconds is a long time. I signaled for the others to drop what weapons could be seen.

The plane was directly behind us.

"Move away!" When we didn't move, he struck Jayne with the back of his hand. "Move away or your pretty little Nazi tart won't be so attractive anymore. He hit Jayne again and shouted, "Move!"

Twenty, I thought, and the two charges at the wheel struts exploded. The Lancaster landed belly down with a crash.

Sebastian shot out of the trees and grabbed Jayne out of the surprised flight lieutenant's grip. Then he punched the man and shouted, "How do you like that you piece of trash? Didn't your momma done teach you that you don't never lift your hands to a lady?"

Blood streamed from Marshall's nose. The turret in the armored car began to rotate and the hatch opened. Not waiting to see who was in the car or what they would do, Jayne tossed a stun grenade into it.

I guessed two or three minutes had passed and we were all still in the land of the living and, somehow, the plane hadn't caught fire. Thank You, Jesus!

We injected the armored car leader and the crewman and dropped them down beside the others. The third member of the crew was still incapacitated by the stun grenade. Sebastian ran to Jayne and put his arms around her. He picked her up, in spite of her protests that she could walk, and we headed back to the trees as quickly as possible. 'Papa' Sebastian was doing a really good imitation of a father. We got to the trees and the RAF station alarm went off. The alarm brought racing fire engines and more boots on the ground. Speculative shots were being fired, and some were in our direction.

We summoned the time car, bailed inside, and hit the "Home" button.

Jayne had been hit with a knuckle duster. She started to cry. "I'm sorry," she stammered. "I let you down. I...I..."

Sebastian looked at me and I realized that one of the tests of leadership is what you say in situations like this. Any fool can be tough; it takes a leader to be tender. Sebastian started cleaning Jayne's face with antiseptic.

"Jayne," I told her, "if you hadn't stayed at your post, we would have all been caught. You letting yourself get captured gave the rest of us the time we needed to carry out the task that may have saved thousands of lives. Well done."

General Carlisle was waiting for us. Squadron Leader Pender said to him him,

"What a team, sir! Thon wee lassie Jayne, she's a real trooper."

"Yes, sir," I told General Carlisle. "Jayne allowed herself to be captured. Her sacrifice gave us the time we needed to disable the Lancaster. The crew were PATCH operatives."

Sebastian said, "Permission to take Jayne to the doctor, sir."

"Yes! Of course!" We watched Jayne's slight figure being guided to the infirmary by the big guy Sebastian.

"Sir," I said. "The whole team worked well. Everybody played their part. Squadron Leader Pender asked the aircrew a question that gave away they were not real RAF. Hera got to...err...exercise her strength, and well, the injections were brilliant."

"Well done, Major Faulkner." Then he addressed our team. "Well done, all. Right, people. Showers and rest. I don't know what you did to them, but you frighten the dickens out of me. A proper bunch of cutthroats. Hera, before you disappear, get Victoria to take over from Sebastian in watching Jayne, if Jayne will let you. He's earned some solid rest too."

* * *

I imagine we all slept soundly that night. Mi-Ling and Libby were asleep when I got to Victoria's flat. I tiptoed in and kissed them. It was good to be alive. It had been a close call, but we had succeeded because we had depended on each other. That's what I liked about time travel; there were no superstars. It was teamwork, no matter the size of the team.

The following morning, we had to debrief. General Carlisle listened to our detailed accounts, as well as to what Squadron Leader Pender had seen.

"Gosh," he said, "I thought flying a Phantom Jet was tough going with some near squeaks, but that's nothing compared to the pressure you time travel types are under."

Sebastian looked abashed. "I nearly killed that sergeant for hitting Jayne."

General Carlisle smiled. "Oh, that would never have done, Sebastian. What if you had killed some politician's grandfather? Where would we be with one less politician in the world?" We all chuckled. The general turned to Jayne, whose usually lovely face was discolored, puffy, and swollen. "I'm putting you in for a gallantry medal. Your conduct was truly courageous. Vanguard and the rest of us are proud of you."

Jayne ducked her head to hide her embarrassment. Strands of auburn hair slipped across her face hiding some of the signs of the trauma she had endured.

"Way to go, Jayne!" Sebastian exclaimed. His enthusiasm affected the rest of us. We crowded around Jayne to congratulate her, which served to make the blush below the bruising spread. We left the office. I headed for the canteen feeling a hunger that I knew from experience was fueled by nervousness.

I didn't realize Meryl was there until I heard her silky voice. "Well, sexy," she said with a southern drawl. "It looks as if I'm gonna marry you after all. Hmmm…and about that honeymoon?"

They must have turned up the heating again, because I suddenly developed hot flashes.

Angus caught up with me when I laterwent for a walk in the car park. "Well done, son. I'm proud of you, Major. Let's hear it from your point of view."

So, as briefly as possible without leaving out any vital points, I described our mission.

"I told Meryl you could lead them. Great work, Major." Angus saluted. I returned the salute. Afterwards, I realized that Angus' salute was the biggest complement I had ever been paid.

I knew we hadn't destroyed PATCH, but we had damaged it and its credibility. It would now seem to possible terrorists that PATCH might not be able to deliver what it promised. All we needed for the big take down was for Bryant to show up at the wedding. We really hoped that hatred would overrule cunning and would cause him to destroy himself.

"Will you take charge of security in the church at the wedding?" I asked Angus. "As much as I would like you as best man, we need to know that someone good is watching our backs."

"Of course, Major. You know the whole team is in this with you. I'll get Mike, Hera, and Sebastian to help me."

I nodded and thanked him. General Carlisle would be there too, of course, and he could easily become a target as well as Mi-Ling or me. "The important thing is to watch out for Mi-Ling. She may be his prime target. It's almost like some kind of obsession with Bryant."

"Maybe," Angus reasoned, "that's because Mi-Ling represents everything that Bryant is not and doesn't have—including faith and trust in God. Maybe Bryant fears Mi-Ling, or fears the God that Mi-Ling trusts. As for you two, we could get you bullet proof vests, but what bride wants to wear body armor under a bridal gown?"

"I just don't want to happen to Meryl what happened to Lucy. Bryant never expressed any desire for Meryl as he did for Lucy. I think you're right that either I or Mi-Ling is the target. Maybe he wants his daughter back. All we can do is wait and see."

As for Meryl, she had to disappear to the gown shop for what was termed a "fitting." Victoria, Mi-Ling, and Libby clucked around about her like a covey of mother hens. To them, everything had to be perfect. Poor Meryl! Half of her loved the treatment, but the other half wanted the big occasion to be over and for us to be together—on our honeymoon.

Anton and I went through to see Reverend Thornton.

"Drew, Anton! How good it is to see you! But it is strange that you should call now when I'll be conducting the wedding so soon. I think there is something deeper on your minds."

I said, "It's about the danger I warned you about when I asked you if you would conduct the ceremony. I have this wild idea that Bryant—I know you remember him—might target Mi-Ling. I believe he wants to kill her because of her faith in Jesus and her love for Him. Apart from her being a girl, she is everything in stellar character and in faith that Bryant is not. And he may resent her even more because his daughter Libby loves her. They have really become sisters since Bryant was killed—or we thought he was—and we adopted Libby."

"Yes," the minister said in his gentle, soothing voice. "Mi-Ling has so much peace and love about her. She is quick to love even those who are cruel or unlovely. She is quick to forgive. She has so much of Jesus that she is an affront to those who are being lost. So it's not surprising that Bryant, and others like him, want to silence her. They know she's right, but they refuse to bow the knee to Jesus. That which you hate, you try to destroy, or to silence as if that silencing it validates your own beliefs. Without the witness of someone like Mi-Ling, you can convince yourself you are right."

Reverend Thornton prayed, asking God to do something unexpected to bring healing where there was only hurt now. "I don't see what God can do in this," the minister confessed, "but that's why He is God. He has His own way of doing things."

Meryl and I finalized the details for our honeymoon and even made motel reservations. We had decided to go back to modern day Waterloo and the battlefield. Our mission there, albeit on opposite sides, had made such a deep impression on both of us that we wanted to see what it was like in peace time. Wartime and close calls we knew only too well.

Just before the wedding, I was summoned to General Carlisle's office. To my amazement, the whole team was there. Meryl seemed barely able to contain her excitement. That portended a surprise—I very much hoped it would be a good surprise.

The General rose from his chair and shook hands with me. He saluted, and I returned the salute. "Well, Major, you are going to marry my daughter, and a wedding requires a wedding present, so here is mine. Whether you thank me for it in years to come, only time will tell." He handed two envelopes to us, and one to Anton. Puzzled, Anton turned his envelope back and forth in his hands as changing the position would allow him to read it unopened.

"Well, open them," General Carlisle said. "Drew, read yours out loud."

I read,

Further to proper procedures being followed and checks activated, and also following your many successful and dangerous missions, you are hereby promoted to head of Vanguard and to the rank of acting Colonel. Miss Meryl Scott, soon to be Mrs. Meryl Faulkner, is promoted to Captain and your second in command. Viewing the seriousness with which this threat is now being taken, and in the interests of international relations, Captain Anton Devranov is promoted to command of the procurement department. Signed Lt. Gen John Carlisle.

I couldn't believe it. I looked up at everybody.

"Well done, darling," Meryl said, coming over to kiss me.

Everyone crowded around to congratulate me. "Well done, chief, we are delighted for you...and for us."

"I can't do this," I protested. "I'm not ready for it."

The General grinned. "Well, for a wedding present it was either promotion or a Hoover. Oh, by the way, you have to take on the diplomatic side now. That includes the American President and any big wig who wants his two pence worth. Try to get on with the Prime Minister no matter the party. American Presidents will change after elections, so you won't always be working with our common sense President Galbraith."

"Will we still get to go on missions?" I asked. Considering the close escapes, I wasn't sure why I was asking that.

"Yes, but not both of you together. Someone has to remain in charge and carry the can—take the blame when things go wrong. So in short, the answer is, yes, but not together. And, besides," he reminded me, "you've got two daughters to consider. That will leave one parent here to love, support, and care for them—you know—do all that parenting stuff that I never got to do with my own daughter when she was lost to me."

I could see the sense in what had been decided.

There was one other happy task: to present Jayne with her gallantry medal. "Jayne we are very proud of you and you are hereby promoted to the rank of Lieutenant," General Carlisle said. Your father, Alan, will be very proud of you."

Jayne looked down at the floor and said quietly, "Thank you, sir, and the rest of you. I don't deserve this, but can I say Sebastian was my role model. He inspired me to be brave when I didn't feel like it and helped give me courage when I had none of my own."

Sebastian had silver tears of joy trickling down his cheeks. "Aww, shucks! Y'all have me embarrassed. Thanks, Jaguar."

Jayne went to stand by him.

"What are you going to do sir?" I asked General Carlisle.

"I will be available in an advisory capacity. That's why your rank is acting colonel. After you become adjusted to your new role, it will become full colonel and I will be totally off the hook. Once the wedding is over, Clarissa and I are going on a long holiday. Then I'm going to build up my model railway so the lovely steam train *The Duchess of Hamilton* can make the run from London's Kings Cross to Glasgow Central in bonnie Scotland on time. That's one of the things about model railways; you can have them run on time as they say."

The general's secretary hurried into the room. "President Galbraith is on the line, sir," she said to me. "Shall I pass him through?"

"Yes, thank you. I hope you will stay on."

She smiled. "I always stay where I'm needed, sir." I smiled back at her thinking that she was a kind of clerical *Mary Poppins*.

So, I had my first conversation with the American President. "*Congratulations, Colonel, on your promotion. We sure are lookin' forward to workin' with y'all and we hope y'all come over and see us sometime soon. Come down to the Ranch and get you some real barbeque and steak and some of the most beautiful scenery on the planet, and that's the God's honest truth.*

"I guess there are rattlesnakes as well? Mr. President."

"*Yup. We've got us a full supply of them varmints. We can take you to see some if y'all want, or maybe, they'll find you.*"

"Thank you, Mr. President, I appreciate the offer."

"*Just kiddin,' Colonel. They normally stay out of the road 'cept if you surprise them. By the way, Colonel, you make a bad liar. You don't like our snakes one little bit.*"

I thought I would get on with President Galbraith just fine.

That evening, away from everything except our memories, Meryl and I sat in a restaurant. As I looked into her eyes and saw her smile I had to remind myself I was the blessed guy who was going to marry this beauty.

"Who would have thought we would have come this far from when we started out?" I commented shaking my head in disbelief. "And now we're starting a new phase in our lives—together."

Meryl was finishing a chocolate pudding. It was proving difficult for her to be philosophical with a mouthful of chocolate pudding.

The music in the restaurant played soothingly in the background. Barbara Streisand's voice sang *Memories* from the film *The Way We Were*. The words seemed so right that it could have been written for us. We had been through extreme danger together. Meryl had nearly died in my arms, then in turn, saved my life. She had engaged me into the adventure of a lifetime—in fact, of many lifetimes. We had a family, Mi-Ling and Libby.

God had kept us and brought us through to two days before the wedding and the joys of a long-awaited and long-delayed honeymoon, which we both looked forward to with equal eagerness. The way we were was not the way we were going to be always. First, there was the wedding. And, it was possible that a snake would show up at the party.

CHAPTER FOURTEEN
The Snake at the Wedding

The Church stood as a constant reminder of all that had taken place in the past with Lucy, Marie, and now Meryl. I prayed that this wedding would go off smoothly, and strangely enough, I was not as concerned about Meryl as I was about Mi-Ling.

It was a day of bright sunshine, as if God sought to remove all trace of darkness, giving bad memories no place to rest or hide…not even in my heart. The multi-colored stained glass windows reflected the sunshine and threw cascades of color across the walls.

In the vestry room at the side of the church, Anton and I waited.

"Are you ready, brother, for the happiest day of your life when you finally get to marry that lovely lady?"

"Suppose Bryant does show up and something happens to Meryl, or Mi-Ling, or even Libby?"

"Ach," said Anton. "You are sounding like an old Russian babushka—a black-shawled grandmother predicting gloom and doom. If you lived in Russia at this time, you would be glad not just for everyday that you were still alive, but for every moment."

Reverend Thornton came into the vestry rubbing his hands.

"Lovely day, full church, and God smiling on the occasion. What more could we want for a wedding? Hmm? Let's pray before we go to the front." He prayed with us, asking for the Lord's protection and asking that the Lord would be honored in our wedding. The phrase *staying alive* passed into my mind. I thought I would settle for that. We then went out to the front of the church. Reverend Thornton had been right; there was sizeable crowd. Some were security, but may others well-wishers.

"One day," Anton said, "I will get round to this…but it's deciding who the lucky girl is going to be. Probably it will be Irja. Wait till I tell her the news."

He said it with such seriousness that I couldn't help laughing.

We got word that the bridal party had arrived, Hymn music filled the air. Meryl and I had chosen a hymn called, *Now Thank We All Our God*. I was only half listening. Suddenly, Meryl appeared on her father's arm. She looked breathtakingly gorgeous. I gasped in awe. Her bridal gown had light blue edges that matched the color of her eyes. The General was in full uniform and looked every part the proud father. Meryl kept looking up at him, and he kept smiling down at her. Meryl carried a bouquet of orange blossom, which I thought was in memory of Lucy. That touched my heart. I felt wetness in my eyes and realized I was crying as they continued up the long aisle.

One thing we had not been able to achieve was to thoroughly search the congregation for Kairon. We had to hide our concerns in case Bryant found out and it scared him away.

I was not going to miss the sight of my lovely bride coming down the aisle. They got halfway up the aisle, just to the point where Lucy had been murdered. There were several movements in the congregation. One tall guy, on a level with Mi-Ling, ripped off a rubber mask and grabbed for her. It was Bryant and two of his chums, thankfully with orders not to shoot—at least until Bryant had made his speech. His two associates went for Libby, and Bryant grabbed Mi-Ling. He put a pistol to her head and wrapped her hair round his hand. We had marksmen in the congregation, but Bryant was too close to Mi-Ling. It made intervention too risky.

"Today you will see justice enacted," Bryant pontificated. "For a long time this murderess has thought she had escaped the justice of PATCH. She killed my first mate, James Lancaster. Now Justice catches up with her."

Mi-Ling had killed Lancaster to save my life. But Bryant wasn't concerned about my life. All his venom was directed at Mi-Ling.

"Now she will be executed..." I had never seen such hateful eyes. They were almost demonic.

"Libby was shaking her head sobbing. "No! Pa, no!"

Bryant ignored his sobbing daughter. He clicked off the safety catch.

"Faulkner," he shouted, look at what happens to those who anger PATCH."

Lord, I prayed, *where are You? Can't You do something?*

Amazingly, we were about to see God's justice at its very best.

Mi-Ling drew her heel back and ran it down the inside of Bryant's shin at the same time she forced her head to one side by about six inches. The force of Mi-Ling's kick jerked Bryant's trigger finger. The gun fired twice. I shut my eyes, which were blinded by tears of frustration. I should have made myself watch. First the shot, then the ricochet. The stone church echoed with the whine. The first bullet returned, hitting part of the wooden balcony. The second bullet hit Bryant in the forehead with a thump. Mi-Ling broke free. Bryant's pistol dropped from his hand and he slumped to the ground. The two goons who were holding Libby were so shocked that they let her go. They were quickly overpowered and handcuffed by security.

Bryant was dying. He sobbed, his body convulsed with heaving.

"Serves him right, "I said through gritted teeth. I had no pity, no forgiveness to waste on the evil thug who had stolen so much of my life from me. Then I realized that Mi-Ling was talking to Bryant.

I crowded closer, wanting to protect my daughter. Amazingly, Bryant's face was devoid of hate and anger now, and the demonic look in his eyes had vanished. Victoria rushed forward to grab Mi-Ling, but I stopped her.

Bryant grunted, "Mi-Ling, I'm going to hell where I deserve to go after the life I lived and the way I persecuted you. I'm sorry. So, so sorry. Please forgive me." Shockingly, the big man was crying, and it seemed to be from genuine repentance rather than from pain.

In my heart I was saying, *tell him to go and rot in hell where he belongs.* I had a right to feel that way. He had murdered my Lucy in cold blood. I was right.

Only in Mi-Ling's heart, something else beat, something else that was much closer to God's heart than my thoughts.

The church had grown so silent that you could hear the rustle of Mi-Ling's dress when she knelt by Bryant. "I forgive you, Captain Bryant."

"God won't. He can't. I don't deserve forgiveness after all I've done."

Mi-Ling took Bryant's hand, the same hand that had held the pistol against her head. "That's what makes Father God so special," she told Bryant. "He forgives us because Jesus paid for all our sins on the cross."

"But I deserve hell!" Bryant gritted. He started coughing. His breath rattled. "I don't deserve what Jesus did."

"But Captain, Jesus died to keep you out of hell. Ask Him. He will forgive you because He loves you." Mi-Ling assured him.

Then, as if He could see an unseen face looking down at him, Bryant gasped hoarsely, "Jesus forgive this foul sinner! I am so sorry." A smile crept over his face. More tears piled into his eyes.

"Thank you, thank you, thank you," he said to Mi-Ling. Then he called in a weak voice, "Libby, my child, come let your Pa touch you one more time. I love you, little Libby. Please forgive me." His voice had dropped to a mere whisper as Libby inched over next to him and reached out tentatively to touch his face.

"I'm sorry for all I put you through, little Libby. I'm not worthy to be your father. But if you can find it in your heart to forgive me as Mi-Ling has, I will die in peace." Libby nodded solemnly and bent down to kiss his cheek in spite of the blood trickling over it from the wound and the frothy blood slipping out from between pale lips. Libby took her father's hand.

Bryant grew so still that I thought he was gone. I was just about to lead the girls away when Bryant looked up at me and whispered, "Take care of my little girl for me, Drew. Please. Please take care of my little girl."

My enemy was dying and I could find no words to speak to him. He had robbed me of love, joy—life. There was a powerful smell of orange blossoms. Lucy stood beside me. "Drew, my love, I've forgiven him—you must also."

"I forgive you, Bryant," I said. He let go of Libby's hand and took mine. My enemy dying at my feet, yet I felt no joy. "I forgive you, Bryant," I repeated, "and I promise...we promise to love and take care of your Libby."

No sooner had I spoken the words than it was like a filthy weight of hate fell off me. I felt release in my own spirit. I hadn't realized how much the desire for revenge had eaten into my heart. Bryant's face was chalk white. Too weak now to talk, Bryant nodded to me and to Mi-Ling. With his remaining strength, he reached for Libby's hand again. Then he was gone.

Lucy said, "You won't see me again until you come home. I have a job to do now, to bring a penitent sinner to the feet of the King Who made it all possible."

"Thanks, Lucy." I said, marveling that I was talking to her and no one else seemed to notice or to see her. Perhaps the scene with Bryant and Mi-Ling had distracted them.

"Don't thank me, Drew, thank Jesus Who made it all possible. Now, go and live your life with Meryl, and may the King bless you both." The scent of orange blossoms lingered, but Lucy was gone.

With touching dignity from someone so young, Libby closed her father's eyes. I had never seen what an angel looked like before, but there was one standing before me now.

"I don't know how to ask, but do you want to continue with the wedding?" Reverend Thornton asked us. He was a brave man. Meryl and I both nodded.

Reverend Thornton sang a verse from the hymn we had chosen, *Now thank we all our God with heart and hands and voices, Who wondrous things has done, in whom this world rejoices.*

"My friends, we have seen more than a wedding today," Reverend Thornton said. "We have seen the wonderful grace and forgiveness of God through Jesus Christ. That is available to all of us no matter what our past."

Going through my freed mind was the phrase, *who wondrous things has done.* We had certainly seen wondrous things.

Meryl and I took our vows of undying love. During the service when nearly everyone had their backs turned, they came to take Bryant's body away. Libby broke ranks and ran down to where her father lay between two men carrying the stretcher. She reached under the sheet and took her still-warm father's hand and escorted him out of the church.

View other Black Rose Writing titles at www.blackrosewriting.com/books and use promo code PRINT to receive a 20% discount when purchasing.

BLACK✿ROSE
writing™

Lightning Source UK Ltd.
Milton Keynes UK
UKOW02f1310221116
288206UK00001B/54/P